Unnatural Selection

Rosana DuMas

Mollusc Media

2016

Unnatural Selection

Lessons of Life and Death on the Paper Trail

A novel

By Rosana DuMas

With a foreword by Sandy Masuo

For Henry and all the creatures who teach us
what it means to be human—when we let them.

Contents

Foreword
Wild Life

A few years ago, my parents uncovered in their storage closet a zoo coloring book from my primary school days that I had carefully completed using my treasured box of 64 Crayola Crayons (with sharpener)—then annotated and indexed using the toy typewriter I had begged for one Christmas. Although the selection of animals in the book was impressive (including such obscure creatures as the kinkajou and the platypus), I felt the text was lacking because it did not explain important morphological features such as prehensile tails and opposable thumbs.

A short time later, when I was about ten years old, I received a book called *Fascinating World of Animals*. It was a *Reader's Digest* one-volume zoology encyclopedia organized into sections that focused on different biomes. I was riveted by the dazzling full-color photos, but what really rocked my formative world was the section on taxonomy. The scientific nomenclature revealed the true names of all known creatures, which had the magical property of being comprehensible in all languages, and the charts were mystical diagrams that disclosed the hidden order of the universe—the connections between flat worms, elephants, emus, and Komodo dragons. It was my initiation into the realm of Nerd.

Other important experiences supplemented my obsessive book learning. During pilgrimages to Woodland Park Zoo with my dad, I learned to be patient and observant because animals are autonomous and have different priorities and lifestyles. Our neighbor across the street was a subsistence gardener, and she showed me that plants have as much personality as animals. Unabridged wildlife documentaries taught me that the harshness of nature is integral to its power and beauty. When I watched the lions at the zoo, I did not think of anthropomorphic cartoon characters, but remembered that female lions hunt in teams and help keep prey species strong and healthy by ensuring that only the fittest survive to reproduce. My parents instilled in me the most basic principles of conservation: clean up after yourself and don't be wasteful. Running errands with my dad, I clearly recall him muttering "No class" with disgust at other drivers who dropped litter out of their car windows.

I left behind a 15-year career as a music journalist when I became the associate editor in the publications division of the Los Angeles Zoo. Many of my colleagues were flabbergasted by this move, but my confidants knew that my fascination with nature had always equaled my appreciation of culture. Despite the primal drama of the music business (at least when I was a part of it), it is not (with very few exceptions) a matter of life and death. The arts enrich our lives, but our lives are only a tiny part of a much larger tapestry, and ultimately the truths revealed in that big picture proved more alluring. All art is storytelling, but the greatest story ever told is the universe unfolding around us. Carl Sagan in his landmark series *Cosmos* explained that "the nitrogen in our DNA, the calcium in our teeth, the iron in our blood, the carbon in our apple pies were made in the interiors of collapsing stars. We are made of star-stuff." That was even more intellectually thrilling to me than was the ending of the 1968 film adaptation of *Planet of the Apes*.

We look to the stars for evidence that we are not alone in the universe, but alien life exists all around and among us. Not in the form of little green men, but the organisms who share this planet with us—from enigmatic slime mold and predatory sundews to whales with their unfathomed depths of consciousness. Great naturalists are able to escape our human self-absorption, observe other living things, and try to understand the world from their perspectives. In so doing they reclaim a part of our souls that often withers within the constraints of civilization.

After pondering such issues for much of my adult life, and working to share some of these insights with zoo supporters for more than a decade, I was delighted to receive the manuscript of this novel as part of my freelance book editing gig. Over the course of my editorial discussions with Rosana DuMas, it became clear that we have much in common. In addition to our professional interests, we share a fondness for cats, John Fluevog shoes, and obscure plants, as well as a loathing of poor grammar. We entertain a similar wry interest in bureaucracy as man's pallid attempt to create a system that functions with the same impartial efficiency as nature. By the time this book was ready for publication, we discovered an even more remarkable connection—a biological one. Due to circumstances that neither of us fully understand, we were separated at birth. Rosana DuMas is the twin I never knew I had.

We grew up on opposite ends of the West Coast, she in San Diego and I in Seattle, and (as has often been cited in twin studies) led eerily parallel lives. I graduated from Brown University, where I designed my own concentration as she also did while attending Amherst College, one of the few other open curriculum colleges in the U.S. After graduating, I spent some time working at WFNX in Boston, while she returned to the West Coast and found work at KCUF, a now defunct pirate radio station that operated from a barge in San Francisco Bay. Eventually Rosana wound up employed at a small zoo in central California at around the same time that I was completing my Master's Degree and beginning my freelance writing career. By the time I found my editorial post at the Los Angeles Zoo, she had already written the first draft of this novel.

Unnatural Selection is the novel that I have never gotten around to

writing. In it, Rosana captures the confluences and collisions between culture and nature that are the essence of human existence and are so perfectly
reflected in the zoological garden.

Criticisms of zoos often revolve around issues of "freedom." Many
perceive life in the wild and life in captivity as diametric opposites. In reality,
animals in the wild are also confined. They live in habitat that only supports
certain numbers of different types of animals. Every day they live within the
statistical laws that dictate whether they will manage to kill another animal
to eat and survive, or whether another animal will kill them. They live with
parasites, pathogens, and poachers that circumscribe their lifespans. They
live with climate change and geological upheaval that shift the parameters
of survival. The wild is simply bounded by different kinds of barriers. Yet
people want to believe in "freedom" and wild animals symbolize whatever
that means to us, trapped as we are within the boundaries of social mores,
belief systems, and, of course, bureaucracy. Over the course of this who-
dunit, Rosana peruses this terrain with a warm irreverence and incisive
satirical edge that I have often felt (and possibly expressed after a few beers)
but have been unable to capture on paper, and for that I owe her a debt of
gratitude.

Sandy Masuo
Los Angeles, California
December 2015

"All animals are equal, but some animals are more equal than others."

–George Orwell, *Animal Farm*

1
The Body
October 15, 2002

Some claim that Southern California has no seasons. But that's not true. Seasons here may lack the meteorological melodrama that takes place over the course of a year in other parts of the country, but they surely do exist. Drenching rains of winter and spring bring flurries of vibrant wildflowers before the patiently desiccating heat of summer sets in, testing the drought tolerance of plants and animals. As summer wanes, the sycamores that whispered softly with lush new foliage in May start to hiss with the arid winds that whip through their crisping leaves. Autumn afternoons may still be toasty, but cooler nights give the morning air a brisk edge that clings after dawn.

For those less attuned to nature's calendar in the wealthy-ish semi-suburb of Santa Narcissa, populated by a disproportionate number of film technicians and animators, yard accessories proclaim the seasons. Animatronic Santas wave stiffly and giant inflatable snowmen swell to signal winter where no snow has drifted since the last glacier passed. Fiberglass, egg-laying bunnies studded with LED lights announce the arrival of spring, then go into garage estivation just as flurries of flags unfurl from May through July.

1

Fall is the domain of faux pumpkins, mock scarecrows, pneumatic skeletons, and instant cemeteries that materialize to herald Halloween.

The Styrofoam headstones were sprouting and the early morning air
was crisp when Randall Willem Wiley arrived at the Santa Narcissa Zoo
compost yard 22 minutes late. He was delayed by a stop in the administrative offices at the front entrance of the Zoo to find out how to obtain
the Zoo forms he would need to file in order to obtain the City forms that
were necessary for him to delay taking the annual "Violence in the Workplace" seminar that all Santa Narcissa City staff are required to complete.
The administrative assistant in the assistant general manager's office lightly
chastised him before presenting him with a copy of the official memo, issued
earlier in the month, that outlined in explicit detail the new procedure for
rescheduling compulsory workshop attendance.

The intricate cotillion of paperwork that unfolded every day in administration generally left Wiley cranky and dyspeptic, but today for some
reason (possibly the snappy autumnal vibe in the air) he was wryly amused.
Driving his battered green truck up to the compost yard, he had a vision of
all the memos he had ever received—an immense column of paper stretch-
ing back in time. It was probably identical to generations of memos before
them, like layers in an archaeological dig site. What had the first memo
looked like anyhow? Was it some Roman dictum on papyrus or a papal
bull on vellum? Did the ancient Egyptians have a hieroglyph for "RE:" he
wondered as the truck sputtered up the hill. He chuckled when it occurred
to him that Moses had probably delivered mankind's first memo when he
presented the Israelites with those stone tablets. Ah, if only they'd had carbon copies back then human history might have been very different. Still
grinning, he parked outside the dingy double-wide that masqueraded as the
compost yard "administrative office" and went inside to brew a pot of coffee. While the machine gurgled and steamed, he started sifting through the
paperwork and mail that had accumulated while he'd been out on vacation.

As the only staff member left in the composting division, there simply
wasn't time to do everything, so his morning ritual was to prepare the cof-

fee and perform triage—cull the critical paperwork and let the rest return to the recycling circle of life. The aroma of French roast expanded to fill the room, and Wiley inhaled deeply. At fifty-something (and several years away from early retirement) he was still holding steady. Relatively clean living had left him well-preserved and in good health. He had most of his hair and only enough gray in his beard to give him an air of rugged wisdom. There were occasional bouts of gout and an enlarged prostate, but aside from that he had few complaints. Over the years, his bad habits had dropped away one by one. Coffee was the only vice he had left and it was like a holy sacrament to him. But this morning something was askew. There was an odd olfactory note in the air.

He went to the coffee maker, which had completed its task, and inspected the grounds in the basket. Nothing amiss. Up close, the contents of the carafe smelled normal. He looked in the wastebasket next to the table and found nothing but paper towels and yesterday's grounds. Sniffing intently, he went to the middle of the tiny office. There it was again. Something unpleasantly sweet. Something spoiled. Something wrong. Two years earlier, a rat had expired somewhere in the ventilation system, out of reach of the custodial staff or any helpful scavenging critters. For weeks, the aroma of decomposing rodent had permeated the office until an enterprising construction staffer discovered vintage building schematics with a diagram that showed how to access the ancient duct. This was like the ghost of that odor seeping in from somewhere distant. Wiley went to the screen door and found the smell ever so slightly stronger. He stepped outside.

A dry, fitful breeze carried the scent in from somewhere in the compost yard itself. Wiley made his way up the hill systematically inspecting the huge mounds of compost. Though animal dung was a vital part of the mix, which was mostly plant matter, only herbivore waste could be composted and even the most pungent camel, kudu, or okapi droppings lacked the taint of rotting flesh. He eventually found a massive, fairly new pile of leaf litter that seemed to be the source. Grasping a nearby pitchfork, he turned over a few forkfuls. It was the third that revealed a discolored human hand.

A wave of queasiness welled up in Wiley's gut and he staggered backward muttering a few choice expletives before running back to the office to phone security. He hated cell phones and refused to buy one for work. The City would not compensate him, and it wouldn't have made much of a difference in any case, since only patches of the Zoo had coverage.

It took close to an hour before anyone arrived. Calls made from the phone in the compost office, for some reason that baffled every IT technician who'd examined it, would only connect to the voicemail of other Zoo extensions without actually ringing, so Wiley had grown accustomed to leaving messages and waiting for responses until the recipients got around to checking them. He had submitted a request for a radio months earlier, but since he was the only person remaining in his division, and was prohibited from acting as his own supervisor in order to approve it, he was still waiting for the powers that be to inform him of the proper procedure for requisitioning one.

A pair of security guards eventually arrived, confirmed that the hand did in fact belong to a deceased human being, radioed for the police, and then instructed Wiley to report to administration. There would be paperwork to complete.

Miles Patagonia had been the director of the Santa Narcissa Zoo for about eight years, and in that time led the staff through more than a few dire straits, but this suspicious death had come at an exceptionally bad time. The Zoo was up for renewal of its accreditation by the National Association of Zoological Parks and Aquariums (NAZPA), which meant about two weeks of intense scrutiny by the Accreditation Committee. A group of five zoo directors and five accountants would evaluate animal care, education, accounting, communications, human resources, information technology, grounds maintenance, horticulture, security, and concessions, then issue a report several months later. On the heels of the NAZPA inspection, a group of dignitaries from China would be arriving to inspect the facility as part of the lengthy negotiation process for the Zoo to eventually receive a pair of giant pandas.

The Chinese government retains ownership of all giant pandas on loan around the world, and charges roughly a million dollars annually per pair, with the money going toward conservation of the country's endangered, endemic flagship species. Since pandas are such a rare and valuable commodity, before any foreign facility can even be considered for a loan, it must meet a number of rigorous qualifications, and in most cases prove itself worthy by first demonstrating the ability to keep and care for a trial species such as golden monkeys. So the Santa Narcissa Zoo had invested heavily in a new exhibit space for golden monkeys, in hopes of a panda return on it.

Additionally, animal rights activists had been increasing their pressure on the Zoo to release its polar bear to an Alaskan animal sanctuary. Though the Zoo had grappled with many such groups in the past, the persistent leader of the pack was Defenders of Animals, aka DofA. (Due to a premature approval of the documents for incorporating the nonprofit, the official name was registered before the board of directors realized its unfortunate acronym. Since they did not want to be recognized as DOA, they filed an addendum that stipulated the official acronym as DofA and hired a part-time publicist whose only responsibility was to monitor media for correct acronym usage.) The group, which was campaigning to have all zoos release their polar bears to sanctuaries, had found fresh vigor in its new leader, Peter Manley, a former actor and game show host turned animal advocate.

Complicating matters was the three-year-long hiring freeze implemented by the mayor. As a City facility, the Zoo had to apply for special dispensation to bring in any new employees, so the staff roster had been dwindling, schedules had been tightening, and the stress levels gradually increasing for the past few months. The police investigation was moving forward amid all this, but not as quickly or efficiently as Patagonia would have liked—which is why he had his executive administrative assistant have the assistant general operations manager's administrative assistant phone me. It seems the volunteer office director, a long lost friend of mine, had suggested to him that I might be able to offer some insights on the case.

It had been years since I last set foot in the Santa Narcissa Zoo, and frankly I hadn't missed it. My days as a volunteer and part-time research assistant were long gone, but no matter how assertively I tried to deny the request to come in and take a look at the situation, the assistant general operations manager's administrative assistant kept insisting that my unique background would be invaluable. It was the training I'd also had as a private investigator that doomed me. Between my knowledge of the Zoo and my experience as a PI, the director was convinced that I'd be able to shed light on recent events. My trump card was that my PI license had expired, but I was assured that that was not an issue. Finally, I got off the phone, my ability to politely argue exhausted, but only after I was locked into an appointment to be at the assistant general operations manager's office at 8 a.m. the next day.

2
The Hand

October 30, 2002

I had been instructed to see the assistant general operations manager about visitor credentials and parking. But in order to see him, I had to go through his administrative assistant, Ingrid Handy, also known as the Hand, who had been working at the Zoo for several decades and was something of an institution within the institution. She possessed an encyclopedic knowledge of the inner workings of the System, a relentless attention to detail, an icy calm under the most stressful circumstances, and fierce loyalty to her immediate supervisor. Even the most powerful personages in the Zoo and City government lived in fear of being stopped by the Hand, who could detect paperwork anomalies with all the fervor and accuracy of those specially trained dogs who can literally sniff out melanomas. In all the time I had worked at the Zoo I had never had to tangle with the upper levels of administration, so my familiarity with the Hand was limited to brief phone contact and word of mouth.

Rather than the Teutonic Valkyrie I had been expecting, she was, surprisingly, a Weeble-like woman, small and ovoid with an expression of grim serenity on her round brown face, accentuated by straight mahogany-colored hair that curved gently on either side of her head like parentheses. She handed me my official visitor pass and moved to block my progress to the inner office with speed and agility that were quite shocking. She was a blur of daisy print forming a human force field.

"Miles Patagonia's assistant sent me to see the assistant general operations manager."

"You don't have an appointment."

"I thought this was my appointment."

"No. This is when you pick up your credentials."

"Don't I need some kind of briefing?"

"I don't know. I was only asked to provide you with the visitor pass."

"Then I can't see him?"

She slowly, firmly shook her head once, left to right.

"You need to set up an appointment."

"With you?"

"Yes."

"All right then. How soon can I see him?"

"He's out of town."

"Oh. When will he be back?"

"Next week."

There was a long pause during which we faced off like Old West gunslingers.

"Can I make the appointment for next week then?"

"I'll have to check his schedule when he comes back."

"OK then. Do you think—"

"Where did you park?"

This twist threw me.

"In the lot."

She clucked at me. "I mean, which one?"

"The one in front of the Zoo."

Touché, I thought, but then what I assumed was a sigh of resignation turned into an expository tsunami.

"Oh. Well, that's OK for today, but if you're planning on being back here often, you'll want to park behind the administration building, which is usually something only senior staff can do (unless you are handicapped or pregnant) but since the parking lot repairs have closed off the area in the main lot that used to be reserved for special permit parking (which you normally have to request at least 30 days in advance, but since these are special circumstances I can probably expedite it), we've been having to issue temporary special permit parking passes for parking behind administration, but if you want to come back within the next week, then I'll have to issue you a short-term employee lot pass because it will take at least five business days for the temporary special permit parking pass to park behind the building to be authorized, so in the meantime, I'll give you a short-term employee parking lot validation card that you have to display on the dashboard of your car at all times because if the security officers see you parked anywhere but the general public parking lot without any pass at all, they will give you a citation that will cost you $85 and count as a regular municipal parking violation—in case that's a problem because of any outstanding parking tickets you might have."

I was with her until roughly the 30-day advance request for the special permit parking pass that would have allowed me to park in the regular special permit parking section that was currently closed off due to parking lot repairs, and then my mind balked. There was a fleeting moment of mental vertigo, but then I caught hold of "anywhere but the general public parking lot."

"Why don't I just park in the general public parking lot?"

"Why would you want to do that?"

"Because I don't mind the walk."

In a car town like Santa Narcissa, you are what you drive, and every time you cruise down the highway, you broadcast your social class, attitude about the environment, and sexual status—plus any more explicit opinions you may choose to express with bumper stickers, flags, vanity plates, or other accoutrements. Where you park is almost as important as what you drive—it's an analog for your station in life.

Once during the peak of my private detecting career, I had been hired by the wife of a mid-level media mogul. He had suddenly upgraded his car from a high-end Volvo to a starter Lexus, and, suspecting that gambling was the money source for the new car, she wanted me to follow him. After several weeks, I could find no evidence of gambling or any other untoward behavior. Finally, one afternoon after his gym workout I tailed him and his exercise buddy to an upscale coffee shop and managed to score the booth adjacent to theirs where I was able to eavesdrop with ease by nursing an enormous cup of overpriced drip coffee and writing in my "journal" with great concentration.

The demi-mogul spent about an hour explaining the burgeoning inferiority complex he was developing because one of his subordinates had been assigned a parking space that was not only closer to the office building than his, but was also a full ten inches wider. "Ten inches!" I remember him exclaiming loudly enough to make heads turn. Obviously, he said, his voice catching, this indicated a lack of confidence in him on the part of management. The new car was an attempt to stake his claim and prove to management that he was prepared to take the initiative of leaving Volvo behind and stepping up to Lexus. Choosing a low-end Lexus showed that he was not overconfident. Paranoid about his new luxury car payments, he had been cranking up the amount of overtime hours he was racking up to demonstrate his commitment to the company and value as a team member.

So telling the Hand that I was perfectly comfortable parking my Toyota Tercel in the main lot was clearly suspect.

"Oh," she said looking at me askance. "Whatever."

It was a draw. I made an appointment to talk to the Hand the following week about whether I needed to schedule an appointment to see the assistant general operations manager upon his return, and then the Hand took me to security, which was holding photos of the body for me.

The cinderblock hut that housed the security staff had all the charm and detail of a Lego building. Just inside the door was a "waiting area" furnished with two folding chairs and a plastic table equipped with a five-year-old issue of *Fly Fishing* and last week's *Santa Narcissa Mirror* Sunday edition. A weary, rotund woman in a form-fitting flesh-colored tank top and peach leggings that, unless you were looking directly at her, created the uncomfortable impression that she was nude, sat in one chair ignoring a preschool-ish aged child (presumably hers) who was wailing and intermittently grasping at her legs and arms. Two oscillating fans at opposite corners of the work area behind the counter created a rhythmic rustling of papers as they skimmed the desks. A towering hulk of a man encased in a snug bicycle cop uniform was behind the counter, a phone clamped between his shoulder and the side of his head. His dermabraded face wore an expression of pained concentration as he jotted down a long series of numbers and letters, repeating them into the phone one by one. After a hearty chuckle and a thank you, he hung up the phone, then turned to where the Hand and I were standing. Flashing the preternaturally white smile of someone who has invested heavily in dental bleaching, he leaned up against the counter and folded his arms, causing the stretchy shirt sleeves of his uniform to strain over his beefy biceps.

"Why hello Ingrid, and who have we here?" he boomed, and all at once the repressed memories came back to me. He had once been the security shack centurion, and every time I arrived at the Zoo I had had to sign in with him. He had a portfolio of pick-up lines that he rotated like the cafeteria menu at a hospital: Monday was "It's a fine morning now that you're here!" Tuesday was "What's a beautiful girl like you doing in a place like this?" Wednesday was the wildcard fashion compliment. Thursday was "Whew... did we just have a little heat wave or is it you?" Friday was "Welcome to work! What can I do you for?" At the time I left the Zoo he had been working on his third divorce and was furiously rebounding, though I began to suspect that he was in a perpetual state of rebound. I cringed inside as I grasped his meaty outstretched hand.

"Sandy Lohm, meet Phil Pinata," the Hand answered as he gripped me in a too warm, too firm handshake. "She's a private investigator."

"Really?" he said with an uncalled for glint in his eye. "Say, you look very familiar. Have we met before?"

Cursing the impulse to be honest, I answered, "Um, yeah. I used to work here. And volunteer. A while back."

"I see," he said, finally releasing my hand and giving me a once over. Thankfully, before he could launch any more clichés, the Hand intervened.

"She's looking into the recent *incident*," she said, raising her eyebrows at the last word. The screaming waif had exhausted herself and in the blaring silence, the depleted mom's gaze was following our conversation. With a complicit nod of her head in the direction of mother and child, the Hand discreetly indicated that we should avoid any mention of death. Pinata turned to her and smiled knowingly.

"Ah, yes: the *incident*," he said with a wink.

"So could you please get the files for her?" the Hand asked.

There was a pause while he added two and two.

"Indeedy-do," he grinned. "Coming right up!"

And with a squeak of his rubber-soled shoes he disappeared into a back room on the other side of a two-way mirror. There was a low murmuring of male voices and moments later he returned with a manila folder, which he handed to me in such a way that his fingers brushed mine during the handoff. I twitched a smile at him and opened the folder.

For about a year, the Zoo had been grappling with the Sniper—someone with a background in graphics and sign fabrication and a grudge against the Zoo. The local news media would use the Sniper's latest antics as filler when space allowed, but the only information revealed by Zoo administration was that the perpetrator had been sneaking in and defacing signs with "snipes," corrections or changes that are inserted after a sign or banner has been fabricated. Occasionally, a source would leak the latest species targeted by the Sniper. In the grand scheme of things, it was a minor annoyance, but no matter how vigilantly Zoo staff sought the Sniper, he or she kept eluding them. The media eventually began prowling the Zoo in hopes of glimpsing new handiwork before it could be removed. The folder contained full-color photos taken by Zoo security of all the attacks so far. On top was a before and after picture of the latest victims—the koalas. The bottom line of the sign outside their exhibit had originally read, "The newborn koala joey is blind, hairless, and roughly the size of a kidney bean." The Sniper had created a snipe that exactly matched the lettering and background, and had carefully affixed it to the sign so that it now seamlessly read, "The newborn koala joey is blind, hairless, and tasty, too!"

I could feel the Hand and Phil scrutinizing me as I snorted and coughed to cover my inappropriate laughter, when a second security officer (the bleached blonde beach boy counterpart to Phil, complete with puka lei and enhanced tan) appeared from the back office with another manila folder.

"Dude," he said, whacking Phil on the back and handing him the folder. "These are the pictures of the dead guy."

Phil, the Hand, and I all slowly turned to the waiting area where the mother and child were impassively watching us. The woman suddenly muttered something in what sounded like cranky Slavic, grabbed the girl's hand, and dragged her out of the office. With a shrug, Phil exchanged folders with me (sans contact this time). I took a quick glance, saw the bloating ghost of an older man's face half buried in soil and leaf litter, knew that I now (unfortunately) had the correct folder, thanked Phil and the Hand, then headed out the door.

At home, I got a beer to fortify myself, then cleared my coffee table so I could spread out the contents of the Claude Hopper file.

Looking at the dead is always creepy—a reminder of the fate that awaits us all—but a dead body is basically so much meat. Personally I find the earthly remains less haunting than the vestiges of the lives left behind.

People surround themselves with artifacts that tell their life stories. Mementos acquired during travels, awards for work well done, curios that are valuable only because the person who gave them is cherished, dusty self-help books, obsessive collections of random items—thimbles, matchbooks, action figures, cars. I'd seen all sorts of scenarios. The fatalities I'd investigated were just more dramatic than the average adulterer or garden variety disability scam artist—accidental deaths that seem hardly accidental in homes with unsecured guns and abundant liquor, or at the end of lengthy medical files documenting chronic burns and broken bones.

The photos of Claude Hopper didn't offer much in the way of context. They were strictly shots of the body as it was found (no morgue shots): a stiffened hand in the leaf litter, then a shot of his grimacing face framed in leaves and grass clippings like a green man caught in the act of screaming. Then a shot of his body freed from the compost—the rumpled, dirty uniform clinging to him like a shroud, his arms and legs akimbo and his silent scream expression anchored to a crushed skull.

It's funny how a single detail can trigger a cascade of memories. Looking at his large gnarled hands, the fingers curling inward suddenly transported me back to the last set of crime scene photos I'd studied like this.

3

Family Ties

Possibly the most famous photo ever taken of primatologist Jane Goodall is a shot of her with a juvenile chimpanzee in Gombe, Tanzania. It was taken right around the time she made her landmark discoveries about chimpanzees' talent for making tools and penchant for eating meat. In the photo, Goodall is crouched on the ground with her hand stretched toward the youngster, who reaches out to her with an intelligent gaze and an inquisitive finger.

The first time I saw that image, as a precocious preadolescent, I thought of Michelangelo's famous image of God and Adam from the Sistine Chapel. Only instead of the stern, patriarchal deity bestowing the spark of life on the erstwhile mud puddle that would become mankind, the contact between Goodall and the chimp was the spark of interspecies communication, a gesture that symbolized *Homo sapiens* and *Pan troglodytes* bridging the slim 1.5-percent gap in our DNA blueprints. That was pretty much the beginning of my interest in anthropology and primatology. The end of my interest in the field came almost as suddenly and much more shockingly some 25 years later with a very different image of our cousins.

I'm not sure how much you know about chimpanzees. Probably your impressions are formed by the images we get through the media, which depicts chimps about as accurately as it depicts people. They are our closest living relatives in the animal world. Chimps are genetically more similar to us than they are to gorillas or orangutans. But the similarities go far beyond our genomes. Chimps live in societies that are every bit as complex and dynamic as those of humans. Which is why their lives in captivity were so awful for so long. Their genetic and physiological similarities to us made them test subjects for pharmaceuticals and surgical procedures. Many people have tried to raise them as if they were human children, and for several years they develop much as a human child would, but then adolescence sets in, just as it does for humans, and the adult chimpanzee is a very different animal. Innovative zoos have always tried to maintain chimp groups as naturally as possible, which means family groups with at least one adult male. Multi-male groups (as chimp societies are in the wild) are very challenging to manage, and few zoos keep groups that include more than one male. The average male chimp is more than five times stronger than an adult male human. Add to this the complicated political alliances and social intrigue that permeate chimp troops and you can have a recipe for disaster, as the Eustace Scrubb Zoo discovered.

For many years that zoo had been home to one of the largest chimp groups in the world—28 individuals including three sub-adult males and three adult males. An interesting facet of chimp society is that although there is an alpha male who presides over the group with all the authority of a commander in chief, it is frequently the secondary male who plays a significant role in the installation and support of the alpha.

Over a period of five years, a series of political alliances and conflicts had unfolded among the males. In a nutshell, it began when the long established alpha male, Franklin, lost his standing—a combination of simian faux pas among the males and loss of sexual status among the females. (Does that seem familiar?) However, it was Franklin's pal Harry who then ascended to alpha status, largely due to the support of Franklin, who, although he was no longer at the top of the social ladder was still well connected. It was something like primary presidential elections. It's a boon to the winning nominee if the loser concedes and then endorses his or her former opponent, thus presenting a united front against the opposition party.

This dynamic worked for a while. With Harry in power, Franklin still enjoyed lots of sex and solid social status. But then they had a falling out, which allowed the third adult male in the troop, Lyndon, to seize control. This was a volatile situation. Lyndon was insecure because he lacked the support of a good beta male. So he started to pal around with Harry, grooming him (literally) for what was basically a VP position. And as anyone who has been subjected to election year media coverage knows, it usually falls to the running mate to act as attack dog. This angered Franklin. Not only was it a violation of the alliance he'd clearly established with Harry, but it meant a significant drop in sexual activity. But then, Franklin and Harry reconciled. It was as if Harry suddenly recognized his friendship with Lyndon as a betrayal of Franklin, but rather than negotiate, he exhibited a classic case of transference and attacked Lyndon, as if he were the traitor. The other males, who had never developed as strong an alliance to Lyndon as they had to either Franklin or Harry, quickly joined in the attack. Part insurgence, part mafia hit, the assault took place sometime during the night. Shocked keepers discovered the gruesome aftermath in the morning.

It was a murder as grisly as any gangland slaying, and the report that the vets, keepers, and curator wrote up read like a crime scene investigation. Despite the most heroic efforts of the vets—nearly ten hours of treatment including some 200 stitches, Lyndon died. He had lost an eye, four toes, and two fingers. The lobe of one ear had been ripped off, he had suffered anal lacerations and been castrated. Piecing together the events of that night in as dispassionate a way as possible, the vets in their official report theorized that because the scrotum was still attached to the body, the testicles must have been extracted through precise incisions most likely made with teeth while he was restrained. Which implied that rather than being a spontaneous and volatile "crime of passion," this had been a deliberate and planned attack.

In the final analysis, the curator cited several examples of such murderous behavior that had been documented in wild chimp groups. I read in horrified fascination that this incident was in all likelihood not a result of captive conditions, but rather an indicator of normal social tensions that had tragically and unexpectedly escalated.

I found the report while searching for a file about climbing behavior in orangutans in the then-research director's office. Her administrative assistant had been out on maternity leave for more than a month, so the information flow had been slowing and I had a deadline to meet. When I asked the director about it for the umpteenth time in passing, she exasperatedly told me to go to her office and just grab it from her desk top. The chimp file was on her desk next to it, open. The report was on one side and a stack of 8-by-10 photos on the other. Reading the report was bad, yet as horrified as I was, I could not resist the urge to see the pictures. The top photo was a shot of the males grouped together, apparently relaxing with no signs of aggression. The Lyndon photos, before and after death, were next, and grisly as they were, I was prepared for them. It was the pictures of the night room that sent me over the edge. There was blood everywhere—smeared on the walls, pooled on the floor, spattered on the ceiling. The edge of one hammock had a desperate brownish red handprint on the edge. I was suddenly in the bathroom heaving into the toilet.

Under normal circumstances I am impervious to even the most graphic images (as long as the subjects are dead). But the death of Lyndon had a dramatic effect on me. All my life I had staunchly believed that man's inhumanity to man was a question of nurture over nature. It was a product of "civilization," and therefore could be cured because it was an artificial construct. Staring at the images of the irreparably maimed chimp and the bloodbath he had endured made me realize that the pathology was in fact part of our programming as a species. It had been coded into us long before we diverged from our chimp cousins on the old family tree.

I snuck back to the office, hoping no one had seen me snooping or heard me barfing, grabbed the orangutan file and carefully replaced the chimp file.

I tried to get the horrible images out of my head, and went back to business as usual—observations, analysis, insights, but it was as if a veil had been lifted and now when I watched our chimp group, I kept having unsettling visions of what really goes on in human society behind our fancy linguistic and behavioral subterfuge. What are the increasingly strident accusations during the final weeks of a presidential election if not an elaborate, abstracted form of shit flinging? (A gesture for which chimps are notorious.) Even watching normal, positive behaviors such as grooming and play began making me anxious and I found it more and more difficult to complete my observational research assignments. When I looked at the chimps, all I could think about was how the observational glass was really a mirror, and except for the fortuitous twist of DNA that provided us with opposable thumbs and hence the ability to build the great pyramids, the Gutenberg press, space ships, and nuclear bombs, we could just as easily be the research subjects.

Before a year had elapsed, I left the Zoo, the detective agency, and my volunteer post, and I never looked back. I downsized, temped, and eventually earned an Associate's degree in horticulture, which enabled me to find gainful employment at a small, private botanical garden. Plants, though they can be every bit as insidious, noxious, and manipulative as any primate, are at least reassuringly alien, and that was a comfort. I had chosen *The Day of the Triffids* over *Planet of the Apes*. So it was with trepidation that I found myself becoming enmeshed in the suspicious death of the Zoo docent.

4

Trick or Treat

October 31, 2002

The next day, I got up at the crack of dawn and went for a brisk walk. With the approach of Halloween, my route had become the customary horror show in varying degrees of scary. Almost every yard was decked out in its phantasmagoric finest with tombstones, gallows poles, humungous hairy spiders suspended in menacing rope webs, skeletons, scarecrows, zombies, and ghosts of many persuasions. But all was still and quiet—the calm before the storm. The sound effects, light shows, and banks of dry ice fog wouldn't start until dusk, when the mobs of trick-or-treaters hit the streets. Despite my aversion to groups of children, I confess that most years I lurk at a nearby coffee shop to watch the spectacle. I suspected I'd have too much on my mind for it this year.

When I got back to the house, I whipped up a three-egg cheese omelet while my trusty old stove-top espresso pot sputtered. Fueled with food and caffeine, I headed for the Zoo. My first interview would be with one Randall Willem Wiley, the unfortunate soul who'd discovered the body. The Hand told me he could be found at the compost yard.

Those who don't understand compost tend to think of it as stinky piles of rotting waste—which isn't the case. Composting is like cooking. It combines the best elements of science and artistry and when it's done well it is efficient, relatively odor-free (or rather stink-free), and imbued with the sort of spiritual wholesomeness that one imagines Tibetan monks achieve. Not everything can be composted (as with cooking, you need to start with quality ingredients) and the process takes time and attention. Temperatures and moisture content must be maintained within appropriate ranges, and proper timing, turning, shifting, and sifting are required before the rich and nourishing final product is ready to blanket a bed of plants.

The Santa Narcissa Zoo had been bold and assertive in establishing its composting program, and it was the template for many similar programs at zoos around the country. Not only did it reduce by about one third the amount of waste produced by the Zoo, but it also yielded enough high quality mulch to meet the Zoo's needs and then some. "Zoo Poo" was a hot commodity every spring during the Poopapalooza charitable auction, and it was snapped up cubic foot after cubic foot by eager area gardeners—generating extra revenue for education programs. Almost all the staff and volunteers knew the Zoo Poo saga and shared it with guests at every opportunity. It was one of the brightest feathers in the Zoo's cap. So it was a somewhat bitter irony that the murder victim had turned up in the compost, putting a grim twist on something that had always been a source of lucrative levity.

The compost yard was located on top of a hillside that commanded a spectacular view of the whole Zoo—a panorama that was almost worth a long, dusty hike up a winding dirt road. Almost. I had been there before, back in my volunteer days and my memory of it was of huge, well-tended mounds of decomposing organic matter. Things had become a little less organized since then. Haphazard piles of used straw animal bedding, tree trimmings, leaf litter, and manure formed a lumpy and intermittently pungent swath around irregular humps of compost and the sifting apparatus that is used to separate the finished mulch into different grades. At the remote end of the yard was a small olive-drab portable structure (sort of a glorified double-wide) that was throbbing with the syncopated crunch of distorted guitars and a titanic rhythm section. I cautiously made my way around the dunes of debris toward the tumult. When I got near enough, I could hear, amid the musical din, the sound of someone cursing. I approached the screen door and through the gray, frayed mesh I could see a bearish man crouched at a desk. The computer screen in front of him glowed with a paralyzed progress bar. He stopped cursing and bowed his head. I waited for the gap between songs and knocked. He turned, cut the music off, and came to the door.

"Yes?" Polite curiosity replaced the angst, though he was still gripping a pen in his hand as if it were a stiletto.

"Hello. Are you Randy?"

"No," he replied with a bemused glimmer in his eye. "But that could change. Who are you?"

"Hi. My name is Sandy Lohm and I'm investigating the death of the docent—Claude Hopper," I began with what I intended as a disarming smile. "I was hoping to ask you a few questions. If this isn't a bad time."

"Oh," he said, the mirthful moment dissipating. "Sure, that's fine."

He opened the whiny screen door for me. "Call me Wiley."

The weathered wooden desk behind him was a miniature analog of the yard outside with mounds of papers gently merging into one another. A space had been cleared in front of the computer terminal, like a staging area, where the desk lamp illuminated what appeared to be several stacks of receipts and an array of forms that were an urgent goldenrod color. Gutted on the floor lay a large gray inter-office envelope that looked like it had seen more miles than my 18-year-old Toyota.

"Have a seat," he said, gesturing toward a spare chair parked next to the desk. "Do you want some coffee?"

"That would be great," I replied, relieved that we would have the common ground of caffeine to start.

He grabbed a chipped mug with a faded Santa Narcissa Zoo logo on it and filled it from a fresh pot.

"Do you need milk or sugar?"

"No, black is fine," I answered and he promptly added a skosh more to the mug, set it down in front of me, then settled into the creaky wooden desk chair. "What would you like to know?"

Interviews are as varied and variable as their subjects, and the amount of information you glean from one has nothing to do with how pleasant or smoothly the exchange seems to go. I learned early on that unless the person I'm talking with is pathologically wigged out by the presence of a tape recorder, the best thing to do is record the conversation, which allows me to concentrate on extracting information and picking up clues from my subject's body language. Now that I'd established the coffee bond, I reached into my bag and pulled out my mini tape recorder. Wiley's brow furrowed.

"I hope you don't mind if I tape our conversation?"

"I guess not."

"It's just that taking notes isn't one of my strong points. This is the best way to get all the facts accurately."

"OK."

I could see him warming up to the idea. People often balk at first, then soften up when they feel the warm glow of the audio spotlight settling in.

"I understand you found the body?" I asked and set the recorder on the desk next to him with the tiny window on the cassette facing me so I could monitor it at a glance and make sure it was running. There's nothing quite like the heartbreak of realizing your tape recorder didn't catch a word of your epic conversation or the furtive revelations of a cagey witness.

"Yes."

"Could you tell me exactly what happened that morning?"

He described arriving at work, settling into the routine, making coffee, grappling with paperwork, mapping out how much he could realistically accomplish, then noticing an odd odor that he decided to investigate. After finding the body he had called for security and left a message.

"I'm sorry," I cautiously interrupted. "You left a message?"

"Yes," he said with an impatient sigh. "The phones have never worked properly up here. Calls don't actually ring through to other extensions.

They go directly to voicemail, so yeah, I left a message."

"I see," I said feeling the mild sense of absurdity I remembered about the place return. "And about what time was that?"

"Probably around 6:45. I was running late that morning because I had to stop in administration on my way up here. I'd been out for a week on vacation."

"Did you notice anything unusual before you discovered the body?"

"I had been on vacation. That was my first day back."

"What about before you went on vacation?"

"What do you mean?"

"You know, strangers on the premises, unusual activity, equipment out of place."

He looked at me with an expression of mild incredulity and laughed the edgy laugh that says, "Are you kidding me?" Then he took a sip of coffee out of a hefty blue mug decorated with dainty white flowers and replied in a measured tone, "There really wasn't time for me to notice anything odd. About once or twice a week I have a chance to get out there and try to manage the yard. I generally spend all my time filling out paperwork to get staff I can't have, or attending meetings that don't really pertain to me."

"I see," I answered with genuine empathy. During my tenure at the Zoo I had spent more than my fair share of time attempting to navigate the Byzantine proper channels that separate point A from point B. "So you run this program by yourself?"

"No, I don't," he answered tersely. "I barely keep it alive. I would need an actual staff to run it and I can't have that. Actually, I'd really rather have a boss who could run it so I could go back to being a gardener."

"But aren't you the Compost King?"

He cringed.

The composting program had been around for years, but when the manager who built it injured his back and went on disability leave, Wiley, who was technically, by title and job description a gardener, was tapped to fill in as an "interim" until they could start the City hiring process, something that even under the most ideal conditions often unfolds in a geological time frame. Then the hiring freeze went into effect, locking the situation into a holding pattern. Wiley had now been the interim compost program manager for three years. During that time, the staff had been whittled away by early retirement and transfers to other departments in the City until he was the only person left—full-time and still interim where originally he'd put in only a couple days a week as the Compost King and spent the rest of his time cultivating and maintaining the Zoo's diverse botanical collections.

The moniker had started as a joke when the composting staff of 12, affectionately known as the Dirty Dozen, had split their time between the Zoo Poo program and the horticulture division. He had always spoken of composting with a religious fervor, so they started calling him the Compost King. Then the marketing division jumped on the nickname and had the graphics division design a superhero cartoon character based on Wiley, to his everlasting chagrin. Every flier in the office that featured the cartoon Compost King had a big red circle/slash drawn onto it. Now he was saddled with it all—the alter ego, the program, everything.

"Can't they just promote you?" This was veering off topic, but I was getting sucked into the commiseration bonding that seemed to link everyone who had ever spent any significant amount of time working at the Zoo.

"No," he replied with a heavy sigh, as if he had explained this a few hundred times too often. "Technically I would have to spend at least six months as a gardener/horticulturist level three and another six months as a senior gardener/horticulturist before I could take over as manager. Which I don't really want anyhow since that basically means dealing with HR crap most of the time." He paused and added with a wry grin, "I'd rather deal with the actual crap."

"Or you could leave?"

"And sacrifice my retirement fund and benefits?" he asked, aghast. "Plus, I still live in hope that I'll get back to the gardens one of these days."

I nodded. Hope does indeed spring eternal in the human breast. "So did you know Claude Hopper at all?"

Wiley's expression soured. "Oh yeah."

"And you weren't fond of him?"

"No," he said sharply, then glanced at the tape recorder.

"Why?"

"He was too nosy for his own good."

"What do you mean?"

He hesitated for a moment.

"Well, he didn't snoop around here because he was mainly interested in the animals. He liked to pal around with the keepers so he could get behind the scenes and then show off how much he knew about everyone and their animals when he was taking special tour groups around. It used to drive Les nuts."

"Who's Les?"

"Les Moore. He's the bird keeper who's in charge of Raptorama. That's the closest exhibit to the compost yard. We sometimes have lunch and he's always complaining that Claude would sweet talk his way into getting back in the holding area, trying to convince everyone that because he used to be a master falconer a few decades ago he knows how to handle raptors. He does food prep, so that gets him into the keeper areas, but the only birds they're allowed to handle are the outreach animals—a cockatoo, a conure, a macaw, and a raven. I guess some of the keepers would give in and let him hang around with the raptors, but Les had a bad incident with a volunteer getting injured by a hawk once, so he's particularly touchy. And I think Claude just rubbed him the wrong way. I mean, I wasn't particularly fond of the guy, but once Les got going on a tear about Claude it was hard to clear the air."

"Interesting," I said, making a mental note to ask the volunteer programs director about Les Moore and Claude Hopper's history. "So aside from yourself, who else has access to this yard?"

"I have to open the gates in the morning. If I'm not here for a short time, like a day or two, then the green waste and manure basically sits in the bins behind the exhibits until I'm back—or sometimes they just dump it. Since I was out for a week, they sent a security guard with a master key up here to allow for a load to come in on Friday."

27

"So is there a regular schedule of waste delivery?"

"Yeah. Normally, there are two big trucks that make the daily rounds picking up waste from behind different exhibits and other green waste bins. They usually show up here before 10 a.m. Sometimes they come earlier."

"So the only load of green waste that came up here while you were away was on that Friday—October 11."

"That's what I said."

"How long would the gates be open?

"That I don't know. I assume it was just long enough to unload the compost. Maybe half an hour? Same as usual."

"Could someone have snuck in?"

"Carrying a body?"

"Yes."

He chuckled. "What, up the service road? In a sack? Like Santa?"

"No, of course not," I laughed in spite of myself. "Someone could have moved it in a cart or another vehicle."

"Yeah. That's possible. But the security officer is supposed to wait until the truck has been unloaded and then lock up again. So if there had been some suspicious character lurking around with a body, it would be a little tough to go unnoticed."

We sipped our coffee in silence for a few minutes. I could hear gibbons' piercing calls in the distance.

"Could someone have dumped the body into a green waste bin?"

"Yeah. I guess. Someone could have dumped him in a bin out in the Zoo. He wasn't buried too deeply. I had to move about three forks of plant matter before I saw his hand. I suppose he might have been in a bin and dumped here. That would explain why no one saw anyone deposit the body here."

"Are there any access points other than the main gate?"

"No. We had some problems with equipment being stolen, so they forti-fied the fencing and limited access to that gate," he explained, gesturing in the general direction of the yard entrance.

"Could you tell from the type of plant matter around him what area of the Zoo it might have come from?"

"Maybe. Not for sure, though. There's no way to know how tousled up it had been in the truck."

"If I bring you photos, could you have a look?"

He furrowed his brow. "Yeah, OK."

"And are you usually up here all day?"

"That's hard to say. It depends on what projects are going on with grounds maintenance or the special events division."

"So you were out of town until the day before you came into work and discovered the body on October 15."

"Yes. I have an alibi. I was on vacation from Tuesday the 8th until the evening of October 14, when I flew into SNX."

"Somewhere fun?"

"Yes. I was about 3,000 miles away from here, visiting family in Nova Scotia."

"Good," I chirped, trying to sound friendly and chipper. My least favorite part of questioning was having to remind people that they weren't beyond suspicion no matter how helpful they were being. I sipped the last of the coffee and stood up. "Well thanks for your time, and the coffee. I really appreciate it."

"No problem," he said, also standing.

"OK. So I'll try and bring those photos with me the next time I'm here," I said as matter-of-factly as possible.

"Sure," he said evenly, opening the screen door.

As I turned to start back through the yard and down the hill, the brazen guitars exploded in the trailer behind me.

The volunteer office director, Corinne Flaherty and I had been good friends during my tenure at the Zoo. She had a fine appreciation of the absurd that helped make even the direst straits seem amusing. Once upon a time she had been an animator with a flair for caricature. She had prevented many a dull staff meeting from becoming a mental embalming session with

29

hilarious doodles that lovingly lampooned our esteemed colleagues.

After my jarring primate epiphany and departure from the Zoo, I cut all my ties to the place, including my friendship with her, for which I'd never stopped feeling guilty.

Leaving the Zoo was like going through a bad breakup where I had to just turn away from it all. Corinne was part of the collateral damage.

My anxiety level grew with every step up the long stairwell that led to my past.

The Volunteer Office was nothing like I remembered it. For one thing, it had been moved to a new, opulent, ultra modern building all gleaming glass and metal on the periphery of campus. Before, it had been located in a dingy basement space in the administration building in the heart of the Zoo. The foyer where I waited to meet Corinne was bright and airy and offered an impressive view of the surrounding park.

Her assistant had pulled Claude's file for me and I studied it while I waited. In my day, all the information that was required from a volunteer would fit on a five-by-seven index card. In the years since I'd been away, it had evolved into a mass of forms with details about work experience, interests, references, evaluations, personal history, plus a card with an identification photo that looked like a passport mug shot.

In life, Claude had been a dapper fellow with twinkly blue eyes, wavy silver hair that had probably once been very dark brown, a square jaw, and, judging by his stats (6 feet-4 inches and 190 pounds), a stately presence. He had signed on as a docent just as I was making my exit from the Zoo. He was born in 1937 and graduated from Santa Narcissa High School in 1955, after which he studied biology at California State University Santa Narcissa, where he completed his Bachelor of Science degree (with honors) in 1959. In 1961, he got a job at Imperator Pharmaceuticals and moved to Texas. He worked there for 30 years as a lab technician and then a research supervisor before he took early retirement in 1991, when he was just 54 years old. (The prescription drug trade was very good to him.) He then returned to the Santa Narcissa area and began volunteering at the Zoo in 1992. It looked like he had dabbled in many avocations from falconry and fencing to freelance photography. There was a photocopy of a lengthy letter Claude had apparently written to Miles Patagonia at the beginning of the year on the tenth anniversary of his volunteer tenure at the Zoo. There were a couple news clippings about Imperator Pharmaceuticals and its development of Povenda, the diet wonder drug that about one in four Americans are now taking. As commonplace as it has become, there had apparently been some controversy during the clinical trials for it. I had just started reading the first clipping when Corinne arrived.

"Hey you," she said, brightening as she made her way across the room. Unlike the offices, she hadn't changed a bit. Tall and statuesque with wavy auburn hair and a bright smile, she conveyed an air of polished enthusiasm. I had seen her dealing with the thorniest personalities with the kind of composure that air traffic controllers have at Thanksgiving. She was wearing an oversized black and yellow striped sweater, black leggings, and a bobbing antennae headband that was conjoined with a rhinestone encrusted crown.

"It's been too long!"

I stood up, relieved that there seemed to be no ill will lingering, and found myself awkwardly trying to decide if a hug was called for. She solved the dilemma by embracing me quickly and putting a hand on my shoulder.

"Yes, it's good to see you," I replied, my gaze drifting to her head gear.

She grinned. "Halloween."

"I see."

"I'm a queen bee."

"I thought so."

"Let's go to my office," she said and led me across a huge room filled with milling fifty- and sixty-somethings in various color-coded uniforms. Several of them took notice of her and began drifting in our direction. She picked up the pace a bit so that we stayed ahead of them. Upon reaching her office she shut the door quickly and firmly behind us, then indicated the chairs opposite her desk and invited me to take a seat.

Glass walls on two sides offered a view of the park through the main room where the volunteers gathered, and opposite, a view of the courtyard below. The furniture was the kind that pretends to be Danish modern but is really mass-manufactured bland, yet what might have been an aseptic space was festooned with a curious array of items—personal photos of pets and family plus an assortment of what could only be party favors. A mound of colorful plastic leis lay entwined in one corner next to a box of tiny tiki idols grimacing in tight quarters and a large bag of grass skirts butted up against an arsenal of beach umbrellas.

"Pardon the luau accoutrements," she said, taking a seat behind her paper-strewn desk. "Our annual volunteer appreciation bash just happened and I am, for better or worse, the guardian of the party booty remainders."

"No problem."

"So how have you been?"

"Well, that's a long story."

"The Cliffs Notes version?"

I thought for a moment. It's always awkward when people you haven't seen in years want to know how things have been. My departure from the Zoo was abrupt and I had basically stopped returning calls from my Zoo friends after I left. She probably thought I'd had some kind of breakdown. Which was basically true.

"Good. I kind of had a premature midlife crisis and decided to change career tracks."

"So I gathered," she said with a genuine, cautious smile.

"Yeah. I wound up getting an Associate's degree in horticulture and I work at Holcomb Botanical Gardens now. I meant to get in touch again, but it was just hard. I was working through a lot of things in my head."

"Well, you can tell me more about it over a beer sometime," she replied and I was starting to feel a little choked up at the total lack of resentment I was sensing over my bad behavior.

"That'd be great."

"So how can I help you?"

"Do you mind if I tape our conversation?" I said and retrieved my tape recorder from my bag and flipped the cassette over. "It's easier for me to concentrate on what you're saying if I know I can go back and get the specifics later."

Her brow furrowed for an instant, but she nodded and smiled. "Go ahead."

I pressed play/record and plunged in. "Well, as you know I'm looking into the death of Claude Hopper."

"Of course! I was so happy that they took my advice and got a hold of you."

"I'm a little rusty at this—it's been a while, but I need a little background on him and I learned some interesting things from Randall Wiley."

"The Compost King?"

"Yeah."

"What do you want to know?"

"I see Claude had been volunteering here for ten years."

"Yes, he was practically an institution himself."

"Did you know him well?"

An odd tension rippled over her otherwise bright and forthcoming expression. "Well, he was one of our more—distinguished volunteers."

"Distinguished in what way?"

"Have you spoken with anyone else about Claude yet aside from Wiley?"

"No."

"Well, as much as he was a cherished member of the Zoo family, he was also kind of, um, challenging at times. Especially in recent years."

"What do you mean?"

"A lot of times people who have been volunteers here for long stretches of time become a little, shall we say, proprietary about the Zoo."

She seemed suddenly distracted and I realized that somebody was gesturing at her through the window behind me.

"I'm sorry. If you'll excuse me for a moment."

She slipped outside and I heard a murmuring of voices through the closed door. After a few minutes, she returned and drew the soft beige drapes behind me to shield the office from prying eyes.

"Sorry about that," she said and blew an errant strand of hair off her forehead. "I'm always on call here."

"This has all changed so much since I was here."

"Yes, the program has grown a lot. In some ways for the better. In some ways I'm not so sure."

"Did Claude adapt well?"

"Nice segue," she said with a grin. "Yes and no."

"You were saying that some of the veteran volunteers could be a bit proprietary?"

"Well, in addition to being a general volunteer, he also was a docent, and that made him even more privileged because education outreach is such a priority here. The public schools depend on us to augment their science curriculum now that the budgets have been whittled away so much, and we have to play that card to make sure we still get funding from the City."

"How was that a problem in terms of Claude?"

"Claude had a healthy sense of entitlement, and of course he had been a biochemist and research scientist. At times, he behaved as if he had staff privileges because he probably had more of a formal science background than a lot of the staff have. So that really rankled with some people. He had no difficulties dealing with boundaries. He never acknowledged that they were there. He could be very charming and persistent, and he was very enthusiastic about his responsibilities here. In fact he was even enthusiastic about responsibilities that weren't his."

"Yes, that's what Wiley mentioned."

She nodded emphatically, sending her antennae bobbling back and forth. "He had a tendency to be omnipresent, getting into areas where he shouldn't have been during events that were really intended for staff eyes only."

"Examples?"

A quiet tapping had started at the door.

"Do you need to get that?"

"Just ignore it."

"Some examples of Claude's over-enthusiasm?"

"OK. This is strictly confidential," she said, casting a wary glance at the tape recorder. "I mean, I'm telling you this in case it will help you investigate this case, but I hope it won't go any further than that."

The tapping had grown more urgent.

"I'm so sorry," she interrupted herself. "Will you excuse me again?"

"Sure," I answered, appreciating once again the fact that I work alone for the most part, and never have to manage anyone.

There was more murmuring outside the door. When she returned, she switched a "Do Not Disturb" sign from the inside doorknob to the outside where it faced the milling volunteers in the big room.

"It won't work for long, but it will repel them for a while," she said and sank into her chair.

"You were saying?"

"What was I saying?"

"Intrusive incidents with Claude."

"Oh yes."

Claude, it seemed, had a way with people. Despite all the clearly stated, liability-conscious rules about where volunteers were and were not allowed on Zoo grounds, Claude knew no boundaries. Suave and glib, he made his rounds every morning in an ever-crisp uniform (accented with a variety of non-regulation ascots) bidding each person he met a chipper "top of the morning." The trick, apparently, was to nip the greeting process in the bud, before it could blossom into a full-blown conversation. Corinne personally found that pretending to have a cell phone call worked well. She had a system worked out when she needed a rescue whereby she would discretely press the memory dial for her husband's office number, then hang up when he answered and he would know to phone her back right away so that she'd have an important call to take immediately.

Although he had indeed led a fascinating life, Claude was just a bit too eager to share his reminiscences, which were actually fairly interesting—the first time through. Adaptations in the animal world were a favorite topic of his when lecturing school groups, however, Claude was not terribly adept at improvising his tales and so he tended to repeat them with the unerring faithfulness of a DVD player. Corinne had begun to suspect that the real reason he was so invasive was not because he talked his way into restricted areas, but that people were trying to avoid talking with him by simply letting him go where he wished.

Most recently he had used this dubious gift of gab to slip into an authorized personnel-only area during the necropsy of one of the Zoo's best loved gorillas. Though he had only hovered unobtrusively, the point was (as the chief veterinarian emphasized rather stridently at a subsequent senior staff meeting) that he might have been exposed to pathogens, or been injured, or injured someone else inadvertently, or distracted the veterinary personnel from their work. This was perhaps the most egregious incident, but over the many years he'd been at the Zoo, he had sweet-talked his way into exhibits and holding areas, behind security lines and caution tape, next to bodyguards, and into motorcades and photo ops.

"Why didn't you just ask him to leave?"

Her eyebrows made two emphatic arches.

"Are you kidding? He'd been here longer than any of the Zoo directors had. Like I said, I would have if I could have, but many donors loved him. He was really a heartthrob to many of the older ladies and he golfed with all the men. The only people who didn't seem overly fond of him were actual Zoo staff."

Ah, the irony, I thought.

"And then there was the money."

"Money?"

"Yes, he probably donated a few thousand a year."

"So he was well off."

"Yes, I'd say very well off."

"How did he come by it?"

"Well, he was one of the lead researchers behind Povenda. And that seemed to be a healthy enough cash cow for him to retire early."

36

"I saw the articles in his file, but didn't see his name."

"He might not be mentioned by name, but it was his baby. He was very proud of it. That's why the articles are in there. He submitted them along with his application to become a docent. His running joke was that America's weight loss was the Zoo's great gain."

"Clever," I said as our eyes met with the same incredulous expression and we laughed. "He must have made a mint. You know money is the root of all evil—and lots of murders."

"Yes. But he shared that wealth, which was really his saving grace. He was incredibly generous, and over the years he stepped up to pay for all kinds of incidental needs—a new refrigerator for the commissary, video recording equipment for monitoring nocturnal animal activity, a van for the outreach staff who visit schools. And people generally did appreciate what he did."

"But not everyone."

There was a somber pause.

"No. Not everyone."

"So who benefits monetarily from his death?"

"That I'm not really sure about. You would have to find out if he left a will. I can't imagine he wouldn't have."

"Who would have wanted him dead?"

"Well, between the money and the nosiness and his kind of know-it-all attitude, he was good at stepping on toes. But just because someone is annoying you don't go and kill them."

"Most of the time. Do you know if Les Moore ever filed any complaints?"

"Les Moore?"

"Yes. Wiley said that Claude was particularly effective in rubbing him the wrong way."

"I'd say that's an understatement. There were several Raptorama incidents where Claude had schmoozed his way behind the scenes, and that was not good. He had actually been a falconer once upon a time, but that was no excuse. And then there was the luau incident," she said and looked down at her desk blotter.

"Luau incident?"

"Well, I had to go out of town unexpectedly because my husband's father had taken ill, and I left Marti in charge of the final arrangements for the volunteer appreciation dinner. She's pretty new and it slipped my mind to mention that she should under no circumstances seat Claude and Les anywhere near each other. They had each filed complaints about one another, but those are only accessible by senior management. You know, confidentiality and all that. So she had no idea that they can't stand each other and thought they might have a lot to chat about. Oy."

"And what happened?"

"I had just gotten home the morning of the dinner, and when I got to the event, I was busy with the certificates that were being awarded and all of a sudden I heard raised voices. And there were Les and Claude at the same table shouting at each other. I managed to diffuse the situation by enlisting Claude to help hand out awards, and I tried to make nice with Les and told him to go get a sundae."

"What?"

"There was a sundae bar for dessert, and he's got a terrible sweet tooth, so I thought that would be a good diversion. I really wanted him to stay for the slideshow finale because it included some really amazing photos from Raptorama, but the next thing I knew, Les came up to find Claude at the side of the stage, called him a son of a bitch, and belted him."

"Really?"

"Yes."

"How come Les is still at work? Isn't that an assault charge in the making?"

"Well, it wasn't much of an assault. Les tried to hit Claude from across the table with all the service pins and certificates on it, so he couldn't really work up much force. His punch kind of missed the mark, and he mostly scraped up his knuckles on Claude's name badge. And you know how civil service is. To be suspended, he would have to have attacked Claude during business hours, on Zoo grounds, in front of children, while sober, sane, and naked. I think he did get written up because someone reported it to security, but Claude refused to file any charges or even a complaint."

"Why? After all that one-upmanship in the complaint department?"

"Beats me. He claimed he was big enough to overlook the incident."

"Could I talk to Les about it do you think?"

"You could try," she said doubtfully.

There was a scuffing sound at the door and then a muffled "Cora? Cora?" began seeping in like a draft.

"You know, I really have to go and tend them," she said with a conciliatory smile.

"Sure thing," I answered, once again glad for a job that is mostly all solitude. "I'll leave my card. If you think of anything, call me," I paused. "Or call me anyway."

She smiled. "Sure."

I went back to administration and made arrangements to meet with Les Moore. He was off on Fridays and Saturdays, and the best time to find him at Raptorama would be later in the day after the last of the raptor shows.

5

The Post-It Girl

When I got home, my neighbor Trudy was having a little get-together on her porch. I had to go past the party to get to my guesthouse out back, so when she spotted me and waved, I altered course to stop in. There was time for a beer, which would make transcribing Wiley and Corinne less tedious. Trudy is maybe ten or so years older than I am—fifty-something but spry and athletic. Her girlfriend, Bess, is a good ten years younger than I am, which makes them a classic Hollywood couple, though neither of them is involved in Hollywood. Trudy is a union attorney and Bess teaches special needs kids. I am always a little apprehensive about their get-togethers because they're often dominated by Bess's young gal pals, most of whom have grown up in an era when it's titillatingly cool (at least on prime time television) if not entirely acceptable to be lesbian, and a couple of them are always very flirty with me, which makes me uneasy. Not because they are women, but because they are young and kind of fresh, and I am weary of that game.

The man of my dreams crossed paths with me relatively early in life and I had many blissful years with him. He was handsome and funny and the passions we shared for such hopelessly arcane things as Holy Land ephemera and Turkmen rugs sealed our fate together. We didn't finish each other's sentences because we were always thinking the same thing and much of the time never needed to speak. He was the kind of person with whom I could feel perfectly comfortable sitting in a silent room. For a loner like me the highest compliment I can offer is that being with you makes me feel like I'm by myself, only with company. We spent most of our non-working time together but never married because we both needed lots of personal space, and because I never put much stock in marriage. I'm not one of those women who grew up with a fantasy wedding in mind, and I never liked children much even when I was one. I had settled into a solitary and stable, if slightly bitter, existence when he came along and jarred me to life. I wasn't unhappy before I met him, but the way I felt with him made the whole world somehow less annoying and more beautiful. Even after he was gone, and I went through the whole grieving process, the lasting gift he left me was that sense of joy.

Eventually he finished his doctorate in Egyptology and almost immediately found a post at a university in Australia. There was a horrible, agonizing time while we both got used to the idea of being apart. He warned me that once he left we'd probably never be in touch. It was just his way, and I understood that. The options were simple: go with him or let him go. And I chose to let him go. I guess I was afraid of the unknown, or commitment, or being uprooted. And of course, I had been glibly reminded so many times about the preponderance of fish in the sea.

I'm also not one of those hopeless romantics who believes in fate or destiny. Or at least I didn't think I was. After he left, time passed, and then some more time passed. I kept thinking about the laws of probability and how many men there must be out there who could fill that void in my life. I went to parties and concerts and conventions and weddings and funerals. And none of these hypothetical men showed up. I honestly don't know what makes me feel more bitter—having lost him or being wrong about the laws of probability.

I looked him up on the Internet not that long ago. He is still at the same university, now as a full professor. I emailed him and we had a cordial correspondence for a while. He's not married either, but he mentioned a girlfriend more than once. I don't remember who sent the last message. I guess we kind of trailed off like when a film fades to black. So I have had a while to re-evaluate probability. I still believe in it, but what I concluded is that probability determines your fate. I don't play the lottery because I know how the numbers work, and they always favor the house. And if I had appreciated the scale of the bet and the wispy thin odds of ever loving someone that way again, I'd be gazing up at a different set of constellations and driving on the left.

Despite all the pep talks that well-meaning people (including Trudy) offered periodically, I retreated into my own life, which seems to bother other people more than it bothers me. Although Bess had told her flirty friends that I like boys and being alone (not always in that order), they ignored the info thinking (with their youthful enthusiasm) that maybe it's not that I'm solitary but that I haven't found the right gal. So, after greeting Trudy and grabbing a beer from the cooler I spent a few minutes chatting with a winsome, olive-complected brunette who had the type of lovely androgynous features that I always imagine elves, angels, and other creatures who have transcended gender must bear. I felt dusty and cumbersome as we discussed water conservation and she twinkled at me, occasionally touching my arm to emphasize a point. It made me wish I could be interested in her. Then Bess joined the conversation and broke the tension, asking me about what I'd been up to.

"Well, I'm detecting again."

"No kidding? That's great!"

"Yeah. Kind of."

"How come 'kind of?'"

"Eh. I've kind of moved on."

"Why are you kind of on the case then?

"It's a favor. Kind of. An old friend at the Zoo recommended me for an

43

incident they had there."

"Is it The Sniper?" she asked brightly, holding up that day's *Santa Narcissa Mirror*, which featured the latest attack: this time the double-wattled cassowary.

"No, no. More serious."

"A murder?"

"Well, that's what I'm supposed to determine."

"What happened?" Trudy joined in.

"One of the docents was found dead."

"That's awful."

"Yeah."

"Any idea what happened?"

"It looks like it was blunt force trauma, and the body was dumped in the compost yard."

"Ew," Bess wrinkled her nose.

"Well, you know the compost is just plant matter breaking down. It's not like sewage or anything." They had heard my compost sermon more than once and were both nodding emphatically. I spared them. "The body wasn't too far gone."

"Did you have to look at it?" Trudy asked with rapt revulsion.

"Oh, no. I saw photos. They'll probably send me the coroner's report when it's ready. I hope."

"Well, what's that rule about the last person to see the dead person alive is the best suspect?" Bess suggested perkily.

"Well, yeah. But that's like saying when you find a lost item it's always in the last place you look."

"Oh."

"I think what you're thinking of is that the first person to report the dead person dead is the best suspect," Trudy offered. Bess and I both looked at her.

"Why?"

"I don't know."

We nodded, affirming the inconclusiveness.

When my beer was gone, I politely declined a second bottle and head-ed home. My cozy little house (the "granny shack") was built in the 1920s and has the type of details that no one puts into homes anymore without a smarmy, self-conscious "retro" attitude. There are numerous problems with it, but none of them are so awful that I'd give up the warm charm for cold modern convenience. I have no effective heat. There's a small floor heater but it only really heats one corner of the living room so I keep a portable radiator in the bedroom and a space heater in the bathroom. These old Southern California buildings rarely have any insulation, so even if I did have more effec-tive heat it would just dissipate anyway. It's a minor problem considering that there are only a couple months of really cold weather (nighttime lows in the 40s with a potential dip into the upper 30s), and in the Midwest or Northeast you'd die of hypothermia during a winter in my house. The plumbing is also temperamental. After hours and hours of systematic experimentation I figured out how to adjust the water temperature in the shower and became acclimat-ed to the splashy kitchen sink since the water only becomes warm if you turn the tap on all the way. But I love it none the less... the hardwood floors and crown molding, the decorative faux fireplace (no actual flue) with ornamental tiles, the creaky valence windows and secret cupboards designed to conceal spices and an ironing board.

After making myself some tuna salad and crackers under the watch-ful gaze of my cat, Henry, I set out a dish of tuna water for him. When he had lapped it up, he sat in front of me and meowed the meow that indicates it's now time for me to pick him up. I had gotten him ten years earlier at one of those kitten adoptions that they have at pet supply stores. He was in a big cage with several other kittens, sitting in a corner, singing in a tiny raspy voice that would later mature into a semi-Siamese yowl. The other kittens were all sitting as far away from him as possible. It was love at first sight. He's orca patterned with amber eyes that are beautiful though slight-ly crossed. At least once a day, he insists on being picked up and carried around for a tour of the apartment so that he can survey his realm from a better perspective. Once we had circulated through all the rooms, a toilet paper tube snagged his attention, and that was my cue to put him down. He batted it around the bedroom for a few minutes before retiring for a nap. I then had no choice but to set about transcribing.

Back in my PI days, we had a freelance transcriptionist who did a lot of business with people at the agency, but I always preferred transcribing my own tape. On the couple occasions I'd had other people do it, there were so many typos and other errors (no fault of the typist—if you're dealing with odd names or jargon that he or she doesn't know, it often comes out with bizarre phonetic spelling) that by the time I tweaked it all I might have just typed it myself. Also, I find I often have insights into the character of the subject when I can listen to our conversation from a safe distance. Someone's verbal ticks might increase in frequency or intensity when talking about a touchy topic or when lying. The downside is that I have to hear my own voice, often blabbering nervously or sounding pompous. This tape wasn't so awful. The Compost King was a bit cranky, but helpful. He didn't know about the luau incident—or he wasn't offering up any information that he did have. And I was surprised to realize that the tone (if not the content) was kind of flirty in places. The second interview, Corinne, made me twinge with nostalgia. Of course we were talking formally, on the record, but it felt like all the bantering I remembered from the old days. When I was done, I set the transcripts aside for the time being. After transcribing I always find it helpful to let the words rest for a while. It's easier to be analytical if you let the emotion of a conversation air out so it can settle into a black and white diagram of what was said. I pulled out the old box of Post-Its that I still kept stashed in the back of a desk drawer.

At the Swift Detective Agency, where I'd worked for five years on a contracted basis before my primate epiphany, my boss had a fetish for Clara Bow and the centerpiece of his office decor was a reproduction of a promotional poster for "IT," the 1927 movie that earned her the nickname "The It Girl." At the time I'd been keeping my hair in a vaguely '20s-esque retro bob and had just pioneered my personal note-keeping method. One day I was absorbed in rearranging sticky notes of various colors on the side of a file cabinet. I heard chuckling behind me and he announced that I was "The Post-It Girl." The nickname stuck, and so did the note system.

Information about suspects goes on yellow Post-Its. Information about witnesses goes on blue. Sources are green. Connecting points go on hot pink. I cleared the Euphorbia of the Month calendar from the living room closet door to make a space for my investigation diagram. It was pretty sparse, and there was a lot less pink in the mix than I had hoped, but that would change soon enough.

6

Ladykillers

October 11, 2002

"What was she thinking?" Don Wanderly murmured as he auto-piloted the Versalift truck across the equipment yard. "What the hell was she thinking?" Silent explosions detonated all around him—like that *Rocky & Bullwinkle* episode about the Hushaboom bombs, only instead of tiny mushroom clouds, they produced pink pulsating fetuses. "What the *hell* was she thinking?" This mantra reverberating in his head was not entirely drowning out the deeper, more annoying question, "What was I thinking?"

He rolled down the window and punched his security code into the number keys in the small box at the main gate and waited for it to slowly slide open as he had done some 3,000 times in his six years at the Zoo, only this time the gate started to glide shut again before he realized he had to press on the gas and move.

What was she thinking? She had assured him that she was on birth control. She had showed him the small round pill case like a little clock with most of the little blisters empty. What was she thinking? He thought about all the times he saw her working the coffee stand after they'd started seeing one another and noted how attractively luminous she looked, and then the slow realization that the glow was all too familiar and the zebra print smock was getting more and more snug around her belly. Finally, a week ago, she'd broken the news to him by the time clock at the end of the day as they were both signing out. She'd waited to tell him until after it was too late to do anything about it. When had it happened? They hadn't even hooked up that many times. His current girlfriend had been in a home improvement frenzy, trying to fix up the kid's room before school started, so the past few months had been full of painting and furniture shopping and fiddling with Allen wrenches and cams to assemble "engineered wood" items with funny Scandinavian names. He kept trying to tell her that the kid was too young to care about having the right ambiance to study—he was starting kindergarten for cripes sake. Was it that time in the car after that awful chick flick? What was she thinking? (What was I thinking?)

It was very early still and there weren't many vehicles about, so he coasted bumpily around the curves of the service road much faster than he should have. (Lost in thoughts of impending fatherhood—again—and annoyance at having been fooled—again—he did not pay any attention to the unusual crunching noise coming from the back of the truck.) Would she want child support? What was the deal with that? He was already paying child support to his ex-wife for their two kids, whom (he thought with a mixture of bitterness and relief) he rarely saw anymore now that they had moved to San Diego. What was she thinking?

Although all the City vehicles were serviced regularly, this particular truck had actually been decommissioned two years ago, so it had not had a maintenance check in three years for fear that it would be impounded and removed from a fleet that was already far too sparse for all the tasks that needed to be completed at the Zoo. It was the only "cherry picker" truck left, so it was still used to install and remove banners and change light bulbs in the high overhead lamps that dotted the parking lot. Over the years, the big hydraulic arm that lifted and shifted the bucket containing the operator had developed a very bad case of arthritis. The joints were stiff and didn't always completely extend or contract. The last time he'd used it to take down some signs, the arm would not fold fully, so he had had to shut it down partly extended as it was and then clamber out of the bucket and down the arm. But it wasn't jutting beyond the bed of the truck, and as long as he didn't have to drive through any low clearance areas, he figured it would be fine until he could find out whether it was possible to repair the truck even though it was technically out of service.

Had she told anyone it was his? He knew people knew about them, but how much did they know? An entirely new scenario of worries unfolded. Absorbed in speculation about how this pregnancy would impact his day-to-day existence at work, he almost forgot that he had to pee. Once he was out in the parking lot changing bulbs there would be no options other than the scant shrubbery in the planter beds, so it was now or never. "Shit," he huffed, and screeched to a clattering halt behind the administration building, parking illegally across three spaces, two of which were reserved for handi-capped staff. Due to budget cuts, security had eliminated the shift that mon-itored this area, opting to concentrate on the main entrances, so there were no public safety officers to ticket or admonish him. He slammed the door and started scurrying up the wide, winding steps, passing a group of keep-ers who had just signed in and were on their way out into the Zoo. Was it his imagination or was there a hush in their chatter as he approached? Was there a knowing glance between the two women in the back? He twitched a smile and waved weakly as he hurried past them and took the last section of stairs two at a time. He was reaching for the door when a ghostly white-and-khaki-clad figure appeared through the frosted glass and swung it open sharply. It was the annoyingly chipper docent who was always poking around in the morning. No matter who you were or how aggravated or antisocial you seemed to be, he would inflict his relentless cheeriness on you. It was too late to avoid eye contact. Taken by surprise he found himself face to face with "Mr. Blue Sky," all tidy and dapper and radiant.

"Well," Claude Hopper boomed at the anxious truck driver. "The top of the morning to you!"

"Yeah," he muttered as he slunk past and headed for the men's room just inside the door. Apparently custodial had not gotten to it for at least a few days. The urinal cake was a small pink nub, none of the four different soap dispenser models contained any soap, and the warm air hand drier was out of order, so he blotted his hands on his pants and headed back to the truck.

Lost in thoughts of resurgent paternity, and thinking, almost subconsciously, that his mother had been right after all when she told him that his penis would cause him nothing but trouble, he didn't notice the repositioned Versalift arm until he was reaching out for the door handle. "Shit!" he spat and started to go back to inspect the bucket. The arm seemed to have shifted from its frozen partly-raised position and was now poking out over the back bumper. "Oh, the hell with it." He slid into the driver's seat and decided to take the truck back to the equipment yard. This time, he'd file the paperwork to have the thing serviced. If it was impounded, that would be his supervisor's problem, not his. The light bulbs in the parking lot could wait until the City requisitioned a new truck for the Zoo. No one comes to the Zoo at night this time of year anyhow, he concluded. "And it's not worth me breaking my neck."

Claude simply couldn't understand cranky civil servants. Why bother staying somewhere if you really didn't care to be there doing your job? Life is too short to waste time on uninspired (half-assed) endeavors. He could look back on his long life and say that he had no regrets. He had pursued all his goals, personal and professional, to their fruition. Whenever he saw an ad for Povenda he knew he'd made a difference in the lives of countless people. Claude loved the Zoo and wanted it to thrive. He had been donating his time and money for so long that he felt he really had had a hand in making it what it had become—and that was no secret. When the latest Zoo director, Miles Patagonia, had settled into his new post, Claude wrote out his mission statement in a letter welcoming him to the fold. He wanted to share his enthusiasm with everyone—staff, other volunteers, the public, old, young—and especially, the ladies.

Middle school is the harshest, most unforgiving social terrain on earth. Those who thrive in it are able to do so because they've developed special adaptations that enable them to cope with the treacherous emotional landscape. It is where valuable adult behaviors are instilled: the instinct to fight, flee, or faint, the comfort of safety in numbers, and all the complex grooming and posturing gestures that will determine where individuals wind up in future pecking orders.

In the springtime of his adolescence, Claude Hopper crept into junior high a lamb and emerged a lion.

He was the younger of two boys raised by a shy and soft-spoken widower whose wife had been killed in a traffic accident when Claude was ten. Although they were as close-knit as a preteen, a 16 year old, and a 40-something can be, it was a challenged household. The senior Hopper was an accounting instructor at the local junior college and taught a couple extra night courses to help make ends meet. Consequently, the boys were often left to their own devices. Which was not so bad thanks to big brother Leif's sense of responsibility and post-World War II food technology. There were always three square meals, though they often involved cans of Campbell's cream of something soup, Velveeta, Miracle Whip, and Wonderbread at varying stages of freshness. (The most bizarre was a crouton casserole that incorporated all of the above. Claude's favorite, the most-hoped-for weekend lunch was the grilled Velveeta sandwich with tomato soup. Over the bumpy course of his three marriages later in life, he would insist that each wife learn the technique from Leif, who grudgingly humored him.)

Another unfortunate casualty of his mother's sudden death was a certain measure of personal grooming. His mother had been in charge of cutting hair, and once she was out of the picture, his dad assumed the responsibility and thus began the bowl-cut era. Leif somehow pulled it off by slicking his hair back and hiding it under a variety of hats until he got a part time job that enabled him to pay for real haircuts at a barber shop. When

Claude complained once too often about his hair, the very next Christmas brought the arrival of the Wahl electric trimmer. Loud and aggressive sounding, he was terrified during the inaugural cut, but his father had a steady hand and the end result wasn't great, but it was better than the bowl.

Leif had coached him in the importance of regular showering and deodorant, and somehow the laundry managed to get done every week, but Claude suffered from the scourge of hand-me-down clothing. If he was lucky, he would inherit something of Leif's that was actually reasonably cool and practically new because it had fallen out of favor and into the corner of a drawer or closet. The worst-case scenario was when his father– not exactly a trendsetter–decided to purge his wardrobe. Although it would have been more cost effective to buy Claude new, inexpensive, mass produced clothing, his father had never recovered from the rationing and heroic conservation efforts on the home front during World War II. Determined to get as much wear as possible out of each article of clothing, he had most of his cast-offs altered to fit Leif or Claude.

At first, adapting to life at James Clerk Maxwell Middle School was only mildly traumatic for Claude. He had become accustomed to being innocuous in elementary school, performing adequately academically and seeming pleasant enough to teachers and his fellow students. The first term of seventh grade put him through his paces. There was more of everything–classes, homework, kids, and demands on his social skills–and he was negotiating it all while still maintaining the low profile he'd been accustomed to all his life. And then puberty hit. Leif had warned him vaguely about it when it became clear that their father was too distracted with work to address the birds and the bees, but the onslaught of hormones was much fiercer than he could have imagined.

Suddenly he seemed to be sprouting hair everywhere and his voice often slipped out of his control, cracking and lurching from one register to the next like the times his brother drove the car and shifted abruptly from one gear to another. And then suddenly there were girls everywhere. Even when they weren't physically in his presence, distracting him, they were on his mind, drawing his thoughts away from geometry, Spanish grammar, and *Silas Marner*.

There were the bouncy cheerleaders who visited the homerooms every week during football season to give everyone pep talks punctuated by the papery rustling of their pompoms. He knew they all wore those gymnastic trunks under the short, pleated skirts, but speculating about what was hidden underneath as they stalked past his desk was almost more arousing. There were cute nerdy girls with glasses and stacks of books pressed up to their brainy bosoms and a few rocker chicks, also—showy and brash with their dyed hair and fire engine red lipstick. One day Eva Buxton dared to wear an off-the-shoulder blouse with a leopard print pencil skirt. At lunch that day he had been so transfixed trying to figure out how her bra stayed on without any straps that he had walked into a trash can, sending his lunch flying. (It took weeks before the tittering about that died down.) Even the Bible study girls were alluring. He wondered if they were as pure and virtuous as they seemed, concealed in carefully buttoned pastel blouses and tastefully matching twin sets. But the apple of his fervent teenage eye was Cassie Waverly. She was in honor society and played saxophone in the school band, but she was also known to run with the detention hall crowd, and it was rumored that she had smoked marijuana. Lean and leggy with a mane of auburn hair and a perpetual wisecracking grin, which was occasionally broad enough to make her dimples show, she was, in a word, hot. And mildly aware of his existence, too, since he had handed her a pencil one day when she was waiting behind him in the lunch line and needed to write down her phone number for one of the extremely fortunate guys who interested her.

It took him two years to master middle school, figuring out how the system worked, always with Cassie the glimmering goal on the horizon. His father couldn't afford to buy him a musical instrument, so he joined chorus, which often performed with the band. He took up smoking so that he would be prepared to expertly light her cigarette, should the occasion arise. He had come a long way. And yet, as desperately as he desired Cassie, his practical upbringing had instilled in him the understanding that he must also get into a good college, so there was a lot of studying and homework to ace in between the smoking breaks, concerts, and trips to the local Dairy Queen in hopes of glimpsing her. His friends, mostly music geeks who wanted to be in band but also couldn't afford instruments, teased him about his unrequited love, but also envied the single-mindedness of his pursuit.

And then it happened. During his "senior" year before transferring to the big three-year high school, Cassie asked him to the spring Sadie Hawkins Day dance. He had been waiting in the cafeteria line with his tray when she sauntered up to him, her hair all shimmery and exuding some kind of spicy shampoo fragrance. She was wearing snug white pedal pushers and a lemon yellow blouse tied in the front, just high enough to allow her navel to wink at him from between the knot and the waistband of her pants.

"Hey Claude," she said.

"Cassie," he said. She was the center of gravity and everything in the room began orbiting around her.

"How's it hanging?" she asked with an insouciant smirk.

"Oh, you know," he replied, the language circuits in his brain shorting out.

"Hey, are you going to the Sadie Hawkins Day Dance?"

"Uh, no," he answered, perplexed.

"Well, do you want to go with me?"

"What?" The line had moved on ahead of him and the annoyed girl behind him, the editor of the school paper, jabbed her tray into his back. He dazedly shuffled forward. Cassie sidestepped next to him.

"Would you, Claude, like to go to the Sadie Hawkins Day Dance with me, Cassie?" She was being flirtily impatient.

"Oh, yeah," he finally managed to speak. "Absolutely. Sure. Of course."

"That's peachy." She grinned with her perfect carmine lips, snapped her gum, and turned to go.

"Oh!" he almost shouted in a panic. She swung back.

"Yeah?"

"My phone number, you know, so we can plan."

"I know how to find you," she winked ever so faintly and strode off.

The impatient editor gave him a restrained whack on the back of his head with her tray. "Beep beep! Move it or lose it, Claude."

He smiled at her and meandered out of line, no longer hungry for food.

For two weeks he was in a subdued frenzy. What to wear? His brother lent him an old suit that was too small for him but worked for Claude. It was almost new, and with his awesome new Chucks, he felt his ensemble conveyed a formal yet irreverent attitude. Just the match for "Sassy Cassie" as she had come to be known.

The night of the dance, his dad sprang for the kids' cab fares for the evening, and Claude ventured out to see what fate had in store. His breath was minty fresh, he had carefully shaved the few sparse hairs on his upper lip that were slowly proliferating into a mustache, and he swept his dark, wavy hair back while waiting for her to come to the door. At last she appeared in a devastating slinky red dress with artfully deployed gathers that made her all fleshy curves and angles. He barely managed to say hello and hand her the camellia corsage he had made from the shrubs his mother had planted around the house when she stepped onto the porch, shut the door behind them, and started to the waiting cab. He thought the protocol was to go inside and meet the girl's parents so they could evaluate him as a match for their daughter, but she murmured something about her parents having a tiff and got into the back of the cab. Inside, she smiled her sassy grin and offered him a cigarette, which he accepted even though the smoke in the back of the car made his eyes water.

They went to dinner at the Raging Bull Steakhouse, which was far more expensive than he had anticipated. Thankfully, Leif had insisted on giving him an extra $20, so there was enough to foot the bill and leave a polite tip. The dancehall was fairly crowded by the time they arrived, and as smug as he felt to have Sassy Cassie on his arm, he was also self-conscious, so it was a relief to slip in, wave at the chaperones, and settle at a table. It was really too loud for conversation, so they smiled awkwardly at one another until Cassie told Claude that she would really love some punch. While filling the cups, he saw a couple of the guys from Cassie's crowd hovering nearby. He smiled at them and gave a half wave. They nudged each other and smiled back, then bolted. That should have been a tipoff. He should have been suspicious, but was too deep in euphoria to question the incident. He quickly forgot about it over the course of a few dances.

The music wasn't bad—the Forget-Me-Nots were former students who had gone on to beat the odds and form a working (money earning) band. Watching Cassie moving to the music in the clingy dress and the spiky heels, he had to remember to move his own body and avoid gaping. And then the inevitable happened: the slow dance—"Only You." Slow dances had the advantage of requiring little skill. On the other hand, they were awkward and intimate, and the chaperones were watching with eagle eyes for any unacceptable migrating hands or excessive frontal contact. With rapt concentration, he placed one hand on her waist and took her hand in the other. To his befuddlement, she put her other hand on his shoulder and pulled him close. When he looked down to try and see what his feet were doing, all he could see was her cleavage nestling up against him. The music receded into the remote corners of his awareness, occupied as he was by her perfume and alternately, her intent gaze, her breasts, and mild concern over his spontaneous physical response to them. He was too distracted to notice that she was leading and slowly navigating them to a remote corner of the dance floor. Suddenly, his reverie was shattered by a series of bright flashes. When he could see again, the circumstances came into crashing focus. Cassie and her friends giggling and guffawing at him with the boys he'd seen earlier, one of them brandishing a camera with a flashbulb attachment.

Later, he found out that Sassy Cassie had lost a bet and he had been the payoff. Which added insult to the injuries of that night. A photo from the incident—a perfect imitation of the celebrity exposé shots that appeared on gossip rags like *Hush-Hush*—eventually made its way to the school paper, where the editor prudently destroyed it.

Humiliated, Claude brooded in the back of the cab all the way home. Leif was asleep and his dad was embroiled in tests he had to have graded by the next day, so he bolted upstairs, stripped off his clothes, and got into the shower where no one could hear him cursing and crying. Neither dad nor Leif asked about the dance, other than a cursory "How'd it go?" that was easily deflected with an "OK, I guess." Neither of them had any idea that it was probably the most significant event in Claude's young life.

Those flashes initiated his transformation from wounded prey to relentless predator. His father marveled at his sudden motivation to earn money delivering newspapers and mowing lawns. But Claude had a powerful agenda that required funding. The paper route and yard work were the respectable side of his income, which wasn't quite lucrative enough for his purposes. In addition to his legitimate income, he cultivated shoplifting skills. By the time summer waned and the new school year loomed, he had reinvented himself almost entirely, making his Santa Narcissa High School debut as a dashing clean-cut charmer. Leaving the arts behind, he signed up for student government and the debate team, and also dropped in on the Youth For Christ meetings every once in a while. Surprised at how easy it was to infiltrate various social groups, and still stinging from Cassie's cruel deception, he experimented with some vengeance dating, going after one or two cute semi-popular girls, teasing them, and then inexplicably giving them the cold shoulder. By the time his senior year arrived, he had perfected his game, having discovered that girls are complex, like coffee or beer. He learned to play on their insecurities, which was tricky because they were often as good at being manipulative as he was. Sassy Cassie was still around, mildly puzzled and somewhat amused at his metamorphosis. But she was now invisible to him. He never acknowledged her again.

College at the California State University Santa Narcissa opened a whole new world of insecure women. Previously, he had targeted the cute and the popular. Now he focused on the vulnerable, cute or otherwise, and joined a bevy of clubs to find them. College students seemed much less judgmental about the type of extracurriculars one chose to dabble in, and he was successful at most all of them—falconry, fencing, pingpong, birding. This set a precedent for life. Claude graduated with a degree in biochemistry and a dazzling dating record. Eventually he became a well-off research scientist, a job (and salary) that impressed many women.

His first marriage, to a college classmate, was the only legitimate attempt he made to truly "settle down." It was the only one in which he had bred, and that had quickly lost its appeal. He waited long enough to be certain that parenting was not a skill set he wanted to develop, and then moved on. Fortune smiled on him, and as his marriage dissolved, he was offered a plum job at the pharmaceutical giant, Imperator. He packed his bags and headed for the Lone Star State.

The second wife was purely a question of aesthetics. She was smokin', drop-dead gorgeous. A model caliber face with high cheekbones and big brown eyes, the best silicon breasts that money could buy, legs that wouldn't stop, and the intellect of a cabbage. He didn't need his women to be terribly engaging, but even the sum total of her considerable physical charms was not enough to make the tedium of her company worthwhile. Completely impervious to his emotional needs—needs of which even he wasn't fully aware, she was unable to gratify them. He wasn't quite domineering, but he had to feel a sense of superiority and know that the woman in question knew that he had the upper hand in all things, that he determined the course of their relationship. And Legs was oblivious, so in 1966, they said their goodbyes and almost instantly she found an elderly Texan oil magnate who became besotted with her eight months before sloughing off his mortal coil and leaving her enough money to keep up appearances for a very long time. Claude moved on to greener pastures with no regrets.

The third one had really rankled. It had been as close to a perfect relationship as he had ever found. She was attractive, but not too attractive. It had been gratifying to be with Legs because he knew most of the men envied him with her on his arm. But then he also saw a lot of hungry gazes that made him feel mistrustful of the gazers and Legs. Number three wasn't bad looking, but he didn't feel he had to be on his toes at all times. She was bright and could make all the right cocktail conversation, but was not ambitious—until the women's libbers got to her and he found her reading books by Betty Friedan and Simone de Beauvoir, the latter in French. Then one day he came home to find her gone, without leaving a note or taking a thing. He discovered the massive engagement and wedding rings he had given her sitting in the bottom of the toilet bowl when he went upstairs to take a leak. After destroying much of the furniture, he decided he would never let one of them get that close ever again, and he returned to his strict regimen of date and dump.

After his early retirement, he returned to Santa Narcissa and discovered the wonders of volunteerism, which enabled him to tap into fresh pools of women. The best was the Santa Narcissa Zoo, though, and he worked his way through every one who had anything to offer in terms of nourishing his ego. And then he met Regina Pearl.

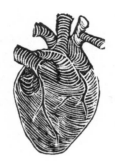

7

Heartthrob

February 12, 1993

The Wild Sex event at the Zoo was a perennial Valentine's Day hit. People just couldn't get enough lurid details about the many ways that animals go about getting it on: male Etruscan shrews that are ignited into a mating frenzy by the females' pheromones and essentially copulate until their hearts explode and they die; hermaphroditic slugs that change sex to suit their partners; wrestling male rattlesnakes with their hemipenes—one penis divided in two? Or two penises united by a single purpose? Claude was adept at making it all seem both naughty and nice, and invariably there were eligible ladies in the audience who tittered and blushed in all the right pauses, then waited to bathe him in attention after his presentation was through. But Regina Pearl was not one of these.

Garbed in a conspicuous caftan made of shimmering red fabric, with her hair wrapped in a matching turban pinned with a Swarovski crystal peacock pin, she was seated dead center in the front row, and whenever he scanned the audience to punctuate a scintillating fact with eye contact, he met her increasingly hostile glare.

Afterward, she approached him as he was mingling with the prey, and challenged almost every mating scenario in his presentation.

"Where do you do your research?" she demanded. "The wall of the men's room?"

"I beg your pardon?"

"You have taken some of the most interesting adaptations in nature and made them into parodies! What kind of docent are you?"

"I'm sorry you feel that way," he replied as his retinue began receding in order to avoid the embarrassment of watching the altercation. "But these are facts of life that are open to interpretation—and for the purposes of this talk I am interpreting them as amusing comparisons and contrasts with what we know to be true of ourselves."

"No, you are cheapening the dignity of these animals with junior high school potty humor."

He paused, struggling to find a mature response to her prudish attack. Just as he was about to suggest that she lighten up (though he had a different prescription in his head), one of the Shrew's minions swept her away.

"Now, now, Regina. It's just a little Valentine's Day fun," the wiry gray man next to her said, patting her arm. "Everyone here knows that he is dressing up the facts a bit."

"Dressing up the facts?!" Claude sputtered. Somehow this was worse than the Shrew's potty humor pronouncement. But the moment she could see that he had been riled by the comment, she grinned triumphantly and stormed off with her cronies.

He did not cross paths with her again for months until one morning when he showed up at his food prep assignment for Raptorama, and there she was, weighing frozen mice.

There were three or four awkward shifts, full of tense silence and excessive politeness. Then one day, an unfortunate mealworm mishap occurred. A large dish of the brown, squirming larvae tipped off a table and suddenly the floor was alive. Both Regina and Claude immediately dropped on all fours and began gathering up the mealworms. In a classic moment that might have been ripped from a breath mint commercial, their faces were inches apart and they suddenly made eye contact. They stood up in tandem, placed their bowls, filled with the last remaining mealworms, on the table, and then fell into a furious embrace and vehement kiss. It lasted only a few moments and they broke apart as if they'd planted their lips on live wires.

"Oh," Regina gasped.

"Yes," Claude responded.

"I'm sorry I attacked you at Wild Sex."

"It was a bit startling."

"I was forgetting that it was supposed to be an entertainment event more than an education event."

"Yes. And I'm sorry I got so upset at your friend."

"Oh. He's not my friend."

"But you were there together?"

"Oh, no."

"It's just… " he trailed off into one of those sudden reminiscences that sometimes crop up from a moment in real time. In Claude's case it was the Povenda research flap, which he had carefully compartmentalized and stashed away. Like an oyster forming a pearly coating around a piece of irritating grit, he had successfully swathed the incident in cultivated memories of it being a minor disagreement. It had become a clear black and white picture of events that were in fact murkily gray. There had been problems in the data from the clinical trials—evidence of some potentially serious side-effects. But he knew they were anomalies. He was so sure, in fact, that he had felt completely justified in proactively adjusting the data. And then there had been the unfortunate lab fire that destroyed all the files—and killed hapless Wolf Faigl. A tragedy, really. The only bright spot was that it had occurred after Povenda had already secured approval on the FDA fast track.

"Yes?" she said, smiling faintly.

Claude returned to the present. "It's just, I was in clinical research for a long time, and when he said I was 'dressing up the facts,' it really rubbed me the wrong way."

She was so brassy and direct, and somehow that made him feel confessional. And over the bumpy course of their romance, he often found himself on the verge of confessing the truth about what happened at Imperator.

"Well," she said, gazing intently at him. "Maybe I can make it up to you by rubbing you the right way?"

8

Gods and Monsters

November 1, 2002

Before returning the Claude Hopper file to Corinne, I had to go to work. I figured three or four weeks of intermittent sleuthing would be enough to work through the case, and my boss was OK with me using hourly increments of the huge backlog of vacation time I had accrued so that I could split time between my job and the case. The plants, however, were less forgiving than she was, and the conservatory was really demanding my attention. Although the volunteer garden assistant was keeping the weeds and watering under control, there were many propagules clamoring to be repotted, plus a big lot of donated plants had arrived and someone needed to separate the wheat (unusual specimens or exceptional examples of common species) from the chaff (plants in poor condition or over-represented in the collection). So, on Friday, November 1–Dia de los Muertos–I arrived at 7 a.m. and waded into the tasks at hand. Before sorting the new arrivals, though, I checked on some of my experiments.

The pet project that I'd been working on for about a year or so was called Magnificent Monsters–a garden full of plants whose names were almost as dramatic as their forms and habits: *Cereus monstrose* (the monstrous cereus), *Aloe ferox* (the fierce aloe), dragon's blood tree (*Dracaena draco*), Gollum's finger (*Crassula argentea monstrose*), *Encephalartos horridus* (the bristling cycad), various Medusa head euphorbias, *Cryptocereus anthonyanus*, *Calibanus hookeri* (named for the creature Caliban in Shakespeare's *The Tempest* and the great English botanist Sir William Jackson Hooker), creeping thyme, and nightshade, to name a few. There was an entire section of satanic plants named for various parts of Old Nick's anatomy including backbone, fingers, claws, hair, and horns.

Most of my monstrous and satanic plants arrived already grown from nurseries in the area, and I had bartered for a few rarer specimens from distant botanical gardens. Others I was growing from cuttings and seed I had collected on my own. My latest cuttings were dearly bought. I had to pull over on a busy foothill highway and scramble out into the sage and sumac to get it, so I was elated to find it rooting. Though weedy and common, no nursery I could find carries *Cuscuta californica*. Known by a slew of whimsical common names including witch's hair, angel's hair, devil's hair, devil's guts, hell bine, and love vine, the commonest common name I know for it is dodder. Like devil-in-the-bush/love-in-a-mist (*Nigella damascena*) I find it amusing that this plant evokes both love and hell. I guess both can be a torment.

There are many species of dodder. This one is native to California and basically looks like yellow Silly String attacking shrubberies. A true parasite, it produces no chlorophyl and so must drain all the nutrients it needs to survive from its host plant, in this case, a sacrificial tomato plant that the dodder was already gripping in its spindly tendrils. I sometimes muse over the *Convolvulaceae* family reunion. Morning Glory is showy and attractive but pushy and invasive. She takes over the personal space of every garden she visits. Cousin Dodder is more demure and kind of bland, but more truly insidious, leaching everything she needs from her hosts. High John the Conqueror (*Ipomea jalapa*) is always on the make, looking to get lucky. Sister Sweet Potato (*Ipomea batata*) is the golden child, economically successful and a bastion of good taste. Once I tried to explain this scenario to a marketing executive at one of the Holcomb Gardens benefits that staff are all required to attend. He told me, only somewhat jokingly, that I need to get out more. I very earnestly replied that he needed to spend more time in the gardens.

Midday Monday, I glided through the volunteer office to Corinne's open door and cautiously peered inside. She was on the phone, her brow pinched with concentration and a dose of mild annoyance. The remains of a burger and fries were next to her computer keyboard. I caught her eye and she signaled me into her office with a big swooping wave and as I settled into a chair she rolled her eyes and made the chatty mouth gesture with her free hand.

"We do have that information on our website. Do you have Internet access?"

A tiny tinny voice squeaked out of the earpiece at length.

"So you do?"

More squeaking.

"OK. Then if you go to our website and click on 'volunteer' there will be a form you can complete online and submit so you can attend our orientation next month.'

More squeaking.

"Yes. On your computer."

A brief exclamatory squeak. Corinne hung up, breathed a deep, brain-clearing sigh, then looked up at me. "What's up?"

I held out the Claude folder. "I came to return this."

"Was it helpful?

"What a character!"

"Yes, he was."

The phone rang.

"I'm sorry—my coordinator is out today so I have to take this."

"Sure thing."

While she tried to politely repel someone who was apparently mostly interested in playing with tiger cubs, I cautiously peeked into the main room. There were a few stray volunteers studying bulletin board information or newsletters and a strange man in a green jumpsuit. He was probably no more than 40 years old, but his portly build and thinning hair made him seem older. He had grown the remaining fringe into a very long sheet of hair which he had wrapped around his skull like a turban, secured in place with a gleaming coating of some kind of hair control product. Wearing oversized sunglasses tinted a pale yellow that seemed like it would actually make the world brighter and more glaring, he stood over a wastebasket trimming his nails with a tiny clipper protruding from a Swiss Army knife. I stared in morbid fascination until he glanced up suddenly and looked right at me. I actually jumped and lamely tried to disguise it as a yawn just as Corinne hung up.

"Oy."

"Another non-prospect?"

"How'd you guess?"

"Should I come back another time?"

"You know, it's going to be crazy like this all week," she said glancing at her watch. "Why don't you meet me at the Sasquatch Lair after work—say, 5:30—and we can talk at leisure."

"Fantastic."

As I left I could have sworn that the green jumpsuit started to veer after me, but when I turned to look behind me as I made my way through the glass doors into the parking lot there were no signs of him.

The Sasquatch Lair is like a lost piece of Disneyland that grew up on the wrong side of the tracks. It is cozily dark and full of cave decor ("petroglyphs" and faux-torches), taxidermied wildlife, giant fiberglass toadstools, and creepy gnomes. I made my way to the back room, which features a fairly convincing fake fireplace and comfy chairs arranged in twos and threes with small side tables among the staghorn lamps. Bluegrass music was twanging softly in the background. I ordered a Newcastle (on tap), picked a small table with two chairs that were off in a corner, and sat down to wait. Someone had abandoned a *Santa Narcissa Mirror* and the small box story on page one proclaimed, "The Sniper Strikes Again!" American river otter pups were the latest target. Apparently there was a leak at the Zoo, because the blurb featured a photo of the sniped sign, which read, "These playful animals are natural swimmers—and tasty, too!"

I was nursing a second pint of Newcastle and had read the entire paper, finishing both the word search and the crossword puzzle, when I started to suspect I'd been stood up. Corinne was an hour late at this point. I ordered the Crispy Critters Basket (a melange of deep fried chicken strips, shrimp, and calamari) and began mulling over the classified ads (an astounding number of exercise bikes are available for free to anyone willing to pick them up) when she gusted in. If we were cartoon characters in an animated world, everything in the room would have swooshed as she passed. She scanned the room urgently, the tan knit scarf around her neck and over-sized sunglasses creating an aviator effect. By now it was surely dark outside and in the dimness of the Lair I wondered how she could see anything. I waved and she swooped to the table, looming over me from her high altitude platform boots.

I opened my mouth to say hello, but before I could make a peep she made an imploring gesture with her hands.

"I am sooo sorry!"

"I was—"

"Wait—not a word until I get a double Happy Camper." She turned on her four inch heels and vanished into the crowd at the bar. When she returned, she had in one hand an enormous glass mug filled with a steaming brown beverage. Sticking up out of it was a long skewer of toasted mini marshmallows giving off delicate wisps of sweet smoke. In the other hand she had what I assumed was my order of Crispy Critters—a large red plastic basket lined with paper and heaped with miscellaneous fried shapes. Tucked in amongst them were cups of ketchup and ranch dressing.

"Crispy Critters?"

"Yes," I said, suddenly famished. "What in the world is that?"

"Mmm... delicious therapy in a cup." She let me have a whiff and I thought I felt a wave of instant wooziness from the aroma. "Coffee, chocolate, brandy, Kahlua, a shot of vanilla syrup, and a big skewer of toasted marshmallows. Want a sip?"

"Sounds delicious, but I think I'll stick to the beer and fried things for now."

"Suit yourself," she said sipping carefully and sliding the sunglasses to the top of her head, where they collided with the regular glasses already parked there. Then she folded them and started to hang them from the neck of her shirt, only a pair of reading glasses hanging from a beaded chain was in the way. She looked up and laughed as she put the sunglasses away in an enormous satchel glittering with tiny beaded beetles.

"Occupational hazard."

"I understand."

"Again, I am so sorry about being late. You wouldn't believe the ridiculous raging fire I had to put out."

"Who was the arsonist?"

"It was a group effort," she deftly used the rim of the cup to scrape the gooey marshmallows off the skewer and into the steamy elixir.

I nodded. The Crispy Critters were delicious, coated in a crunchy breading that was light, perfectly seasoned, and not at all greasy. What I thought was ketchup was actually cocktail sauce with a zippy dose of horseradish.

"So what did you want to ask?" she said, swirling her Happy Camper around in the cup.

"Well—"

"Hey, where's your tape recorder thingy?"

"Thanks for reminding me." I fished it out of my small, drab handbag, switched it on, and placed it on the table.

"Better safe than sorry," she grinned.

"I need to piece together as much of Claude's last day as possible," I said, trying to refrain from scarfing down the food. "So he would have signed in at the Volunteer Office?"

"Yes. Or possibly at the admin building. We have an auxiliary computer sign-in monitor up there so if people are in a hurry to get home they don't have to detour to the VO."

"Could you tell me which one he used and at what time?"

"Sure," she said, reluctantly setting the drink down. After a moment of rummaging around in the beetle bag, she produced one of those handheld electronic devices that still aren't part of my quantum reality. She flipped some flaps and pressed some buttons and frowned a little before answering.

"What's wrong?"

"Oh, nothing much. I had had several conversations with him about coming in early and spending too much time chitchatting with people. His food prep shift at Raptorama was supposed to start at 9 a.m. but I see he signed in at 7:35 a.m. on Friday, October 11—from the admin computer."

"And did he really spend an hour and a half making small talk?"

Dunking the gadget back into her bag, she took another sip of the Happy Camper and looked up with a pained smile. "Oh, yes."

"If he was such a social dynamo, then why did it take four days for anyone to notice him missing?"

"I don't know. His regular food prep shift is at Raptorama on Fridays and/or Saturdays, and he had stopped touring the school groups a short time ago, so no one would have expected to see him at the Zoo on any weekdays. He lived alone, and not close by, so it's not like the Zoo was in the neighborhood. Also, just because he was a social dynamo doesn't mean he had a lot of close friends."

"So people really just tolerated him?"

"Well, he had been a donor for ages. Not massive amounts, but regular as clockwork—a couple thou a year maybe. He even briefly served on the board of trustees once. So he felt very—entitled. And most folks here don't like to look a generous gift horse in the mouth too closely."

"So people tolerated him."

"For the most part, yes. He had his fans, but they were generally people who only saw him when he was 'on,' giving tours or talks. Not actually working with him."

"And what was it like actually working with him?"

"He was a man who was used to having things his way. I don't want to say he was a control freak, but I could see him being a total micro-manager. And he could talk you to death if you weren't careful."

"And who didn't tolerate him?"

She looked into her dwindling drink. "God, I feel like a tattletale."

I waited. I could tell she wanted to talk, but was hesitant due to an over abundance of tact. If she felt guilty for tattling, then I felt guilty for manipulating her into tattling. But not guilty enough to give up. While she weighed her conscience, I excused myself to go to the restroom, but stopped at the bar first to add another Newcastle to my tab and to make sure that an endless queue of fresh double Happy Campers would always be at the ready for Corinne. When I returned to the table, she had just extinguished the next round and was swirling the marshmallows around with the skewer.

"So tell me," she said, "why did you leave the Zoo?" She looked like she was bracing herself for some terrible confession about sexual harassment or office politics, or, worse, something she had done.

"You know, I don't think I've ever really tried to explain it out loud to anyone before, so it may sound kind of crazy."

"Try me. I've got all kinds of experience with crazy."

I laughed, took a deep breath, and recounted my discovery of the file about the incident at the Eustace Scrubb Zoo and the strange simian epiphany I'd had. I tried to explain why I had to cut myself off from everything and everyone in order to get my bearings and find a new direction, one that I was still exploring and still enjoying. There was a pause while we both sipped our drinks.

She looked at me intently, then leaned forward.

"Between you and me and the Happy Camper, there were a lot of people who were annoyed by Claude. Way past the tolerance point."

"Like who?"

"Well," she said hesitantly. "There's Les Moore for one."

"Well, that's pretty clear. So you have no idea what might have set off the fireworks at the volunteer dinner?"

"No. It could have been anything. Or nothing. All I know is that I had fairly regular complaints. Apparently, the relief keeper who covers for Les when he's out was perfectly happy with Claude. So Claude would come in and do food prep for the next day and Les would find the food and invariably something was wrong with it. Peeled when it shouldn't have been or not peeled enough. Chopped instead of diced, shaken, not stirred. Whatever. I tried to move Claude but he can be, um, how shall I say, challenging. So it was hard to place him anywhere else and like I said, the relief keeper—Trixie Lockhart—liked him. So I tried my best to keep him scheduled for days when Les wasn't in."

"So it was a vicious circle—Claude prepping for Trixie and annoying Les."

"Generally."

"How often did they cross paths?"

"As seldom as I could arrange it."

"So aside from general personality conflict, did you ever get any impression that there were more specific issues of contention between them?"

"Wow. These Happy Campers are super strong!" she said, placing the empty cup on the table. "My forehead is starting to get tingly."

"Are you OK?"

"Oh, yeah. I'm fine until the tingly spreads to my lips," she said, beaming at the waitress who replaced the empty cup with a fresh flaming drink, which Corinne extinguished with a little less flair and more care.

"Do you want to get something to eat?," I suggested. "That might take the edge off the Campers." The waitress hovered. Corinne glanced at the bar menu on the table tent.

"Maybe some french fries?"

The waitress nodded and dashed away. Corinne continued. "One time I had to take some paperwork up to Raptorama and Les was there with Claude and Trixie, so that was weird because Claude was in top form chatting up Trixie, who was kind of flirty and Les was just glowering at them. A lot of it revolved around the whole falconry thing."

"Was it something specific?"

"Hmmm," she murmured into her cup. "Les thought Claude was a poser."

"What do you mean?"

"Oh, you know. Falconry is like this whole subcultural thing with lots of codes and stuff. You know, social rules. Like becoming a Mason. And Claude hadn't been an active falconer for years but he still acted like he was part of it—offering his opinions about how the birds are trained and managed—and that was annoying to the people who really are actually active. And I guess he would still go around saying he was a master falconer, which Les always pointed out is kind of cheesy. You know, like when you go to a really ritzy restaurant and they have a menu that doesn't have any prices listed and it's like 'If you have to ask, you can't afford to be eating here.'"

"That's cheesy?"

"No," she scoffed with a grin. "Asking how much everything is is. It was cheesy for Claude to go around announcing himself as being a master falconer. I'm not sure how long it had been since he had actually gone hunting with a bird. He had pictures of himself at one of those medieval fairs, but that was in the '70s when he lived in Texas, I think. And you know you're just going throught the motions if you're only flying the birds."

"You are?"

"Yeah. I didn't know that either. I thought it was all about flying displays and the birds were trained to be like aerial retrievers. But it's really the birds that do the hunting. The human hunter just flushes the game and the bird does the deed."

The waitress arrived with Corinne's fries and she dug right in.

"But surely that can't have been enough of an issue to kill him."

"Maybe not. They just had clashing personalities and that was enough of an issue to set off tempers."

"OK, and do you know what days Les is in?"

"Sunday through Thursday. There's a Raptorama staff schedule up in administration. You can check that the next time you're at the Zoo to make sure he's not out on vacation or jury duty or anything like that."

"All right. So Claude signed in at the admin computer and then headed up into the Zoo. Do you know which route he took?"

The service road is basically a ring road encompassing the Zoo campus. At three points it connects with public area—one was at Raptorama. The service road was more direct, but the public path wound around past almost every exhibit.

"Knowing Claude, he most likely took the service road to the first junction at Billy Goat Bluff, then blabbed with the children's zoo staff before heading into the Zoo to check in with all the animals—and keepers."

"I see. Well, maybe what I'll do is just retrace his steps. Since the Hand got me my official credentials I should be able to reenact his last day, yes?"

"Hmmm. Yeah. Just be sure someone lets security know what you're doing. They're training a bunch of new recruits who seem super eager to take care of business. Even when there isn't really any business that needs taking care of." She giggled.

"Gotcha. OK, so based on the info in his file, he seems like he was quite the man about town. What about personal relationships? Did he have any best friends? Girlfriends? Boyfriends?"

An involuntary eyebrow arching signaled a big affirmative before she slowly nodded.

"Well, he was quite the schmoozer. That's partly why he was so popular with the public and donors. He was a silver-tongued devil and could make comparative dentition sound about as sexy as, you know, sex. He really loved to schmooze the ladies—and I would say that in the world of volunteers, the ladies outnumber the gentlemen by about two to one."

"Was there anyone… special?"

She sighed heavily. "You could say that."

"So who was the lucky gal?"

"Oh, boy! Now it's time for… " she drummed the table. "The Ballad of

Claude and Regina!"

One of the things I'd missed after leaving the Zoo was the watering hole gatherings we used to have. Despite my generally morose nature, I'm a pretty happy drunk, and so was Corinne. We'd happily sloshed our way through many a happy hour. I chuckled partly at the memory and partly at what I knew would be a colorful explanation.

"Pretty epic?"

"In a word... yes!"

"How long had this been going on?"

"Oh, probably since about your time. But it kept picking up momentum. It went in cycles. He was such a ladykiller, he couldn't resist chatting up any women he encountered, and Regina Pearl was so possessive, she couldn't stand the flirting, but he loved to push her buttons—" big wink "—and then there would be the big explosion—" pyrotechnic hand gesture "—with lots of tears and fiery words and occasionally damaged furniture or food projectiles, and then the calm, followed by the reconciliation with lots of googly eyes and cooing of sweet nothings. It was a drama in four acts that played out again and again and again and again. You know. Star-crossed yadda yadda—Romeo and Juliet. Liz and Dick. Sid and Nancy. Kurt and Courtney."

"Good Lord—how did I miss all that?"

"Well, you had to be in the right place at the right time," her brow furrowed fleetingly. "Or the wrong place at the right time. And it did kind of escalate over the years."

"When is Regina in?"

"She should be in tomorrow, but you'll need to prepare yourself. She is very much the drama queen, you know, and totally devastated by Claude's death."

"Genuinely?"

"I think there is a tiny, pointy kernel of truth under the many layers of blustery anguish."

"Do you think he really cared for her?"

"Maybe, maybe, baby."

I opened my mouth to ask what Regina was like but she cut me off.

"Speaking of babies, you know Claude, Junior is a volunteer, too."

"You mentioned him before, but not that he is a volunteer."

"Yep."

"So how old is the kid?"

"Well, not a kid. More of a goat!" she poked my arm and winked—a gestural rimshot. I laughed and rolled my eyes.

"Yeah. He's fully grown, and actually very goat-like. He has a long scraggly beard, and he often smells like he's in rut. But he is really dependable. Just too eccentric for interacting with the public. Claude had been a volunteer for years when all of a sudden Junior showed up at a volunteer orientation."

"So Senior didn't know about Junior?"

"Well, obviously he knew about him. He is the only child Claude had, but since Senior was totally estranged from the mother, he hadn't seen Junior since he was a baby." She paused. "Senior hadn't seen Junior since Junior was a baby, not since Senior was a baby. You know what I mean."

"Yes."

"It was just sort of an odd coincidence."

"What does Junior do?"

"He's the head librarian at the City of Integrity main library."

"That's kind of far."

"Oh, he has a teeny little solar-hybrid car that gets like a thousand miles to the gallon. It looks like a shoe."

"Like a shoe?"

"Yes! Not like one of those fiberglass, you know, marketing shoe cars that's shoe shaped, but it's just sort of accidentally shaped like one of those sneakers. A Converse high-top."

"His car looks like a Chuck?"

"Exactly."

"Wow. That's unfortunate. Unless you like that kind of thing. I guess."

"He got it from a shop that customizes cars with solar panels. Claude, Senior, told him about it."

"So they got along?"

"Oh, yeah! It was kind of sweet, actually. They met at a briefing for an event and it was like they were long lost family." She paused. "Which is actually what they were. There was that kind of awkward formality, but it was like volunteering together gave them an excuse to get to know each other."

"What about the mother?"

"I don't know. Junior is an adult and on his own. If he said anything to her, it never came up. I don't even know if she's in the area."

"Do you—"

"But I think he listed her as an emergency contact! So maybe she's local. I can look it up!" She started to dive back into the enormous beetle bag, but I stopped her. It was a possibility. Estranged ex-wife resents horrible ex-husband for reconnecting with their only child. But it seemed a long shot. There were better prospects to follow up on first.

"It can wait."

Volume-wise, I'd say I'm about two-thirds of Corinne, but then, her Happy Campers probably packed twice the alcoholic punch as my Newcastle, which added up to a very fuzzy edge at that point in the evening, and I decided that it was time to call it quits as far as drinks were concerned. I turned the recorder off and we had a less focused conversation about shoes, reptiles, the tendency for people to pee just about anywhere, and how impossible it is to underestimate people's inability to read signage. Eventually I offered to drive her home, which she agreed was a good idea. The staff at the bar knew her and wouldn't mind the car staying in the lot. Her husband could bring her back to get it in the morning.

When I parked outside her house, Corinne leaned over and gave me a huge hug then leaned back and sighed. "I missed all those happy hours."

"Yeah. Me, too."

"So when the case is over, we should still hang in the Lair."

"It's a plan."

She smiled, got out of the car and wobbled to the front door, where she was greeted by her husband, who waved vaguely at me, and a very happy Irish wolfhound named Thor.

9

Circle of Life

When I was in the Zoo's research department, I spent hours each week engaged in observational research. The procedure is pretty basic. You watch a particular animal or group of animals for a certain period of time. At regular intervals you write down the behaviors in which they're engaged. The various activities—grooming, playing, eating, mating, fighting—are defined and coded, and you basically jot numbers down every minute or two minutes or however long the interval is. After you accumulate enough codes over a period of time you have statistics that can be converted into any one of a number of exciting graphic representations of your subjects' lives.

We had produced a lot of valuable studies about behaviors in different species, and yet there were times when it all seemed pretty pointless. No matter how many astonishing insights are gleaned from empirical data, superstition always seems to prevail. One day I was working on a study designed to determine whether tortoises would demonstrate substrate preferences, given a choice. It involved watching the animals for hours and noting how much time they spent engaged in various activities in different sections of their enclosures, some covered with bark and others with sand or pea gravel. It was slow work. Over the course of an afternoon, I heard numerous people reacting to the enormous king cobra in the neighboring exhibit. A bearded gentleman with a timid son stared at the snake for a while and when the animal began to roam around the enclosure flickering its tongue, the man explained that serpents are cursed animals because Satan had taken their form to lure man into evil. Snakes have no remorse and do not even blink an eye when striking their victims. I marveled at the ease with which he inverted symbol and symbolism, and fought the urge to point out that snakes have no eyelids, so they they are physically incapable of blinking, and that this adaptation has nothing to do with good and evil, which are human constructs. But stopping my observation would have invalidated my data and I'd have had to do it all over again. So I bit my tongue and focused on the tortoises.

A while later, after the tortoises had begun to demonstrate a clear preference for approaching their dish of food from the sand side rather than the bark side or the pea gravel side, a woman told her two children, who squealed with delight when the snake "hooded" briefly, that it was an enormous snake like this one, named Muchalinda Nagaraja that sheltered the Buddha when he was struggling to meditate during a bad storm, and this is why the king cobra is a sacred animal. Even though this wasn't any closer to truth than the previous parent, it made me happy because snakes generally get such a bad rap, particularly among the faithful, when they are guilty only of fulfilling their biological destiny, which is to kill and eat animals who are not fast, wary, or clever enough to escape them. Nature can be brutal, but it's never anything personal. Conscience makes it cruelty.

People have always done this—interpreted animal behavior in human terms. I guess self-awareness makes us self-centered. The ability to attach abstract meaning to the world around us is our greatest gift (aside from our massively overrated—in my opinion—opposable thumbs). Ever since we lived in caves, we've used ritual to try and absorb the desirable qualities we see in other animals and exorcise the unpleasant ones we find in ourselves, and we used to be infinitely more imaginative about it. Nowadays we drive Jaguars and Mustangs and Tiburons, and we live vicariously through sports teams with bears and lions and rattlesnakes as logos, but it's all window dressing. How many screaming football fans have ever gone swimming with sharks or encountered a live bear? How many nine-to-five commuters have seen, let alone ridden, a mustang?

Our relationship with animals used to be much more intimate. Before they were reduced to logos and tamed into companion animals, they were hunters that we feared, revered, or exploited. (Yeah, we look down our primate noses at scavengers now, but humans stole their fair share of pre-killed carcasses to get where we are today.) Or they were prey that challenged us. They were sustenance and we worshipped them for giving us life, and sacrificed them to deities because they were precious to us. They died for our sins and nourished us with their milk, eggs, flesh, and blood. We domesticated them and built civilization on the strengths of their backs. In 1900 there were about 100,000 horses living in New York City, pulling carriages, cargo, and carts; mobilizing police and fire trucks; carrying fares and commuters. The Association for the Prevention of Cruelty to Animals got its start trying to prevent people from working horses to death and beating them into submission. Abuse is the dark side of objectification, and it's easier to objectify animals when we forget (through carelessness or intent) our own animal nature.

Nowadays, aside from companion animals, people mostly encounter domestic animals, and most of the domestic animals around us die anonymous deaths behind concrete walls in factory farms and laboratories or in shelters we build for surplus creatures that only exist because we thought we wanted them and then changed our minds.

I watched a David Attenborough film of bushmen hunting a greater kudu using the most ancient method known to humans. It unfolded like an epic dance—ritualized and elegant. The hunters pursued the kudu relentlessly over the course of a day and many miles across dry scrubland. The quarry was out of visual contact much of the time, but the hunters' pursuit

83

was the very definition of dogged, running and following on foot a trail that was all but invisible to "civilized" humans. They almost lost track at a watering hole, but the lead hunter, after slaking his thirst (just as the kudu had done not long before), paused to channel the animal, think like the animal, be the animal long enough to choose the direction that the kudu had chosen. In the end the hunters and the hunted were spent. The men could have perished just as easily as the kudu but ultimately, they caught up with the exhausted buck, who had collapsed and was in the process of expiring. The lead hunter speared the animal's heart, but this was mostly symbolic as he was already on the threshold of death.

The hunters touched him reverently and said prayers to thank him for his life. They took his saliva and rubbed it on their legs to absorb his spirit and stamina, and then they carried him on the long journey home to their village, recounting the impressive chase the buck had given them, enmeshing him in story. Their actions transformed the kudu into a noble, sacred creature. Unlike the pigs and cows we buy in pieces, renamed pork and beef, priced by the pound and sterilely packaged in plastic and styrofoam. Every time I eat a steak or truss a Thanksgiving turkey, I pause to think about the animal that this flesh was and be thankful for its brief and inglorious life. I've been accused of being a hypocrite and romanticizing the "primitive" (and also of being morbid), but animals have profound meaning to me, particularly the ones I consume, and if that seems hypocritical or romantic or morbid, then so be it.

I could totally understand the concerns of DofA. I had once been a card-carrying member. Inspired by a horrific film I saw of cattle being tortured before slaughter by poorly trained, over-worked, under-paid men wielding captive bolt stun guns, I joined, and spent much of my high school life trying to avoid eating "hidden meat," struggling to quell rampant foot odor from non-leather shoes, and pestering my parents to go vegetarian. The DofA rhetoric was very compelling. Everywhere I looked, I saw animals enslaved to humans, suffering for humans. I saw nothing but accusation in the calm gaze of our family cat, Spot. Yet oddly, it was Spot I credit with my first big existential epiphany.

Though she was an indoor cat, I had observed her on countless occasions staring intently out of windows at squirrels, birds, and other small creatures, making the odd chattering sound that is the physical manifestation of the pent up feline urge to kill. If she had not come to us, she might have lived the rest of her life as a stray, killing other animals (frequently native wildlife) to survive. But as our pet, we fed her prepared cat food made from the undesirable scraps of animals that had been killed for human consumption. So keeping her as a pet seemed to be a zero sum game, and at least as a pet she was eating parts of animals that people might have otherwise discarded as unappealing. Even at the tender age of 17, I hated waste as much as I hated watching those cattle suffering.

One day Spot slipped out of the sliding glass doors that led to the backyard. After a panicky hour or so, she reappeared at the door with a dead lizard in her mouth. I felt a mixture of relief at her return, wonder that she knew how to kill something, and sadness at the loss of the lizard. I waited for her to eat the lizard, but after depositing it at my feet and staring expectantly at me for a few minutes, she went back inside to resume her windowsill vigil. Apparently, the reptile was some sort of offering, which I discreetly buried in the backyard. Since cats are obligate carnivores, the DofA me was in a quandary. I kept thinking about Spot's kill for days. Of course keeping a pet was also problematic in the DofA purview, but I could only deal with one issue at a time and food was simpler. Or so I thought before a heart-to-heart that I had over the course of several dozen coffee refills and some bad menthol cigarettes with my then-boyfriend, whose mission, he declared, was to exist outside of the food chain.

"Yeah," he had said breathing smoke fiercely from his nostrils. "That's the only solution."

"But is that even possible?"

"Well sure! You can totally be vegan."

"Yeah, but I mean, you're still in the food chain. You're just only eating plants."

"So?"

"So killing plants is OK."

"Yeah. They don't feel pain."

"So the main problem is the sensation of pain?"

"Well, no. There's pain and suffering that animals go through on farms."

"But what if you hunt for a deer in the wild."

"You're still killing it."

"But it's wild and free, and if you're a good hunter, then it shouldn't be any worse for the deer than if a wolf or a mountain lion killed it."

"But that's a wolf or a mountain lion."

"So what?"

"That's what they do. It's a natural behavior."

"Yeah, but humans are also hunters."

"Not all of them. What about Hindus?"

"They just don't eat cattle."

"What about Buddhists?"

"OK. But that's also because of a religious belief."

"Yeah."

"I don't think that really counts. My point is, people, before there were formal religions that made it right or wrong to eat meat, were hunter-gatherers who killed and ate animals."

"And plants."

"Right. And plants. The thing is, if it's part of the way that we're wired, if it's something in our nature, then why is it morally wrong?"

"Hmm. I don't know. Because we know better now?"

"What do you mean?"

"We know how to live without meat. You know, complete proteins, beans and rice and all that stuff."

"Yeah but we have to work to live without meat protein. We have to invent things like tofu."

"And we have."

"But what if you were out in the wild without tofu factories. What if you couldn't grow the soybeans to make it."

"Well, I guess I'd starve."

We sipped our coffee in silence for a while.

"Would you eat insects?"

"Maybe."

"But they have faces."

"Yeah," he said staring into the cloud of smoke he had just expelled. "But they don't have spines."

"So killing and eating invertebrates is OK?"

"I guess so."

"Have you ever boiled a live lobster or crab?"

"Ew... no. I'd have to be pretty far down the starvation road to eat that anyhow."

"So they get to survive because you are a picky eater?"

"What's up with you?"

"Nothing. I'm just trying to sort some stuff out. I think there are worse things than being killed and eaten by some other animal."

There was a long pause during which he stared at me so intently that he jumped when the cigarette burned down to his fingers.

"But the point is, the animals suffer before they get killed and eaten."

"I know that."

"And not eating meat reduces the demand for the animals, hence the reduction in suffering."

"I get that," I said impatiently. "But have you ever seen African wild dogs kill a Cape buffalo?"

He warily shook his head.

"They chase it until it's exhausted, disembowel it, and then wait for it to bleed out. Cheetahs suffocate baby gazelles by clamping their mouths over their faces."

"But they're animals."

"So are we!"

There was a long pause, and yet another coffee refill.

"OK. What if you were killed and something ate you."

"I don't think that would be so horrible. It sort of grosses me out more to think about some stranger embalming me or incinerating me than to think of some scavenger eating my flesh. In India, the Parsis are a religious group who leave their dead to be consumed by vultures at the Towers of Silence."

"What?!" He almost shouted. People at neighboring tables were starting to glance over at us disapprovingly.

"It would make more sense than mouldering in a coffin after being pickled in chemicals."

"What about the people who knew you?"

"My remains aren't going to keep them company. It's kind of cool to think of my remains getting back into the life cycle, soaring around in a bird for a while. Everything dies eventually and the only resurrection that we really have is to give life to other beings with our flesh. I mean, that's truer to what Jesus meant by communion than being pickled and preserved in a hermetically sealed box. You know, the bread and wine bit: 'Eat this—this is my flesh; drink this—this is my blood.' Whatever memories the people who knew me have are going to be what stays with them."

His brow was furrowed so fiercely, I was afraid that he'd have a permanent crease.

"What if other people ate you?"

"I don't think I'd really care because I'd be dead."

"OK. Rewind. So are you just trying to rationalize falling off the wagon?"

"It's not rationalizing. I'm just trying to understand why I'm on it. "

"Right."

The waitress came by with yet more coffee and a hopeful expression, asking if she could get us anything else. I ordered the chicken fried steak.

10

Cricket Honey

November 5, 2002

Approaching the Zoo parking lot the morning after the Lair, I noticed a small media commotion. At the center of it was the president of Defenders of Animals, Peter Manley, who was hard to miss since he was nearly a foot taller than the reporter next to him and wore a luminous white suit. I swung past the news van and milling people with signs and parked as far away as possible. It was the "Go For Bear" campaign demanding that the Santa Narcissa Zoo release its 18-year-old polar bear, Suzy Q, to a marine mammal sanctuary in Alaska. This battle had been going on for years. They had a strong emotional presentation, and also lots of unhappy old film footage of Suzy Q engaged in neurotic pacing.

One of the first research projects to which I had been assigned, long before the tortoise substrate preference study, was behavioral observations for Suzy. She had been rescued from a game reserve that sold "guaranteed hunting expeditions" (aka canned hunts) to people who like to track and kill big game animals but don't have the patience or skills to actually learn how to do it. Yes, polar bears are protected, and yes, it's illegal, but that's no obstacle if you have enough money. Eventually the facility was busted and the animals were sent to any zoos or rescue organizations that could take them in. Of course the Southern California climate and the antique exhibit space that was available at the time weren't optimal for the bear, but one of the Zoo's more eccentric (and breathtakingly wealthy) board members had been smitten by Suzy and stirred by her story. She offered to pay all the fees to transport Suzy from the game reserve to Santa Narcissa, as well as the costs of modifying an exhibit space for her. The dividing wall between two old fashioned grotto exhibits, built to the rigorous bomb shelter-like specifications of the '50s, was demolished to make one large exhibit, and the construction crew remodeled it as best they could to create a vaguely naturalistic feel with a pool and some rocky "clearings." But during her time at the game reserve, Suzy had been kept in a fairly squalid "holding area." Apparently she came to the place as a cub (her mother had been shot and killed by a hunter who claimed he had mistaken her for a moose) and the guy who operated the facility planned on keeping her in a behind-the-scenes enclosure until she was big enough to take her chances on the shooting range.

In the wild, polar bears take up a lot of space. They can cover up to 20 miles a day in search of food, which occupies most of their time and attention. The world's largest land predator, and more carnivorous than other bears, their preferred prey is seals which, being slippery, agile, and smart, the bears have to work hard to catch. Polar bears have been found swimming up to 50 miles away from solid ground, and in the zoo world they are classified as marine mammals. Because they are both predators and scavengers, polar bears are pretty inquisitive, which means for many years when they were kept in captivity without sufficient physical and mental stimulation they would develop stereotypic (repetitive) behaviors due to excruciating boredom. Basically it's the same thing as all the foot twitching and leg bouncing you start to see when people have been held captive in a meeting that's dragging on too long—only on a grander scale.

When Suzy first arrived at the Santa Narcissa Zoo she spent much of her day turning in circles or pacing, to the distress of the keepers assigned to her. But the animal care staff rallied and launched into a series of behavioral experiments. Guests were perplexed by the random objects that appeared in the exhibit—road cones, tires, burlap sacks, bales of hay, old fire hoses tied in knots or wrapped into balls, and strange blocks of ice with bits of fish and squid embedded in them. After a while, some of the novel items triggered her curiosity and she began to play with them. To give her more options and the choice to be out of eye shot of strangers, the door to the holding area inside the mouth of the "cave" remained open almost all day and sometimes she would vanish inside (usually to attentively, calmly watch the keepers preparing her food behind a large glass panel—kind of like bear TV), leaving guests grumpily wondering what lived in the grotto. But the enrichment strategy ultimately worked. I know because I spent hours and hours gathering observational data before and after it was implemented. Suzy was a non-releasable animal: too habituated to humans and commanding too few survival skills to make it in the wild. She would have been shot on the range or euthanized if the Zoo hadn't taken her in, and thanks to the hard work of her keepers she was leading a comfortable existence now. DofA felt she would be better off dead, but I couldn't accept that. In the wild, animals fight for life to the bitter end, and she had been spared a bitter end—twice.

Skirting the gathering of protesters, I paused to watch Peter Manley speaking to the reporter.

"So, Mr. Manley," the elaborately coiffed woman in a fire engine red suit began, "wouldn't you agree that the Zoo is helping to save endangered species that are vanishing from the wild?"

He smiled a practiced smile and calmly began his practiced party line:

"Zoos are nothing more than prisons that represent the worst kind of animal exploitation. Certainly factory farms are awful and cause vast suffering, but zoos cannot even make the excuse that these animals are serving a concrete purpose like sustenance. Ultimately it is a great lie that feeds into the much greater lie that is our perverse relationship with animals. Even our pets are prisoners of our own psychological needs, which we use as justification to contain them in our homes and take away their dignity."

The reporter smiled confusedly, and I fled. These were arguments I had heard before and rejected before. I made my way to the gate, showed the membership ambassador my ID and pass, and then headed out into the Zoo to find Les Moore.

Making my way through the Zoo, I was amazed at how much had changed. Whole sections were gone, transformed into bigger habitats that were lovely even without the animals in them. It was like some accelerated geological process had taken over and all the big bomb-shelter concrete grottos had been reclaimed with waterfalls and faux-glades. I made my way to the far side of the Zoo and arrived just in time for the midday Raptorama Show. It wasn't really a show in the sense of a performance where the birds did "tricks." Various raptors (turkey vulture, kestrel, barn owl, peregrine falcon, golden eagle, king vulture, red-tailed hawk, and Harris's hawk) waited patiently on perches eyeing the crowd, while three keepers explained their natural history. Then each was given the opportunity to exercise the special talents of his or her species as part of a carefully choreographed demonstration of the birds' natural behaviors. I'd seen the presentation countless times, but it was still miraculous to watch a peregrine falcon dive after a lure at 200 miles per hour or feel the silent gust of air as an eagle owl soars past you. Afterward, I meandered backstage in hopes of finding Les Moore.

I've conducted easy-going interviews with lots of lively chatter and friendly overtones that were almost fun, only to discover after transcribing them that they contained little or no useful insights. And I've muddled through awful interviews full of tense silences, terse responses, and hostile vibes that yielded really spectacular insights. My interview with Les Moore was the worst of all possible worlds: awkward and pointless—or at least largely pointless. But there's no way of predicting these things, and once I'd waded into the briny deep it was too late to turn back.

The backstory I had gotten from the general curator was that Les had been hired as a keeper shortly after my departure from the volunteer program. He had moved from a small zoo in Texas to Santa Narcissa specifically to take this job, and had been doing fine work ever since he arrived. Though he was mainly interested in raptors, which were his regular charges, he was still occasionally deployed on other sections when keepers were out sick or on vacation.

Les was probably in his late 40s and had a deep auburn mane of hair streaked with silver that he kept contained in a ponytail and under a brown baseball cap. He was one of those rare redheads who don't freckle excessively and he scrutinized me over the chain link gate with shrewd hazel eyes.

"Hi. I'm Sandy Lohm," I said bravely meeting his gaze. "I'm investigating the death of Claude Hopper? Is it OK if I ask you a few questions?"

A fleeting spark of some emotion flashed behind his eyes.

"Oh, sure," he said in a deep, gravelly voice with a touch of twang. "Look, I have some food prep to do. You can talk to me while I work or come back some other time."

I hate playing the omega dog in interviews, but sometimes there are no other options, and I was determined to extract something useful from this exercise. It was time to roll over and beg.

"That would be fine."

I trailed along after him toward the kitchen area of the keeper building. There were birds other than raptors in the off-exhibit space—a couple macaws, a big glossy raven, and a familiar face. I was pleasantly surprised to find Martin the magpie still alive and flapping. Nearly 20 years ago, he had arrived at the Zoo as an adult. Ancient and blind, but still alert and charming, he immediately started swaying his head and crooning "hellooooo" when I greeted him. In addition to the usual bird of prey menu items (mice, rabbits, quail), the food stores included an assortment of fruits and vegetables and invertebrates. Les took the top off of a plastic storage bin with holes punched in it and started counting out mealworms into small dishes.

I took out the tape recorder and asked if he would mind if I taped our conversation. He shrugged and continued going about his business while I asked random questions about the birds, and he responded laconically with information I already knew.

I was rapidly running out of avian small talk while I desperately tried to figure out how to get to the topic of Claude.

He moved on to the cricket farm—a big terrarium with pieces of cardboard and bits of fruits and vegetables in it. Several hundred crickets chirped and clambered around, ignorant of their impending doom. Les caught one and pinched it gently between his index fingers and thumbs, then shot a glance at me.

"You ever had cricket honey?"

I gaped for a moment while I wracked my brain for any references to "cricket honey." Paralyzed, I couldn't decide if he was genuinely trying to engage me in a conversation or making fun of me.

"Uh, no," I said.

"Just like wheat grass juice, only sweeter," he explained and in the blink of an eye gave the insect a quick squeeze and kissed its posterior. I converted a spontaneous guffaw into a sudden cough.

"Try some," he said, releasing the spent insect back into the tank and catching up a fresh one, which he pinched and squeezed, then held out to me as if it were a match to light my nonexistent cigarette. Thinking only of the stories I would be able to one day tell incredulous listeners, I leaned in and gave the cricket a quick peck on the behind. The tiny drop of fluid was like essence of lawn clippings with a faintly sweet patina. Not awful, but nothing I'd care to repeat.

"Atta girl," Les said with a sly grin. "Now what did you really want to ask me?"

Annoyed as I was, I was even more determined to get to the questioning. He leaned back, amused and waiting. I took a deep breath.

"So Claude Hopper..."

"Was a self-important son of a bitch."

It's hard to come up with a follow-up to an answer like that, but I needed to know more and decided that it couldn't get any worse.

"And what was it about him that makes you say that?" I asked, realizing that I sounded like a market research survey phone jockey.

He chortled. "What didn't?"

"Well, what was most annoying to you?"

"Hmm, let's see. There's his condescending attitude, his stilted manner, his excessive aftershave, his inaccurate understanding of falconry, his subpar animal handling abilities, his lack of attention to detail, his sense of entitlement, that nutty docent girlfriend of his, his relentless forced cheeriness, and those stupid ascots he always wears. For starters."

"OK." I wasn't sure where to go after that. "So about how often did you see him?"

"Too often."

"Hmmm. I meant more like in terms of days a week?"

"He's usually in on my days off. Which suits me just fine."

"And the last time you saw him was... "

"The volunteer appreciation dinner at the end of September."

"Did you talk?"

"Yes."

"Much?"

"No."

"I understand you had more than just words with him at the dinner."

He glared at me. "So."

"Well, something must have set you off?"

"If you say so. I don't recall."

"Did he say or do something that offended you?"

"Look, I lost my temper."

"Over what?"

"Nothing. I had one too many glasses of wine."

"So you just took a swing at him?"

"Yes."

"Your regular days off are Friday and Saturday?"

"Yes."

"So you weren't here on the day he died? Friday, October 11?"

There was a pause during which he bristled.

"As a matter of fact, I was."

"Did you see him?"

"No. I had to pick up forms to fill out for a conference I plan to attend. I was in administration for about 20 minutes and then I left."

"Did anyone see you arrive or leave?"

"No."

An awkward silence unfolded.

"OK. Well, I'll let you get back to your work. I might have a few more questions later on. Is it all right if I come back?"

He scrutinized me for a moment. "Yeah. OK."

"Here's my business card in case you think of anything else you'd like to share."

He took the card and stuffed it into is shirt pocket without looking at it.

I packed away the tape recorder, braced myself for the long walk back, and turned to go.

"Hey—" he called after me, "So I'm a suspect?"

"Well, yeah."

"Shit," he said, and resumed counting crickets.

Marveling at how little I'd managed to glean from the conversation (and vaguely worried about any cricket-borne pathogens I might have just ingested), I started walking down the dusty gravel drive to the service road and administration. One of the freakish fall heat waves that always seem to shock people here (even though they happen without fail every year) had gripped the region and it was probably pushing 100 degrees. I could feel a film of sweat developing as I crunched along in my less-practical-than-anticipated shoes. I was relieved to get back to the cracked asphalt road and had just settled into a purposeful pace when I heard a vehicle slowing down behind me. It was a weathered green truck with Randall Wiley behind the wheel.

"Hey there," he said with an abbreviated wave. "You headed for administration?"

"Yes I am," I replied, suddenly concerned about whether the sweat was making me look waxy and flustered.

"Want a ride?"

"Sure." I made my way over to the passenger door and climbed into the cab. It smelled of white sage and "piney woods" air freshener. The dashboard was littered with an assortment of forms in various stages of completion and between my feet was a smattering of rocks.

"Did you just finish talking with Les?"

"How'd you guess?"

"I can't imagine why else you'd be this far up in the Zoo unless you were at the raptor show or the compost yard—and I just locked up the yard."

"Hmm. Maybe you should be doing the investigating." I still felt a little guilty about the end of our previous conversation. But he seemed to harbor no ill will at the fact that he was still a suspect, albeit not a strong one. I was relieved when he laughed at my little jest.

"So how'd that work out for you?"

"Not so much."

"Did he tell you all about his home bird?"

"His home bird? Like homegirl?"

"That's what he calls the peregrine falcon he keeps at home."

"No. But I did learn a lot about meal worms and crickets."

He glanced over at me with a grin. "Did he offer you cricket honey?"

I was beginning to suspect I'd just been the butt of a practical joke. "As a matter of fact, he did."

He chuckled. "Don't worry. You might get some good info out of him yet. He only offers the cricket honey to people that he finds worthwhile. So that means he thinks you're OK."

"Well I hope it's not going to take much more cricket honey to get the info I need."

He smiled, bemused.

"What were you trying to find out? Whether he had an alibi?"

"Well, there's that," I began, trying to decide whether I wanted to tip my hand to the Compost King. He was still a suspect and the cops were still verifying alibis including his. I decided that if he did do it, then it would seem to

97

be to his advantage if I started barking up the wrong tree instead. "It seems to me there must be some reason he had such antipathy for Claude."

"You mean other than the fact that he was pompous, overbearing, and thought he owned this place?"

"I think there has to be a more compelling motive than Claude's annoying personality traits. I mean, there are annoying people everywhere. And something tells me Claude wasn't the only person who annoys Les. What would make Claude more than an annoyance to Les?"

"Well, I think old Claude might have known Les's dad."

"Oh?" My heart skipped a beat. He looked at me with a quizzical expression and paused the truck at an intersection. A slow-moving flatbed carrying two mini forklifts crept in front of us, and while we waited for it to negotiate the turn he explained the Povenda connection.

"I've been to Max's place with Les a couple times, and I'm pretty sure he mentioned working for Imperator—you know that's the company that makes Povenda, the diet drug."

"Well that's a pretty odd coincidence," I said, then felt a wave of dismay. "Crap."

"What?"

"I don't think Les will talk about that no matter how much cricket honey I suck down."

After a hearty laugh, Wiley smiled. "Yeah. You're probably right about that. This could be your lucky day, though. Les's dad, Max, is a really nice guy. He lives in Toyon Canyon, not too far from the coast. He has a big Veteran's Day barbecue every year. Les usually invites a bunch of us. It's on Monday. You should go."

We had finally arrived at the administration building and I told him I'd think about it. What I was really thinking was how the hell I could invite myself to the barbecue. I'd have to kiss a lot of crickets over the next few days if I wanted to get on the guest list. As if he was reading my mind, Wiley told me to let him know if I decided to go and I could go with him. There was a weird moment while I tried to figure out how inappropriate that would be. Again anticipating my thoughts he explained that a group of Zoo staffers were all going together after work that Monday—about 3 p.m.— and I could ride along with them. (Animals don't take holidays, so zoos run on a hospital schedule.) Mentally breathing a sigh of relief, I told him that sounded like a fine plan, and I'd call to confirm.

"Great," he said as I climbed out of the truck. "But sometimes the phone doesn't actually ring up at the compost yard, so if I don't pick up be sure to leave a message."

Pondering the implications of this convenient coincidence, I came home to find Henry at the door, waiting to derail my thoughts. He sang his raspy welcome meow while I picked up the mail from under the slot. I stroked him for a few minutes, wondering how to go about broaching the topic with Max Moore if I could corner him into a conversation. I made my way to the kitchen with Henry excitedly trailing me. He was supposed to eat expensive canned food formulated for "less active" cats, but he would have nothing to do with it. So I had worked out a compromise that involved tuna water when possible, occasionally chicken baby food, and a blend of the special diet food with dried tuna flakes and a capsule of fish oil, which I hoped would spare him from becoming arthritic as he advanced into his golden years.

I murmured embarrassing terms of endearment to him and checked my answering machine. There was a call from Officer Pinata, who wanted to know if by any chance he had given me the set of Sniper photos along with the Claude Hopper pictures, and the Hand, whose message was so long that the machine cut her off in the middle of an update on the delayed return of the assistant general operations manager and an explanation of how to reschedule my appointment with her to schedule a time to see him. I deleted both and made my way to the couch to review my Post-It files. I turned on the news and started jotting down the information about Claude and Max Moore and considering what other details to add to the collage on my closet door. I had just finished when Henry joined me on the couch, muscling his way onto my lap, where he draped his 18-pound furry bulk across me.

After a loud commercial break, the news anchors opened with a story about the "Go For Bear" controversy at the Santa Narcissa Zoo. I found myself looking at another picture of Suzy in the hands of Peter Manley as he spoke to the reporter I'd seen him with earlier that day. I didn't really want to listen to his spiel again but I had not had the presence of mind to move the television remote within arm's reach before Henry pinned me to the couch, and now he was sleeping intently.

The Action News Team cut back to the excessively groomed anchors in front of a picture of Philip Landers, the Santa Narcissa City councilman who had been very critical of the Zoo in the past, though had stopped short of endorsing DofA. They cut to footage of him at a City Council meeting earlier in the year where he pointed out that the taxpayers were footing the bill for this unhappy Zoo bear and he would do everything in his power to work with concerned parties such as DofA to make sure that the Council evaluated the situation.

Stroking the soft sleek fur on the top of Henry's head while he softly snored, I wondered if he felt enslaved by my psychological need to make him happy.

11

Bunny Hop

November 30, 1955

The closet was not musty and mothball-scented as one might expect. Densely packed with clothing on an upper and a lower rack that combined to form a wall of skirts and sweaters, blouses and slacks, it was permeated by perfume—a powdery floral aroma that couldn't be dispersed or dampened by any laundry detergent. It simply absorbed other scents into itself. It was the essence of mama.

The previous owner of the house had removed the hideous burnt orange shag carpeting only to find that the floors had never been finished, and the grainy hardwood felt smooth and worn under his bare feet. A single low-watt bulb hung from the ceiling with a dangling ball chain to switch it on and off; after he had been pressed into the wall of clothing, the light extinguished, the door shut and locked behind him, he could hear the chain, just out of reach, making its whisper of a squeak, gradually slowing even as his heartbeat quickened.

Darkness and the suffocating sensation of the clothing began seeping into him as it always did. One time he had pressed his way to the very back of the closet, vainly hoping to find an escape—like those kids in *The Lion, the Witch, And the Wardrobe* who discovered a way to Narnia. But all he found was the bumpy, cold back wall of the closet. He began to quietly panic as he thought of all the empty arms and hems closing in around him, like ghosts in a crypt. He closed his eyes and tried counting, which sometimes calmed him, but not this time. This would be a very long time-out gaging by his mother's rage.

For much of his eight-year life on the farm he understood what happened to the animals who grew too old to produce milk or eggs. His parents offered no rationalizations. They had grown up on farms, where producing food is a matter of life and death. They told him it wasn't good to name the hens that came and went, and explained that if there are too many male goats in the herd, it's unpleasant for the does, the bucks themselves, and the people who tend them. But then they had gotten some rabbits, and that was different. They were fluffy and warm and when he fed them, instead of greedily plunging into the kibble or aggressively pecking, they would softly nibble. As they started reaching market size, Peter became increasingly anxious. He had tried not to name them, as he had not named the chickens or the goats. But the rabbits had assumed names in his mind, against his will. He tried to un-name them, but that didn't work. And then the day came when he overheard his parents discussing selling the rabbit meat and fur. He knew better than to take issue with them. His responsibility was to be seen and not heard. Yet something about the rabbits ignited a rebellious streak in him.

That night, he snuck out to the rabbit hutch and extracted them, one at a time. Sitting on the ground outside, they hopped around a bit, but made no effort to run away. Peter stamped his feet behind them and flapped his hands at their faces, and they seemed mildly startled, but still did not bolt into freedom. He whispered urgently that they would be killed soon if they did not flee. "Go, go, go!" After ten minutes, he started pushing the luminous white animals, and goaded them to the edge of a small stand of trees nearby. One by one, they leisurely made their way into the brush, noses twitching, eyes alert. (He would never know that all of them were consumed by hungry hawks, bobcats, coyotes, and foxes before the end of winter.)

Just as he got back to the house, his father, having heard Peter sneaking down the creaky stairs, came out of the back door to investigate, found Peter, and demanded to know what he was doing outside in his pajamas. Peter said that he thought he had left a toy in the yard, and his father shooed him inside. Within a few hours, there was hell to pay. His father administered the verbal punishment, and his mother took over from there–pinching his ear and tugging him toward the closet. Eventually, his father released him and Peter promptly wept and begged for forgiveness, but the tears were angry ones and the contrition a lie. The rebellion smoldered, but he learned to suppress it, control it, channel it into other pursuits. From that point on, he led a duplicitous life. He let his parents believe that he had learned his lesson, which was the hard part because he had to accept his role and responsibilities on the farm. He also let them believe that he would eventually take over the farm. With no siblings, there were no other options. But each day brought him closer to freedom.

As soon as he graduated from high school, he fled the confines of his parents' limited expectations and the omnipresent cloud cover of the coastal Pacific Northwest for Southern California, with its big open skies and unfettered possibilities. He discovered a talent for acting, and managed to make a living between waiting tables and bit parts. Eventually he landed the title role on a hit television series, *Detective Quaice*, about a dyslexic investigator who solves crimes with the aid of his nerdily charming personal assistant. After five seasons, that show ended and he found himself hosting a popular game show that had a long enough run for him to buy a house that was comfortable but not showy and to get DofA out of the red. Though he maintained formal contact with his family, he never again set foot north of San Francisco.

To say that Peter Manley hated confined spaces was an understatement. Elevators, phone booths (back in the day), those little rooms where they cover you with a leaden drop cloth and shoot dental X-rays at you, even sub-compact cars all left him in a cold sweat. For years his therapist had been trying to nudge him back to whatever childhood trauma had left him with such debilitating claustrophobia—to no avail. Peter had shut the door on that experience and it would take more than conversational prodding to get him back there. All the shrink knew was that there was some dark menace behind his patient's anxiety, and combatting that menace was what drove Peter Manley in his mission to free all captive creatures.

12

Aloha

September 28, 2002

The annual volunteer appreciation gala had crept up on Les Moore. It was always held on the last Saturday in September so that the newest crop of student volunteers (freshly minted seniors) could be part of the festivities, but this year had flown past with exceptional speed, and it seemed as though Labor Day had only just elapsed when he found himself rummaging through his closet for the one decent pair of non-khaki pants he owned to match the lone dress shirt that spent most of its time in the remote nether region at the back of the top shelf. The theme this year was "Aloha, Summer" and guests were encouraged to wear their fiercest tropical couture. Navy slacks and the trusty subdued plaid shirt would have to do.

As the supervising animal keeper at Raptorama, he was obliged to go every year, and every year he faced it with equal parts dread and anticipation. He had to steel himself to go, bracing for annoying chatter and awkward social encounters, but once he settled in, it was almost never quite as bad as he expected, plus the food was always outstanding—and he had Corinne Flaherty to thank for that. Corinne knew her volunteers, she knew the people who worked with them, and she knew the people who knew how they all got along together. She knew better than to seat Les next to any but the most self-possessed students and only the most low key docents. And she knew to absolutely never seat him at the same table as Claude Hopper. Their mutual antipathy had never ignited into outright confrontation, but Claude's volunteer records included numerous complaints about Les's less-than-appreciative attitude, lack of courtesy, and poor communication skills. It also contained as many complaints from Les about Claude's rampant sense of entitlement, disregard for protocol, and poor communication skills. After the first few volleys, she started keeping score in the back bottom corner of the folder. So far, Les was in the lead, having filed three more complaints than Claude, though with three months to go before the end of the year, anything could happen.

But Marti Hudson, the new volunteer supervisor who had been hired and trained just before Corinne departed on an unexpected trip to visit her husband's ailing father, didn't know, couldn't have known about the terrible twosome (as Corinne thought of them). The grievances were only accessible by senior management. So Marti, thinking the two would have much to talk about due to their mutual interest in Raptorama, had made the ill-fated seating arrangement too late for Corinne to see it until the night of the event.

Claude, in his freshly cleaned and pressed docent uniform, complete with the "aloha ascot"—aqua blue silk festooned with peach colored hibiscus flowers—ambled through the crowd, winking at his lady friends and offering firm, manly handshakes to his male colleagues. Usually Regina accompanied him, but at the last moment before the dinner she had cancelled due to a migraine. Claude suspected she was angry with him about a minor flirtation he'd had with one of the new docents and was punishing him. But his mood was not to be dampened. He looked forward to the annual gala with enthusiasm, regarding it as the Academy Awards of the volunteer set, and he, with an appropriate sense of self-deprecating humor saw himself as the Clint Eastwood of the docent crowd. He had, after all, golfed with Eastwood once. Actually, he had been employed as a part-time caddy during one of the ebb tides of his working life during college, and Eastwood had been at a charity event at the exclusive golf course. But he had spent several hours in the vicinity of the actor and knew they would surely have made a tremendous golf match-up.

Nodding and waving this way and that, he gradually made his way to table number six where his seat awaited, the only empty chair left. It wasn't until he had donned the plastic lei draped across his place setting, grasped the chair back and maneuvered his way into the space that he realized his lefthand neighbor was none other than Les Moore. He looked so different out of uniform and without a hat that Claude only realized who he was when he looked him in the eye. Some inflammatory phrases flitted through his mind, and when the two made eye contact, there was a fleeting moment of mutually hostile recognition before they each turned to the people on opposite sides and ignored one another for the time being. Eventually, though, both parties stepped out to claim certificates, and they were left with each other.

Somehow the conversation went from coolly cordial to corrosive in a matter of seconds, and it all began with falconry, the reason Marti Hudson had seated them at the same table. Falconry is one of the few remaining avocations that still rely on an apprenticeship system. A novice falconer becomes apprenticed to a mentor while learning the craft. The apprentice becomes a general falconer after two years, and a master at seven. This was the point over which the smoldering antipathy flared. Claude had suggested that his past experiences as a master falconer gave him the necessary skills to be able to work with the Raptorama birds.

"A master falconer?" Les said, putting his glass down forcefully enough to send the Chardonnay sloshing. Heads turned, then turned away again. "When is the last time you actually went hunting with a bird?"

"That's not the point. I've flown birds enough for the purposes of the presentations you do at Raptorama," Claude said sternly.

"Yes it is the point. Just flying birds isn't falconry. Do you even keep a bird anymore?"

"Look, I've been to Saudi Arabia," Claude responded, indignant. "They revere these birds there. They have a culture of falconry that is thousands of years old."

"Yeah, they revere them all right," Les retorted. "They're revering them to death. Those people have no idea what it means to respect wildlife. They trap anything and everything and do anything they want. They've decimated the falcon populations there."

"Oh. So now you're making this a cultural argument?" Claude was incredulous. "What a bigoted thing to say!"

"How the hell are you making this into some kind of racist argument? How much time did you spend there? A long weekend at the Riyadh Hilton? I'm making a criticism about conservation policy."

"Of course," Claude responded with barbed sarcasm. "A criticism about how *those people* treat wildlife."

"I'm sorry. Was I not using the politically correct terminology for a group of irresponsible people? Let me rephrase it. In Saudi Arabia, insufficient wildlife conservation policies mean that the unregulated taking of wild raptors for the purposes of falconry is jeopardizing the stability of falcon populations. And not just falcon populations. All their animals. Everything's nearly extinct there."

"I can't believe how spiteful you are. The Saudis maintain game preserves."

"Yeah—bits and pieces here and there, and everywhere else they're out there with Land Rovers and semi-automatic rifles hunting everything to death. For cripes sake they hunt the houbara."

"They've hunted the houbara for centuries. It's a game bird."

"It is not the natural prey of falcons. They trap them and use them for training. They are being over-hunted across their range, and the declines are sharpest in Saudi Arabia, Iran, and Pakistan."

"According to whom," Claude countered.

"According to the International Fund for Houbara Conservation which conducts biannual surveys. That's whom."

"Are you taking issue with my grammar as well?"

"You are such a pompous ass."

"Well it takes one to know one."

All nearby conversation had died and they were left glaring at one another amid the strains of ukulele music when Corinne appeared. She diplomatically asked Claude if he would please help hand out the service awards at the podium and smiled apologetically at Les as soon as Claude indignantly departed the table.

"I'm so sorry, Les," she said once Claude was out of earshot. "Marti made up the seating arrangements because I had to go out of town unexpectedly. Look, the sundae bar is set up. Forget about Claude and get some dessert. I'll make sure he keeps busy until the end of the evening. I really want you to see the Raptorama photos in the slideshow finale—the volunteers put it together and it's really fantastic."

Les glowered at her and then gave in to his insatiable sweet tooth. "All right."

The line for the dessert bar had materialized almost instantly and snaked around the back of the outdoor auditorium. Fortunately, it was moving briskly and he became distracted by the two middle-aged women in khaki ahead of him who were chatting about their weight loss struggles.

"Well, I tried practically every diet that came along. It was so frustrating, going through all that torture and getting nowhere," said the shorter of the two. "I hate grapefruit!"

Les studied them for a moment. One was almost as tall as he was, probably five-eight or so, with an hourglass figure that was fleshy but shapely. The one who was confessing her dieting follies was plump, but not unpleasantly so. He recalled his mother fretting over her figure before she became ill, and countless experiments with low calorie recipes that involved lots of cottage cheese and Jell-O. Shortly before she died, she joked that she had finally slimmed down but wouldn't be able to enjoy it.

"Yes," replied the curvy friend. "But once I gave up dieting, my weight kind of settled. And Dan hated all the food restrictions. He actually told me he'd rather see me zaftig and enjoying my food when I eat with him. Plus, the fat seems to settle in places that he likes to have a little heft."

Les felt himself blush while they giggled.

"Well, that's good for you, but my weight didn't settle, and I just can't get into the right eating habits. My blood pressure and cholesterol were untamable, so my doctor put me on Povenda."

"Hm. I've never tried any weight loss drugs. I'm so worried about side effects."

"It's a gamble I'm willing to take. For me the odds were better than the hypertension. And it worked like a dream for me."

"Well, you should tell Claude."

"Hopper?"

"Yes."

"Why?"

"Don't you know he invented it?"

"No kidding."

"It's true. That's where he made all his money—at Imperator Pharmaceuticals. He was the lead researcher for Povenda."

"Rich, handsome, intelligent. I can't believe he's single."

"Well, I understand he's been married three times before, so clearly that thing about the third time being the charm isn't true. He lived in Texas for a long time—I think near Austin—and he was married to that would-be ingenue who married the Confederated Oil guy."

"Really?"

"Oh, yes. But his first wife is from around here. He's from Santa Narcissa. It's kind of strange, actually. You know his son is a volunteer here, too?"

"What?"

"You probably don't see him much because you only tour the school groups. He's a general volunteer, and I also do general volunteer assignments, so I sometimes cross paths with him. He's rather, um, eccentric. You'd never guess Claude's his father to look at him. He obviously takes after his mother's side, I guess."

"So is that why Claude came back to Santa Narcissa? To connect with his son?"

110

"Oh, no. He made out like a bandit at Imperator. He retired early—at 54."

Les was following the women in line, but had forgotten about the bowl in his hands and the ice cream in front of him. Everything around him had blurred, his mind suddenly focused with pinpoint clarity on who Claude Hopper was. He stepped out of the dessert line and turned to scan the room until he found his target. Claude was busy hobnobbing near the lectern. He was behind the table where all the service pins and certificates of merit were arranged to be picked up by recipients. Les strode across the room and leaned up against the table. Claude, in the middle of an amusing marsupial anecdote, paused and looked at Les, his glib smile fading just a bit.

"What do you want?"

"You conniving son of a bitch," Les growled, then wound up and swung at Claude, who pulled back quickly enough that the punch landed on the cluster of service pins arrayed on the breast pocket of his uniform jacket. There were gasps all around, and a startled yelp from Claude. Before anyone could make a move, Les, clutching his abraded knuckles, took off through the nearest exit.

13

Junior League

November 6, 2002

The cricket honey left me with no ill effects, and the next morning over scrambled eggs with toast and coffee, I studied the colorful but not very cohesive Post-It note array on my closet door. I decided that unfortunate cranky Les Moore was my prime suspect so far. Of course, he was pretty much my only suspect. The Compost King's alibi checked out. He was about 36,000 feet over Lake Michigan on his way home from Nova Scotia during the prime time for Claude's death. Corinne's tale of the tempestuous and potentially homicidal girlfriend kept coming to mind. I wondered again whether he had left money to her in his will, or maybe named her as a beneficiary on his life insurance policy. She was a docent, too, so maybe a perusal of her dossier would be useful.

I walked into the Volunteer Office just as a storm was brewing. A willowy woman with gold blonde hair turning silver gray was standing at the threshold of Corinne's office gasping that she just couldn't understand what she had done to deserve this kind of treatment. The conciliatory tones coming from inside were not having much of an effect and finally the docent stalked off. I'm sure she would have slammed the door dramatically if it hadn't been one of those pneumatic ones that resists such displays of temper. I waited a few minutes, studying the staff newsletter, then crept over to Corinne's office. She looked up with the stern expression of a detention hall monitor, saw that it was me, then slumped and motioned me to step into the office.

"Oy and Vey."

"Sorry."

"Ugh. Not your fault. That was none other than Regina Pearl."

"Really?" I said, glancing outside the door as if I could rewind and conjure her back into the room.

"Yes. If I'd known you were out there, I would have introduced you. And maybe avoided being in the flight path of the shit storm."

"What's up?"

"Oh. I had to revoke some of her privileges and she's not happy about it."

"Like what?"

"Well, I had to take away her cart privileges."

"Did she hit someone?"

"No, not that bad, but she drove off with the vehicle plugged in one too many times. And the last time, this time, she must have floored it out of the parking space because it decapitated the cord so the plug was still in the cart and the live wire was lying on the pavement."

"Yikes."

"In a puddle of water."

"Yikes twice."

"Yeah, we were lucky someone saw it and alerted one of the electricians. But that's kind of the last straw after a lot of other issues. She's almost as bad as Claude in terms of taking liberties."

"She seemed pretty incensed."

"Oh, it will blow over. That's the problem, actually."

"Well, it's Regina that I came to see you about."

"Oh?"

"Do you think I could borrow her dossier?"

"Is she a suspect?"

"I'm not sure. I'll know more after I look at that, and talk with her."

"Give me a second and I'll get it for you. I have to make a phone call first."

I meandered back out into the office and spotted the green jumpsuit guy who had been there on Monday. He was looking at me but not looking at me. The hair turban was slightly askew, and he was wearing a green and white striped rugby shirt and purple corduroy pants. His beard draped like Spanish moss and this time he was wearing untinted glasses that made his eyes look huge and jellied. The silence was beginning to sink into awkward depths when Corinne came out of her office with a manila folder, handed it to me, introduced none other than Claude Hopper, Jr., and excused herself. Trying to not look startled, I shook his hand and managed to not recoil at the touch. It was like gripping an enormous warm gummy worm. He said hello with a gust of halitosis. I stammered that I was sorry about his recent loss and he blinked his watering, far-sighted eyes and thanked me.

"I know who you are," he said in a hushed tone.

"You do," I responded, hiding my confusion since Corinne had just introduced me as the private investigator looking into the circumstances of his father's death.

"Yes. You used to work here, and you were a research volunteer."

"Yes."

"That's why they put you on this case."

"Yes."

"Well, I know what happened to him."

"You do?"

"Yes," he replied and stepped closer. "He had dangerous information."

"About?"

"Did you know he was a photographer?"

"Yes."

"Have you seen his work?"

"No."

"He was an investigative journalist and had some... incriminating photos."

115

"Of whom?"

"Do you know Philip Landers?"

"The City councilman?"

"Yes."

"Not personally. I know who he is."

"Well, let's just say that the councilman knows Peter Manley pretty personally."

"The DofA guy?"

"Yes."

"What are you getting at?"

"You'll see what I mean." He winked at me and touched the side of his nose with an index finger. His nails were buffed to a high shine.

"OK."

"Would that be of interest to you?"

I had to fight the skeptic in me who wanted to dismiss him. Just because he was eccentric didn't mean that whatever information he was offering was irrelevant.

"Sure."

"I can messenger them to you."

"OK," I said and handed him one of my Holcomb Botanical Gardens business cards. "You can send them here."

He carefully put the card into his wallet and shook my hand again with clammy gratitude. I wished him a good afternoon and quickly exited. Settling into the driver's seat, I sighed, smirked, and started the engine. I had backed out of the space and started toward the exit when Regina Pearl gusted out of nowhere, blindly lurching across the asphalt in front of my car, arms cradling her head as if all the injustices of the universe were hailing down on her. I honked and she paused, made a tragic, sour grimace at me and then continued her distraught pantomime across the lot.

It was still early-ish, and there would be a few more hours of daylight, so I headed for Holcomb Gardens. During a trip to Santa Barbara a couple years earlier, I had discovered a nursery with an astonishing selection of garden statuary, all handmade by a local stone sculptor. My big splurge on non-plant expenses for the monster garden was a collection of stone figures—grotesques based on the works of a nineteenth century Italian artist whose quirky figures were reminiscent of the illustrations from Alice in Wonderland.

The first two had arrived and were waiting for me in the yard adjacent to the green house, swaddled in protective wrapping and sitting on a wooden pallet. I retrieved a utility knife and freed them, then stood back and chuckled. One was a bearded, gnome-like man carrying a chimney sweep's brush. He was grinning a leering bug-eyed smile and wearing clogs. The other was a distraught female figure wearing an elaborate wimple with one arm flung up in the classic gesture that proclaims, "Woe is me!"

14

The Man-Eater

November 6, 2002

Regina Pearl hated the annual tuberculosis test that was required in order to work or volunteer at the Zoo. Years ago, one of the elephants had contracted TB from someone on staff and died, so from that time on, everyone had to be subjected to the hassle and humiliation of TB testing. Because she was late with her test, as usual, she had to go downtown to the Santa Narcissa City employees' health center to have it done. The whole building was outfitted in vintage 1970s recession-era institutional decor—beige-green walls with beige-pink trim, cryptically patterned floor tile designed to disguise everything from mud to blood, faintly flickering fluorescent tube lighting in an accousticized ceiling stained with the leaks of several decades of rainy seasons and punctuated here and there by a pencil or wad of gum. It was disgusting. As if she could ever have come in contact with any of the type of people who carry diseases like that, she thought indignantly as she waited for the curt nurse to hand her the forms to fill out.

With the papers in hand, she crammed herself into the uncomfortable combo desk chair (probably enjoying its retirement from one of the nearby public schools) and began the odious process. The worst part was getting started with the form. She actually didn't mind the test itself. The needle prick was far less intrusive than the irksome paperwork—asking for her legal name and date of birth and other personal details that were really no one's business but her own.

She had worked very hard to reinvent herself and complete the metamorphosis from Jayne Paine into Regina Pearl and damn if she wasn't going to make the most of herself. She didn't need these nasty annual reminders of the person she'd left behind.

Growing up in the semi-outback that preceded suburban tract housing in the San Hernando Valley, Jayne was the youngest of four girls. Over the years she met other "youngests" who had become spoiled brats, but that wasn't the case for her. Her parents, after three competitive, quarrelsome daughters, were too exhausted emotionally and financially to lavish much of anything on Jayne. Once she started high school she really felt the skimping. The way the school district boundaries fell was odd and although her family lived physically closer to the more blue collar school, she and her siblings wound up attending the ritzier school that was part of the neighboring district comprised largely of kids from the wealthy side of the tracks.

By the end of the first term of her freshman year she began to loathe the hand-me-down quality of her life. At school she was defined as Bethany's little sister, Katherine's little sister, or Jennifer's little sister. At home there were not only hand-me-down clothes but second hand sentiments… when Bethany was your age… why can't you be as clever/thrifty/responsible as Katherine… you're not nearly as outgoing/academically-inclined/generous as Jennifer… Even her name came up short. As if all the syllables had been used up by her sisters. The best her parents could do was add a "y" to plain Jane—a silent distinction that she spent her life having to explain. "No, it's Jayne, with a 'y'" was the chorus to every introduction.

Her mother had a chronic problem remembering her children's names. She would sometimes call one daughter by another's name and often by an amalgam of more than one: Jatherine, Bejerine, Jatheny, Kamany. As if they were all roughly interchangeable. Even in this, she knew the "J" was always Jennifer, never Jayne.

The nurse rubbed a small patch of skin on her left forearm with an alcohol swab, then, ever so carefully injected the serum under the skin, leaving her with a little blister, instructions not to scratch, and a reminder that she would need to return in two days for a reading. She gave a terse thanks and then gusted out of the building to the parking structure. Putting on her seatbelt, she caught a glimpse of movement behind her in the rearview mirror—two people grappling in a shadowy corner. She started to reach for the cell phone in her handbag to call for help. Then she realized it was consensual grappling. The dark-haired man had the red-headed woman pinned up against the wall. Her stretchy knit skirt was hiked up and one shapely leg shod in a bright red patent leather pump was wrapped around the back of his legs and her hands were raking his scalp. He had one arm around her waist and the other under her mostly unbuttoned shirt. They were kissing ferociously, as if they were trying to swallow one another. Regina was at first disgusted, but before she could avert her gaze, something about the man caught her eye.

For a moment he turned so that she could see him in profile—the short slightly upturned nose, the James Dean hair, and the way he was gripping the woman... suddenly she was back in high school with a boy who looked uncannily similar, in the back of a car at the drive-in to see *Some Like It Hot*. What started as a simple kiss during the film credits became a warm and viscous make-out session. Somehow despite her (admittedly weak) efforts to not let the situation escalate, clothing was slipping off and body parts were merging.

As competitive and bickersome as her sisters were, they were all "good girls" who stuck to the conservative Christian code of modesty and chastity that had been instilled in them—and in Jayne. They had not been allowed to date without a chaperone, and this made them the object of curiosity, disdain, and lust. But as with so many aspects of her childhood, Jayne was not subject to the same parental attention to detail as the others were, so she

121

was allowed to go out with boys, unaccompanied, though her parents had to meet and approve of the potential squire, authorize the proposed activity, and insisted on a strict curfew of 8 p.m. These restrictions were a bit imposing, but not so difficult to circumvent, which is how Jayne managed to finally outdo her sisters in one arena, and how she found herself in the back of a Chevy Bel Air, making out with the president of the Student Council.

She was lost in a heady, swirling mix of pleasure and surprise when suddenly he murmured "Jennifer." She froze and pulled away, as if she had been stung. He immediately apologized. It was a tragic blunder on his part with no cruel intent. He hadn't even dated her sister. It had only been a desperate, unrequited crush on Jennifer. He liked Jayne very much, and she coincidentally bore the strongest resemblance to Jennifer. And unfortunately had a name that also started with a "J." He tried to keep her from slipping out of the car and storming back to the bus stop. But the damage had been done, the fury unleashed—a cold and calculating fury, like an enormous glacier grinding and scraping everything in its path.

And thus began the metamorphosis. Jayne decided she would never again be interchangeable with her siblings. She reinvented herself as a new Jayne who no one would ever think of in the same mental breath as any of her sisters. Tapping into an audacity that startled even her at times, she transformed herself into the school vixen. When she couldn't pilfer money from her sisters or raid the curse jar on the kitchen counter, she would simply shoplift the accessories she needed to maintain her persona—make-up and jewelry and designer clothes. She checked out from the local library a manual for beauticians in training, and gradually her dishwater blonde hair paled and refined into cold platinum. If her family noticed a change in her, they couldn't be bothered to do much more than tease her about it in passing. At school she ascended the social ranks and became one of the popular people. Others watched her hungrily, and she hungrily consumed all the attention she could get. She knew she was OK to look at—nothing remarkable, but not bad. She had a good figure and even features with clear skin. Her allure was her audacity. She flirted recklessly with sales clerks, busboys, fellow students, even some teachers. It was her sheer boldness that got her where she wanted to be. Of course, age tempered the raging minx, though she never stopped seeking revenge for the slight in the Chevy.

Attuned to the shortcomings of every man she met, she became adept at pinpointing weaknesses and exploiting them for whatever ends struck her fancy—dinner and a show, a designer dress, estate jewelry, and purebred Abyssinian cats. As Regina Pearl, she was respectable, with a respectable job managing the accounting department at the local junior college, and though she had never married, she was respectably serially monogamous.

It was quite shocking the first time she went to the supermarket and the cashier called her "Ma'am" instead of "Miss," and it was this seemingly minor incident that spurred yet another reinvention—this one not related to vengeance, but the response to a strange urge to do something of value—perhaps a reflux of the values her parents had attempted to instill in her during her youth. After reading an article in the *Santa Narcissa Mirror* about volunteer programs at the Zoo, she decided to investigate. Though she had never in her life considered the value of the natural world and the need for conservation, she was fascinated by the idea of being surrounded by exotic animals (they had Sumatran tigers there!) and a new audience.

The reality of exotic animals was not as exciting as she had imagined it would be. The Zoo had strict rules about who was allowed to have contact with the animals, and even the keepers had no contact with most of the interesting animals. She could get no nearer to the tigers than the general public, and the only animals docents were allowed to handle were boring (she could see rabbits and guinea pigs at the pet store), intimidating (birds seemed unpredictable and demanding), or unappealing (reptiles of any kind were repellant to her). So she did not apply for an animal handling certification, and instead pursued research (which did not allow her to get any closer to the animals she liked, but did give her a legitimate purpose for observing them) and food prep. It was interesting to talk with some of the keepers, and she found that at Raptorama she could sometimes watch them working with the birds that were in the show. When grumpy Les Moore was in a better mood, he would tell her interesting things about birds.

Once he had explained how the dinosaurs had not all gone extinct, that some of them had survived climate change and the rise of mammals. They were warm blooded and eventually grew feathers and became birds. Regina bristled when he used the "e" word. Growing up, her parents had complained constantly about the public schools teaching evolution, and wanted to put the girls in a private Christian school, where biology would never become speculative in any way that would challenge what they knew to be true about the universe and how God had created it. But thanks to their unrelenting complaints, the high school tamed its curriculum. They conducted an experiment with wingless fruit flies and regular fruit flies that illustrated Gregor Mendell's discovery about dominant and recessive genes, but never considered the larger implications of his experiments. Likewise, they had sprouted beans and subjected the plants to various growing conditions to see how they reacted to different levels of light or watering schedules. Yet there was never any discussion of how different plants had adapted to varying conditions, or how these characteristics demonstrated a larger pattern of development.

Whenever she looked at the inquisitive parrots or the powerful raptors now, she imagined the dinosaurs that Les said were hidden in each one. That intrigued her, and also frightened her a bit. Not just the notion of a scary, alien beast inside the familiar animals, but also the implication that there might really be an alternative reality to the one she had inherited from her parents. One in which the universe was not created as she had always believed it to be, by a benign and omnipotent entity, but through a process that was like a rampant science experiment in which everything happened by chance and probability. Later, after her tumultuous introduction to Claude, she saw that this was his reality. It secretly thrilled her to think of living in his world, and when they were together, it was always in his universe. They had never truly argued about faith and reason, but the rules governing her existence always seemed to bend to the stronger forces of his. When he talked about his work in research and medicine, or about the animals around them, or why people behave as they do, she felt herself swept away from how she had been taught to see the world, and, with a sense of anxious exhilaration, she realized it made her happy.

Lost in her reverie, she did not notice the departure of the grappling couple and was startled when a car honked behind her, the driver gesturing to inquire if she was pulling out of the space. She nodded, started the car, and headed for the Zoo.

15

Photo Synthesis

November 7, 2002

When I left the Zoo world for horticulture, I severed most of the ties to my past, which was a fairly awful process. I'm not a social dynamo by any stretch of the imagination, but over the years, most of my tiny social circle arced through the Zoo. Corinne was the one I missed most. But reinventing myself turned out to be a pretty all-encompassing project. I spent more than a few lonely evenings crying into the sofa cushions while Captain Kirk and his crew saved the universe from luridly clad aliens. But most of the time, between studying and workshops and my own personal field trips to various parks and gardens I was too tired to spend much energy dwelling on what I'd left behind.

My non-Zoo friends assumed I was having some kind of crazy pre-midlife crisis. They watched carefully to make sure I wasn't going to do anything harmful to myself or others, and waited patiently for it to pass. But it didn't. And when I tried to explain how plants are the foundation of life itself, how they changed this planet into a world that would support animal life by converting a noxious carbon dioxide-based atmosphere into an oxygen-nitrogen dominated one, then ingeniously developed clever methods of coaxing animals into helping them reproduce and colonize new territories, I know the diagnosis began to shift from pre-mid-life crisis to early-onset senility. The conversion, however, was genuine. My return to the Zoo reminded me of some of the people and aspects of the place I had learned to stop missing, but also made me thankful for my work at Holcomb Botanical Gardens.

A great garden is a story; a reflection of what's in the mind of the gardener. Conventional plants tell a conventional tale. Edged by predictable Nile lilies and clivia, the manicured lawn, demanding a constant regimen of mowing and edging, frequent water, weed killer, fertilizer, and aeration, sets the stage for pampered roses, always on the verge of rust or mildew, an all-you-can-eat salad bar for aphids. We have an arsenal of power equipment at our command these days, but back before World War II, a massive, meticulously clipped lawn meant an army of groundskeepers to maintain it with hand tools. The lawn, formerly a symbol of landed aristocracy and wealth, after the War became a statement of American post-war affluence. Converting the technology of tanks and the chemistry of explosives into power mowers and fertilizers meant every American yard was an estate.

Similarly, before the evolution of the modern large scale nursery, collecting exotic plants was the domain of eccentric explorers who traveled to distant lands and returned with living treasures to grace the hothouses of botanical gardens and the wealthy elite. Nowadays, bird of paradise, palms, and exotic ferns are available at any home improvement store, as are the watering systems needed to keep many of them growing happily in the middle of the dry chaparral. Both these scenarios are about money, power, and, in Southern California, the politics of commandeering water from distant places. As a public garden, at Holcomb we are expected to create these fantasy landscapes, and the Royal Rose Garden and the Hawaiian Paradise are probably our most popular attractions. My personal tastes are less conventional.

Plants themselves have tales to tell, natural histories that have inspired myths and legends. When humans were more directly at the mercy of nature, understanding plants was as important as understanding animals, water, and weather. Today, people are far less connected to plants than they are to animals, though they depend on them even more for food, clothing, medicines, the air we breathe. Perhaps that's where taxonomy has done us all a grave disservice. By separating plants and animals into different king-doms, we alienated them from us. The compilers of ancient bestiaries listed plants (as well as gems and minerals) alongside animals as entities with distinct properties and magical powers. Mandrake, nightshade, and ginger were carefully described alongside unicorns, lions, and owls.

The curators were happy with the progress I'd made so far in the mon-ster garden, and I was looking forward to tending my beloved monsters after the awkward diversion of the Zoo. Leaving the greenhouse, I was sur-prised to see our mailroom clerk scampering up the hill toward me waving a packet. He was an upbeat, highly caffeinated young perma-temp who had initials instead of a name—EJ, DJ, TJ, ASAP, COD—alphabet soup was slosh-ing in my brain as he approached. I tended to think of him as PDQ. Part of the reason I could never remember his name was that it was so distracting watching him talk that I could never come up with a mnemonic to help me remember. He had a pierced tongue and several lip piercings that were re-cent enough that he had not yet learned to talk without lisping and clicking.

"Thandy!" he halted breathless before me. He had shaved his head over the weekend and to protect his delicate scalp from the elements he was wearing a black knit cap with cat ears pointing up from the top.

"Good morning," I replied while he held out the packet.

"Thith jutht arrived for you via methenger. It theemed important tho I thought I'd bring it up here right away."

"Thanks." I looked at the address label and saw that it was from Claude Hopper, Jr. This didn't bode well, I thought, and, waving absentmindedly at ASAP, I went to the patio area behind the greenhouse where I kept a table and chairs. I sat down and opened the messenger service package and found a sealed manila envelope. Inside that was a hefty stack of eight-by-ten glossy prints: the photos that Claude, Jr. had mentioned. A note written in scratchy pencil on the back of a used DMV window envelope informed me that the files were quite extensive. Junior had included a sampling of his father's work so I could see that he was a legitimate photographer but also some particular, peculiar shots (found in an older section of the archive) that might be helpful in my investigation.

Apparently, Claude had not only freelanced for the *Santa Narcissa Mirror*, but also sold titillating celebrity photos to tabloids and gossip columns. There were some lovely nature shots—landscapes and wildlife in the local mountains, but also a smattering of candid photos of starlets who were inadvertently flashing a bit of nipple or bending over just a little too far in dresses that were a little too short. At the very bottom of the stack were some slightly blurry (as if they had been taken from far away with a zoom lens) and rather lurid pictures of two men *in flagrante delicto*. One, with mussed hair, wearing a studded collar and on all fours was glancing behind him at the other man, who was in an extreme priapic state bearing down on him with a riding crop raised above his head in mid-stroke. It seemed to have been taken from a high angle through open sliding glass doors. Looking more closely at the setting, I could see what seemed to be a menagerie of taxidermied animals grimacing and posturing stiffly in the background. I turned the photo over and saw some extremely back-handed scrawl in the bottom left corner that read "Manley and Landers at Hidden Valley Resort" and dated August three years earlier. I blinked, re-read it, and then looked at the image again. The content was so startling that I hadn't really been thinking about the identities of the parties involved. When I examined the figures again, I could see that the man on top could most surely be Peter Manley. Later on at home, an Internet search for images of Santa Narcissa City Councilman Philip Landers was pretty conclusive. I broke out the Post-Its and set up a whole new line of connections.

Did Manley know about these pictures? Did Landers? If Manley and/or Landers did know, would either one take extreme measures? Was Hopper blackmailing one or both? Was Manley still tied to Landers? Did this have something to do with perceived antagonism on the part of City Council toward the Zoo? This was the most exciting break I'd had yet. After applying a flurry of Post-Its to the closet door, I studied the new pattern, then dug a small cleaning cloth out of a desk drawer and paced around my living room, dusting random objects. It was a good way to distract myself and mull things over. Henry watched me from his favorite window sill. I was shifting the objects on my faux-mantel and wiping away the dust between the clear spots each nicknack left behind when I realized I'd overlooked something. I picked up the phone and dialed Corinne's number.

"Sorry if I'm bothering you."

"No—not at all! Just pleasantly surprised to hear from you. How's the investigation going?"

"I wanted to thank you so much for sharing all the information about Claude and Regina. It's been really helpful."

"Happy to help."

"Yeah..." I didn't want to tip my hand just yet. "I had an interesting conversation with Claude, Junior."

"Yes. He clearly did not inherit his dad's schmooze skills. I was surprised to see him at the Zoo at all. He's actually been in more often than usual since Claude, Senior, you know..."

"How often does he normally come in?"

"Only a couple days a week. It depends on his library schedule."

"Well, some people like to have diversions at times like that," I said. "He mentioned his father's photography."

"Yeah. That was another of Claude's many pursuits. He was a freelance photographer."

"That was definitely the case, and Junior sent me some interesting pictures."

"Really?"

"Yes. I don't really feel at liberty to go into much detail right now, but I was wondering whether you knew of any connections between Claude and Peter Manley?"

"The DofA guy?"

"Yeah."

"No," she relied with curiosity crackling in her voice. "Did they know each other?"

"That I don't know, but based on the photos I have here, he knew *of* Peter Manley, and there seems to be a connection with someone on the City Council."

"Who? What do you have?"

"I don't want to say right now. I don't even know if what I have is legitimate, but if it is, there might be a whole different course of investigation to pursue."

"I see," she sounded disappointed.

"Do you happen to have Junior's phone number?"

"Not on me, but I can look it up for you. Do you want it now?"

"Kind of. Junior sent photos and intimations but no contact info."

She laughed. "OK. Can I call you back in a few minutes? I need to log into my work e-mail."

"No problem. I'll be here."

She phoned back in less than a few minutes with the number and, preparing for awkwardness, I took a deep breath before dialing.

"Good evening. This is Claude."

Having grown accustomed to thinking of him as "Junior," this threw me for a moment.

"Hello?" he asked while I mentally fumbled into action.

"Oh, hi. This is Sandy Lohm—the private investigator?"

"Yes, yes," he replied eagerly, as if he'd been expecting my call. He was one of those people who never seems to find the right position for the mouthpiece, and I felt like I was probably speaking into the side of his neck.

"I'm calling because I received the photos."

"And..."

"They are very interesting."

"I thought you'd agree."

"So did your father tell you what was going on?"

"Well, I thought that was fairly obvious. The DofA guy is in bed—quite

132

literally—with the City councilman."

"So your father was blackmailing one or both of them?"

"No, of course not," he murmured indignantly. "My father wasn't a blackmailer. He cared very deeply about the Zoo, and I think it's not too much of a stretch to see the implications of the photos."

"Which are?"

"That the animal rights contingent is pressuring City Council policy regarding the Zoo. My father was going to blow the whistle on this unethical relationship."

"Did he tell you that?"

There was a pause that might have been him hesitating or repositioning the phone. "Not in so many words."

"What words did he use?"

"Well, he implied that he knew about this relationship."

"So he didn't show you the photos?"

"No. I found them after he had... passed. When I was sorting through things at his house."

"What did he imply about the connection between Manley and Landers?"

"Well, he mentioned many times how odd it was that Phil Landers is so opposed to providing support for the Zoo. It was like he had a hidden agenda."

"That's not exactly evidence of a plot to undermine the Zoo. Even if they were lovers, that doesn't mean Landers was doing anything illegal."

"No. But releasing the photos would probably have discredited him, and that at least would have lessened the negative pressure from the City Council."

That made sense. Claude, Senior wasn't trying to implicate Landers or Manley for breaking the law. He just wanted to protect the Zoo. Manley had come out publicly a few years earlier, so the photos were an issue of invasion of privacy for him, but Landers had a well-heeled wife and kids.

"I see your point. You know what would be really helpful is if I could have a look around your father's house. I need to find something more solid that indicates what he may have had in mind. There has to be a more concrete motive."

"The police have already been there."

"Do they know about these photos?"

"No."

"So they aren't looking for any connections between your father and these two. Can you meet me there tomorrow?"

We arranged to meet at Senior's house the next morning at 10 a.m. It was in the foothills just north of Santa Narcissa.

After we said goodbye, I got online again and looked up the telephone number for Santa Narcissa City Councilman Philip Landers. His field office was on the outer edge of the downtown area, not too far from my house. I picked up the phone and started the process of setting up an appointment to speak with the councilman. Then I placed a call to Defenders of Animals, and was flabbergasted when the woman who answered the call cheerfully told me to come by the offices any time the next day to see Peter Manley. I could go to Claude's house in the morning and still make it to DofA. Then there was the Max Moore connection, and I had to follow up on that one no matter how awkward it might be. It was time to gird myself for the barbecue, which was only three days away. I dug Randall Wiley's card out of my wallet, dialed the number for the Compost Office, and left my message at the sound of the beep.

"Oh, hi. This is Sandy Lohm, the detective from the other day. You mentioned the barbecue on Monday and that I could catch a ride there with you. So I'll be at the Zoo around 2:45 on Monday. I'll wait outside administration."

16

Casa de Claude

November 8, 2002

It was a good thing that Claude, Junior decided to wear the same green jumpsuit he wore the first time I saw him, and that he chose to stand at attention next to the mailbox at the end of the long drive that connected Claude, Senior's residence to the road. Although I had made good time despite the morning rush hour, within a few turns after exiting the freeway, I had lost all sense of direction on the winding residential streets of the foothill neighborhood. I habitually navigate by the omnipresent Southern California sun, but the steep terrain and groups of mature trees made that difficult, and in this neck of the woods, people did not opt to have their house numbers stenciled onto the curbs. It wasn't a posh neighborhood in the showy Beverly Hills sense. People here were paying to live close to nature but still have comfortable access to the city when they wanted a dose of culture. The homes were not mansions and had been situated far enough back to accommodate the massive street trees. The gardens were well tended, but not manicured. Most of these property owners could probably afford to maintain golf course perfect turf, yet many (I was pleased to note) had yards designed to blend into the native chaparral. The few cars parked on the street were luxury makes and models, and a number of signs staked in front yards for the upcoming election all backed Republican candidates. I was definitely out of my element.

Finally, I found Claude's street. As I made the turn, an unmarked police car pulled around a corner and crept up behind me and I wondered if my vintage Tercel prowling the 'hood had prompted someone to call them. My dealings with the police had always been civil and professional in my PI days, but it still made me anxious to be in close proximity to cops—perhaps the result of too much hypothetical criminal thinking on my part. Guilt by association. I had reflexively slowed down and checked to make sure I was under the speed limit when I spotted Junior gesturing for me to pull into the drive. It was a relief when the cop car kept on cruising down the street.

Only a sliver of the house was visible from the road, and I drove carefully along the bumpy cobblestones and around a large scrub oak, then parked in front of the garage and waited for Junior to catch up.

"Hello," he said and eagerly shook my hand when I got out of my car. "This way please."

Glancing around as we made our way down the walkway, it was difficult to tell where the property ended, with landscaping that gently merged into the surrounding hills. The house was mid-century modern and well cared for. The front door was at the crook of an L, with floor-to-ceiling windows creating a glass wall along the shorter lefthand side. The facing wall was windows only halfway to the ground. Inside, hallways ran along each arm. The inner wall along the floor to ceiling windows was adorned with abstract wood carvings. Massive green-and-yellow variegated agaves with spiny leaves that arched and bent as if they were swimming in the warm air lined the path outside so that it seemed the wooden shapes were hovering above them. Along the half-glass wing was a planter bed lined with old bluish columnar cacti standing stiffly at attention behind a row of beautiful blue compact agaves that used to be known as California cabbage. All those spines and serrations were as good as guard dogs.

136

At Holcomb, we had a similar armament planted outside our equipment storage yard. Foolish teenage thieves once tried to circumvent the barbed moat and get over the fence. One of them escaped with shredded clothing. The other skewered himself and left a trail of blood that a police dog was able to follow effortlessly. When the cops caught up with him, he looked like he was suffering from a bad case of stigmata. He had pierced both hands on agave spines and picked up a brow of barbs from the euphorbia called "crown of thorns"—the decorative outer perimeter of our defense system. He wound up with nerve damage in one hand and breaking and entering on his permanent record.

Junior opened the door and we stepped into a foyer that was a huge square of charcoal gray slate. The hall to the right led to the master bedroom and bath. Straight ahead and down three broad and shallow steps was a large open living room with an airy galley kitchen to the left. A door at the junction of the living room and kitchen led to Claude's office and a small bathroom. The furniture was sleek Danish modern with lots of svelte wooden arms and legs that made the place seem uncluttered even with the preponderance of artifacts throughout. Claude had traveled a bit, and had great taste—alabaster carvings from Egypt, ash-glazed ceramics from Japan, beautiful tribal weavings from Afghanistan. One wall displayed a spectacular tent door. The intricate pattern, which told the story of the nomadic people who had made it, was woven in rich madder reds and intense indigo blues. The fringes were tightly braided into tassels with small silver beads at the ends. Once upon a time, it must have been part of a wealthy dowry.

Huge windows opposite the tent door in the living room framed the hillside view and sliding glass doors led to a deck that was a transition space between inside and out. I felt involuntary pangs of house lust. A place like that was far beyond my means, and yet it made me happy to know it was there, just as hideous tract housing could haunt me long after I'd passed it by.

"It's a nice place," Junior said.

"Sure is," I tore my gaze away from the view. "Did you come here often?"

"Not really. A few times. We had both been volunteering at the Zoo for a while before we found each other. But I live pretty far from here, and a lot of times dad's girlfriend stayed here."

"Regina Pearl?"

"Yes. I find it somewhat taxing being around her, so dad and I mostly talked at the Zoo or on the phone. Sometimes we went out to eat."

"How about your mom? Did your dad get back in touch with her after you two met up again?"

"Not really."

"What do you mean by 'not really?'"

"Well, they weren't not talking, but neither of them went out of their way to contact the other."

"So there wasn't any animosity?"

He paused before answering. "Not really."

"So there was some?"

"Some what?"

"Animosity."

"Well, their marriage wasn't great. But my mom always implied that they both knew it wasn't working and they split pretty amicably. I know it wasn't easy for her being a single mom, but we got by OK. It was just the two of us. When I told her that I met dad volunteering at the Zoo, she seemed to be happy for me. But not necessarily for herself."

"So did they ever talk after you and your dad reconnected?"

"Not that I know of."

"I see. Do you mind if I look around now?"

"Go ahead," Junior answered. "The police already looked around and copied some of his files. I think a forensic accountant is going over his books. That's pretty much it."

"Did you tell them about the photos you sent me?"

"No. I thought it would be best to have you look into that quietly first."

Photographs were everywhere, but very few were of people. I assumed he had taken most of the landscapes and animal photos (lots of exotic birds) during his travels. Among the few people pictures was an old black and white snapshot of a young Claude with a toddler (presumably Junior) and a woman who must have been his first wife, Junior's mother. Her dark hair had been coiffed into a fierce bouffant and her strong features were softened by the affectionate smile she wore for her baby boy. I picked it up from the side table, turned the frame over, and lifted out the backing. Letters in fading ball point pen read "With Claude, Jr., and Claudia—Santa Narcissa, 1968." Next to it was a group shot of men in white coats standing around a cake decorated with the Povenda logo. They all held champagne flutes and appeared to be toasting whomever was taking the photo. Claude was beaming in the middle, and someone at the extreme edge of the gathering was cut off by the picture frame edge—half a frowning face and resolutely folded arms. If there was anything written on the back, I couldn't get to it without a screwdriver to undo the frame backing.

Bedrooms are always odd. It's hard not to think of all the intimate things that go on there—sleep, insomnia, dreams, sex, reading. Like the rest of the house, it was immaculate. Dust free, ship shape, and Bristol fashion. The bed was securely made—tasteful olive sheets and a matching chenille coverlet tucked in with hospital corners. I looked under the mattress and found nothing but neat—no porn, no drugs, no stash of cash, or any black-mail notes. On the dresser was a framed photo of Regina Pearl in her docent uniform, beaming at the camera. Dresser drawers revealed nothing unseemly unless you have a fetish for ascots and socks neatly bundled. A colorful assortment of boxers complemented the ascots, all neatly folded as if he had been expecting to have his personal effects inspected by strangers.

The bedroom was large enough to accommodate a queen-size bed, a large bureau, a big trunk, and a wardrobe/armoire full of neatly pressed clothes, which meant he was either a Percheron of a clothes horse or he had repurposed the closet, and I hit pay dirt when I opened it. He had convert-ed the closet into a dark room. It was one of those walk-in closets that was meant to serve as a dressing room—big enough for a chest of drawers or a vanity and with a window that Claude had blacked out and covered with a heavy, lined curtain. In addition to his digital work, he must have still used film because the work space was stocked with chemicals. It, too, was clean as a whistle. I felt silly doing it, but I ran my hands along various surfaces looking for secret storage compartments. Some prints were clipped to a wire, hanging to dry—photos of Claude and Regina apparently at Disneyland plus some shots of eagles, hawks, and vultures in the wild—though I couldn't place where. It seemed like somewhere north. There were redwood trees and rocky beaches in some of the shots. I also found a file of computer discs labeled with subjects and dates. I grabbed them, tucked them into my bag, and went back out into the main room.

The trunk was unlocked, and when I opened it, I thought I had stumbled upon Claude's secret S&M locker, but when I looked more closely, I recognized what must have been his old falconry gear—the thin strips of soft leather called jesses that are attached to the legs of the bird so the handler can tether it; a pair of silver bells that can be attached to the jesses; a beautiful hood that looked large enough for an eagle, made of deep red leather embossed with black paisley patterns and ornamented with silver and faceted red ceramic beads plus a curled black plume; a couple smaller, less ornate hoods; parts of some wooden perching; and a leather gauntlet that looked like it had been well used, but was dry and stiff from its long dormancy in storage. Neatly folded beneath all the equipment was a black silk shirt, black jeans, some black suede chaps, and a pair of cowboy boots that almost matched the fancy hood. There was also a leather-bound photo album that was partly full of pictures from the falconry group he must have once belonged to. They seemed to participate in medieval fairs now and again, and apparently when he wasn't being a cowboy, he was a wizard with a merlin. In a few photos, a youthful Claude was wearing the outfit in the trunk. I carefully replaced everything the way I'd found it, then meandered back to the hall, and onward to Claude's office. Junior was sitting on a chair out on the deck, apparently lost in thought. He did not acknowledge me when I passed.

The office was like a time capsule from an era before metal furniture and "putty" colored machines. The swivel chair and desk were wooden, as was the set of three short file cabinets below the windows. Sitting on the leather desk blotter in front of a green banker's lamp was a computer that should have been out of place, but the sleek white half-dome hard drive and flat screen mounted on a silver adjustable arm seemed right at home in a retro-futurist *Blade Runner* way. He had hidden the printer under the desk on top of a milk crate. I settled into the chair and rolled over the black-and-white floor tiles toward the files.

The photo archive was huge—an autobiography in hanging files, carefully arranged by subject and in chronological order, they went back many years. I found photos from his college days at CSU-Santa Narcissa full of beehived and bouffanted young women in uncomfortable looking clothes and dapper guys with buzzcuts and skinny ties. Clearly Claude had been a joiner: Archery Club, Fencing Club, Campus Youth for Christ, Catholic Charities, Chess Club, Young Republicans. There were family photos—uncomfortable holiday tableaus and vacation pictures from Disneyland—always dad and older brother, no mom in the pictures. Claude was in only a handful of photos. In a folder labeled "Legs," I found photos of a woman who was a dead ringer for Ann-Margaret, though her expressions in all of them seemed forced. Her long auburn hair was carefully styled to seem care-free but was probably secured with a number of hair products, and she was wearing heavy make-up and false eyelashes. The photos seemed to be modeling shots—she was wearing skimpy macrame beachwear in some and in others, filmy lingerie with preposterously oversized glasses that echoed her preposterously augmented breasts. Behind all the 8-by-10 glossies was a small wallet-size print. I turned it over and came across a wedding photo of Claude and Legs. So he had apparently tried a very different marital strategy after Claudia.

About a third of the folders were for specific events that he had covered as a freelancer—press conferences, outdoor music festivals, media events—one apparently at the Santa Narcissa Zoo. There were lots of paparazzi-type shots—movie premieres, celebrity roasts, and awards shows—but no more Manley-Landers pictures. I recognized a few of the stars, but most were just well-groomed enigmas. Tucked behind a folder labeled Poodle Skirt Pa-

141

rade (which was just that—a retro '50s fashion show that took place in 1976) was a box of materials about Povenda. I moved it to the desk and carefully pulled out the contents. It catalogued details of the clinical trials—articles from pharmaceutical industry trade papers, news stories, and a number of fading pages that contained a ghostly correspondence between Claude and Max. Some were typed memos. Others were hand-written notes. It seemed odd that Claude had such an insecure cursive backhand—perhaps the passive counterbalance to his aggressive people skills. Max's writing was clear, firm, and consistent. A copy of the framed Povenda approval party photo was labeled 1981 and all the people in it were identified on the back. The scowler at the periphery abstaining from cake and champagne was none other than Max Moore, whose name was scrawled in a different hand, away from all the other names. Like many of the other men in the photo, he was sporting sideburns and a lab coat that was open in the front to reveal a tie that was almost wide enough to pass as a muffler.

Although I recognized Povenda thanks to the relentless marketing campaign that had made it second only to Viagra on the pharmaceutical hit parade, I was unfamiliar with the backstory of the diet drug.

Apparently, it was a combination of two FDA-approved drugs that had already been in use for many years. Elatadine was the brand name for phelinphyne, an antidepressant, and Habitrex (hyonatrep) was a medication prescribed to ease withdrawal symptoms in smoking cessation. Both had been developed by Imperator, and coincidentally both were about to go off patent. So the company had put heavy pressure on its research and development team (led by Claude) to find a new application or reformulation that could justify a fresh patent. Claude was the one who suggested a combination of the two medications to treat obesity.

After the initial testing and some adjustments to the formula, Imperator submitted four placebo-controlled, one-year, phase III clinical trials on 3,200 obese patients with at least one co-morbid condition, such as diabetes or depression. The Federal Drug Administration's Endocrine and Metabolic Drugs Advisory Committee voted in favor of approval in 1978. But three months later, the FDA rejected the Imperator application for Povenda. This was apparently highly unusual and caused Imperator stocks to tumble. The Europeans wouldn't even approve the two component drugs, so although hardly surprising, the European rejection made the bad news worse. As dry and impersonal as the FDA's response was, I couldn't help hearing an admonishing note in the denial: "Before your application can be approved, you must conduct a randomized, double-blind, placebo-controlled trial of sufficient size and duration to demonstrate that the risk of major adverse events in overweight and obese subjects treated with phelinphyne/hyonatrep does not adversely affect the drug's benefit-risk profile."

Apparently, Imperator complied with the recommendations, because I found more articles dated three years later that reported the additional studies had been completed and submitted, and the FDA still had questions about significant side-effects, which included increased risk of stroke and suicidal thoughts. The FDA gave Imperator a three-month extension to find a solution, which seemed to revolve around adjusting the verbiage on the packaging and the wording of the potential side-effects warnings rather than any reformulation.

The correspondence that documented what was going on inside Imperator was mainly between Claude and Max, who was adamant in his feeling that this combination of drugs was not the solution they were seeking and that they should consider looking at other drug combinations. Although neither scientist made any overt threats, the messages between the lines were quite clear. The company was pressing for a new money maker to increase stock value, and Povenda was going to be that drug. Max disapproved of the "write-around" solution, implying that he was willing to blow the whistle and report to the FDA that Povenda was too dangerous to approve.

There were several news stories from the *Austin American-Statesman* about a major fire that broke out in the Imperator labs. It destroyed a significant quantity of data and killed one employee, a technician named Wolf Faigl. He had been working late and dozed off in the staff lounge—never to wake up again. Investigators determined that the fire was most likely arson,

143

and circumstantial evidence indicated that it was an inside job, possibly by a disgruntled employee. Max Moore was a co-supervisor at the lab, and his key code was the last entered at the lab the night the fire broke out. No physical evidence was found to connect him to the arson, and he had an alibi, though not an iron-clad one—he was home watching television with his son, Lester. No indictment could be made, and he was moved to a research section dealing with less sensitive projects, and as time wore on and no conclusive answers turned up, the media coverage dwindled and stopped.

This was an interesting twist. How much had Max told Les about what was happening at work? Would he have mentioned Claude by name? Les was a teenager at the time, but that didn't mean his dad wouldn't confide in his son. If he did, would Les have provided the alibi his dad needed? One article mentioned Max's bedridden wife. Would she remember Claude? Wiley had only mentioned Max's barbecue and nothing about a wife. I wondered if she was still in the picture. I dug a Post-It pad out of my bag and jotted down some questions.

Though most of his life had been lived in analog mode, it looked like Claude was embracing the digital revolution. The computer was loaded with photo files, mostly newer work. The CDs from the darkroom contained backup files of the photos Junior had sent to me, but offered no additional information. I found files on the computer that had the same date-time stamp, but they were nature photos from Hidden Valley State Park.

Hunting around the computer I found his e-mail. Various passwords were written on a memo pad. I tried them all until I got into his inbox. There were a few sparsely worded exchanges between Claude and Claudia. It seems Claude reached out to her regarding Junior—carefully suggesting that they might both take him out on his 30th birthday. He didn't make any personal inquiries, and she offered no details about her life. After a couple efforts at making arrangements, the e-mail trail ended. There was correspondence between Claude and Junior, but there were probably a couple hundred, and they all seemed to be quick notes about meeting at the Zoo or planning to have a meal. I made notes and printed a few documents. Then I had to heed nature's call, which was an excuse to inspect the bathroom.

It was also tidy, but the older you get, the more medication vials and tubes seem to accumulate in the medicine cabinet, and opening Claude's triggered a pharmaceutical avalanche. There were allergy creams, antacids, laxatives, and sunscreens. Also Placidol, Viagra, and some condoms. He apparently monitored his own blood pressure, and loved to floss. One of the drawers below the counter was almost entirely full of dental floss—waxed, unwaxed, tape, ribbon, plain, mint, and cinnamon, in a range of sizes, from massive economy spindles to tiny metal buttons designed to fit neatly into an overnight bag. After a cursory inspection of the toiletries, I returned to the office and started putting things back in order.

Eventually Junior appeared and asked how much longer I would need, but I was finished for the time being. I asked him about the sibling in some of Claude's family photos and he explained that after college, his dad's older brother Leif had become a successful civil engineer and moved to Alaska where he put down roots and started a family. Claude usually spent the holidays with Leif and his wife and three kids. So the brother probably wasn't going to offer much insight on recent events, but I asked for his contact information anyhow, and told Junior to let me know if the cops found any suspicious activities in his finances—big chunks of money appearing or disappearing regularly. Claude kept meticulous records, but a forensic accountant would know how to look for deceptions with numbers. I have trouble remembering the PIN for my ATM card. Junior said he would let me know as soon as he heard anything. I gathered my print-outs from under the desk and shut the computer system down. Junior followed me out to my car. He didn't speak until I had opened the door and was about to slide behind the wheel.

"Thank you so much for pursuing this."

"Well, I haven't found anything yet."

"But I know you will."

"Here's hoping," I said, and grasped the warm, clammy hand he offered.

145

17

Bedfellows

November 8, 2002

As it turned out, Peter Manley's Defenders of Animals headquarters
was about three miles away from Holcomb Gardens in a bungalow on the
periphery of a municipal park. During my tenure as a DofA member when
I was in high school, I had only known the post office box mailing address.
It was a good thing it wasn't any farther—the traffic was already thickening
up with people fleeing early for the long weekend. I was looking forward
to interviewing Manley about as eagerly as I was anticipating meeting Max
Moore on Monday. My fear was that talking with Manley would rekindle
the guilt that still sometimes haunts me about betraying the cause. But at the
very least it was a diversion from dreading the barbecue.

The building was roomier inside than it looked from the outside. It
must have been a private residence once upon a time. I imagined a park
warden circa 1920 occupying it, with his skinny tie and the old-fashioned
riding britches, his hat hanging by the door. The conversion into offices
wasn't as brutal as some I'd seen. There were still hardwood floors and a
faux fireplace like the one in my house, only this one had beautiful vintage

arts and crafts tiles adorning it. The afternoon light made the white walls luminous around poster sized black and white photos of animals: a lab rat being injected with some compound; a steer in a chute leading to the stun gun; a multitude of chickens crammed into wire cages stacked in row upon row on a farm truck headed for the processing plant; a small, exhausted female dog lying on her side in a squalid puppy mill pen, teats swollen and eight tiny pups greedily feeding; a caged cat wired to some menacing apparatus via electrodes attached to his or her shaved skull. The images were familiar to me despite having leapt off the wagon all those years ago, though I noted that the pregnant mares being drained of their urine to produce estrogen for hormone replacement therapy had been replaced by the purse-dog puppy mill. Two steps forward, one step back.

A youngish man and woman—probably in their 20s and attractively disheveled as only people that age can be, paused from folding fliers and stuffing envelopes when I walked into the room and regarded me with mild curiosity when I announced that I had a four o'clock appointment with Peter Manley.

"Oh," the scruffily bearded blonde responded.

"He's back in his office," the redhead added, nodding toward a hall that led into the house. I smiled and thanked them, then went past the kitchen and a bathroom and found what must once have been a bedroom. The door was ajar and I could see Manley seated at his desk with a phone cradled between his left ear and shoulder. Behind him on the wall was a poster-sized print of the Jane Goodall photo from Gombe with a Charles Darwin quote: *Animals, whom we have made our slaves, we do not like to consider our equals.*

Though I am not a big fan of game shows, and had never watched an episode of *The Million Dollar Question*, I had of course seen Manley on television long before his DofA role. *Detective Quaice* was a late night syndication classic. I studied him while he completed what sounded like a friendly phone interview. He saw me hovering and waved me into the office with a distracted smile.

In person, he looked pretty much exactly as he did on television, only better—if a bit older. Which was quite shocking. Santa Narcissa had become quite a popular retirement enclave for media personalities and afforded limitless opportunities to study the longevity of plastic surgery and efficacy of cosmeceuticals. What I'd concluded from the living mummies I'd seen over the years is that you can only prolong youth for a while. A skilled hand wielding the knife and deft collagen injections can work wonders, especially on a face with good bone structure to start with, but we all lose the battle with time eventually. And the longer the illusion of youth is perpetuated, the harder the fall at the end. I'd rather take my chances with a good diet, regular exercise, and some sunscreen.

Standing in line at an ATM once, I had been studying the strangely taut yet wrinkled, and ever so translucent skin of a platinum blonde in front of me, and barely suppressed a gasp when she stepped forward. She was wearing a pink velour track suit with shorts, and her exposed legs told her true age. Of course, she had probably had some of the veining laser-excised, but they were an orange color that I recognized from my own few failed experiments with canned tanning products, and reminded me of the diagrams of frog leg anatomy we'd studied in high school biology, only wrapped in slack folds of skin.

Peter Manley was no mummy and watching him chuckle and chat with his interviewer, I pondered whether or not he had in fact had anything done. His hair was still abundant and silver, cut in a generic, conservative style that would probably pass muster in the armed services. There were lines on his face, but the skin seemed natural and uncured, and when he smiled the crinkling around his eyes folded and unfolded with an organic suppleness. All the vegans I knew had the same telltale pasty skin, while his looked weathered but robust. I was wondering if he ate a lot of supplements when the call wrapped up and he put the phone down.

"Hi. You must be Sandy Lohm?" he said, extending a hand across the desk. His grip was warm, dry, and firm.

"Yes, I am," I smiled.

"Well, how can I help you?"

Somehow my inner geek got the better of me and I found myself gushing, "I just have to say I'm a big fan of Detective Quaice."

He laughed. "Role model?"

"Actually, yes. In an abstract way. I watched the show growing up, and I don't think I ever consciously thought of being a detective like you, or he, was. But the detecting is part of science, and I loved that."

"Interesting. So you're a science detective?"

"I used to be a research volunteer at the Santa Narcissa Zoo. Now I'm in horticulture. Detective work is a side line."

At the word "zoo," I cringed, waiting for the animal rights sermon, but there wasn't one.

"Did you enjoy it at the Zoo?"

It seemed like a trap. I resisted the urge to fidget.

"I loved it. But I kind of lost my faith in humans, and, ironically, that's what made me leave."

"What happened?"

I found myself confessing to him my chimpanzee epiphany, even as I wondered why the hell I was doing so. He gazed at me thoughtfully while I shared my story.

"It's hard to look in the mirror."

"Yeah."

"You look surprised."

"Well, to be honest, I was expecting a lecture about the evils of zoos."

"Look. I really wish there were no zoos. But I also know that the conditions that would make them obsolete are going to be almost impossible to achieve. Human civilization is spreading like a cancer on this planet. We have created a culture in which people have less and less real experience with the wild, and with wild animals. As a result, we are increasingly out of touch with ourselves. It's a degenerative condition. Even the greatest zoo in the world can't fix that. And most zoos aren't great."

"But... you're so critical," I stammered. "On the news the other day,

150

for instance. All that about our perverse relationship with animals and our enslaved pets."

"We are in a battle to save ourselves from our own worst nature. It's a battle for hearts and minds. Sometimes I have to break their hearts to open their minds. I know I am being manipulative. I'm willing to do that because I am committed to the cause."

Suddenly I understood how he had almost singlehandedly revived DofA.

"So am I—in my own way," I said feebly, wondering if he felt as passionately about trees.

He smiled and leaned forward. "And that's why I don't need to lecture you."

I found myself smiling back.

"Do you mind if I tape record our conversation? It's easier to transcribe than it is to decode my chicken scratch."

He furrowed his brow, then shrugged. "Sure. This isn't for public consumption is it?"

"No, no. This is simply for my own accuracy," I said, hoping to put him at ease. "I'll need to file a report when I'm done with the investigation, but as long as you aren't directly involved, there's no need to bring your name into it."

"OK."

I extracted the tape recorder from my satchel, made sure it was running, and set it on his desk between us.

"So I'm looking into the death of one Claude Hopper. Is that name familiar to you?"

"No," he said slowly, trying to place the name. "Who is he?"

"He was a docent at the Santa Narcissa Zoo."

"Was he. Why would I know him?"

"Well, I have received some photos from his son that suggest he knew who you are."

"Oh?" He seemed suddenly to become remote.

"Yes. I'll show them to you, but I have to warn you that they are rather graphic."

Behind his natural tan, the color faded from his face. "In what way?"

"They are of a sexual nature," I answered and removed the pictures face down from the envelope. I slid them across the desk.

After a pause during which he scrutinized me until I felt myself flush, he slid them to the edge on his side and turned them over. An odd expression crept across his face—recognition, anxiety.

"I know these."

"You do?" Now it was my turn for an odd expression.

"Yes. I received them in the mail about a week ago."

"At home or here at the office?"

"Here."

"Do you still have the envelope?"

"I do," he said and slowly got up to go to a large wooden file cabinet in the corner across from the door to the room. He fished a set of keys from his jacket pocket and opened the bottom drawer. The envelope, sealed in a Ziplock bag, had been stashed in the middle. He brought it over and handed it to me. It was a standard manila envelope, 9 by 12, with a label that had been laser printed. There was no return address, just a sticker from a mailing service in Las Vegas. I carefully opened it, only touching the edges. Inside was an 8.5-by-11 folder to hold the photos. A small yellow Post-It was stuck to it, and in a familiar, spidery, back-hand, it read, "I know about you."

"So you're being blackmailed?"

"No. That Post-It is all there was. Either it's a very inept blackmailer, or someone just looking to scare me. Scare us."

"And who is 'us?'"

"You do recognize the man I'm with."

"Philip Landers?"

"Yes."

"Yeah. I just wanted you to confirm it."

"Yes. He and I have been lovers for about five years. His wife doesn't know, or she does know but pretends not to. She wouldn't want to kill the goose that lays the golden eggs. I take great pains to keep our relationship confidential. To protect him. Personally, I don't really care who knows."

"And you've never met Claude Hopper or his son?"

"No. How on earth did he know about us? The getaway where those were taken is very exclusive, secluded, and expensive."

"Well, he was a freelance photographer, and even though most of his work was perfectly legit, he did pursue some dubious subjects. He anonymously sold quite a few photos of starlets accidentally flashing or sunbathing topless to various gossip rags. I assume he knew how to work the system and grease the right palms to get access to the subjects who interested him."

"What did he want?"

"That I don't know."

"You said his son gave you these copies?"

"Yes."

"What was he doing with them?"

"Well, Claude, Senior and Claude, Junior had been separated for many years. The dad and the mother divorced when Junior was a toddler. Then Claude went to Texas for a job, and worked there for many years, and when he retired he came back to Santa Narcissa. He started volunteering at the Zoo, which is where he reconnected with his son, who was coincidentally also a volunteer. I guess these must have been in Claude, Senior's effects."

"So, Junior sent these to me?"

"That I don't know. It's possible. The postmark is after Claude's death and around the same time he sent these copies to me. I suppose a handwriting analysis might solve that. I don't know who else Claude might have showed these to."

"What do I do?" he asked, his well-preserved brow creased with concern.

"For the time being? Nothing."

153

18

Food for Thought

November 9, 2002

Corinne had informed me that Regina Pearl could only be reached on-line and gave me her e-mail address with a mysterious smile and a hearty, "Good luck!"

After four spare and cryptic exchanges that made me feel like a tabloid reporter intruding on Jackie Kennedy after Dallas, I arranged to meet "QueenP" at one of the Zoo eateries on November 9, after Claude's memorial service.

During the most recent round of concessions upgrades, all the sit-down snack shacks had been reinvented as a set of food-themed thoroughfares: Burger Boulevard, Pizza Place, Enchilada Avenue, and Hot Dog Street. It was marginally more compelling than the previous incarnation in which they had all been a series of "Huts" except the pizza stand, which, due to the proprietary national chain, was the lone "Pad."

It was overcast with a little spritzing, which seemed to have spooked much of the Saturday crowd, so the Zoo was less busy than usual during a long weekend. Making my way to Hot Dog Street, which was at the extreme opposite end of the Zoo from the front entrance, I mentally reviewed what I had learned thus far about Regina Pearl. Her dossier was considerably shorter than Claude's. It seemed she had grown up in Santa Narcissa, leaving the area only to attend college up north. Most of her professional life had been spent in education, though not in the classroom. Her last job was managing the accounting department at the local junior college. Where Claude had dabbled in volunteer assignments throughout the Zoo before roosting at Raptorama, Regina was interested in research and helping craft enrichment items for the cats. She had begun volunteering long before Corinne took over the program, and judging from the notes in the file, Corinne would probably not have enlisted her if it had been her choice. Though she was reliable and punctual, her actual contributions were a bit underwhelming for all the time she clocked in. The research projects that had been completed about ocelot and tiger behavior had had her undivided attention, and enrichment it seemed, was a distant second best. She settled into a regular food prep shift shortly after Claude did.

Passing Burger Boulevard and Pizza Place, I noticed that the stands, which were all still the same uniform pinkish orange colored stucco (the exact color of those waxy-spongy Circus Peanut candies), had not only been renamed, but each had a new sign proclaiming its moniker and a menu mission statement:

Burger Boulevard: Meat you can't beat!

Pizza Place: Top this!

Enchilada Avenue: Cheesy good!

Hot Dog Street: Where the wieners meet!

I was very early, so I ordered the premium Italian sausage with peppers and onions for a premium price. But to Hot Dog Street's credit, it looked and smelled great. The peppers and onions even had the precious charred spots that street vendors on the East Coast always manage to achieve. I found a table and settled in. Arranging my tape recorder, notebook, and food I found that someone had etched into the enamel table top a fanciful artist's rendering of two male pelvises with impossibly huge anatomical fea-

156

tures jousting beneath a banner proclaiming in faux-Gothic medieval script: *Where ye wieners meet!* My inner junior high school student smirked before I covered the scene up with my notebook and downed the unexpectedly savory sausage.

Regina arrived right on time, dramatically arrayed in a draping black ensemble complete with hat and veil that proclaimed grief from about a hundred yards away. She flowed into the seating area scanning for me and I stood and waved. She gusted over to me, driving a cloud of White Shoulders before her. I was glad I had finished eating. She briefly gripped my hand in cool, bony fingers, then sank into the chair opposite me. When she removed her oversized super-dark sunglasses, I could see that she had been crying. Her red-rimmed gaze settled on the tape recorder.

"I hope you don't mind," I said and tried a mild dose of humor. "It keeps me from having to try to decipher my own scrawl later."

"OK," she replied, wearily wary. "If you must." I didn't give her a chance to think about it much and jumped right into the conversation.

"So how was the memorial service?"

"Oh," she sighed with a slight quaver. It was difficult to tell where the genuine emotion ended and the dramatic embellishing began. "Beautiful. Tragic. He was so uncompromising in the way he lived. He wanted no regrets at the end. Dear God, I will miss him!"

"I'm so sorry for your loss," I replied.

"Thank you." She blinked back a fresh wave of tears.

"How long had you known him?"

"We were in the same docent class."

"So that's how you met?"

"No. I had seen him and knew of him. We met at one of the Wild Sex presentations on Valentine's weekend several years ago."

"You were both attending it?"

"No," she blushed faintly. "He was the speaker, and I went up to talk with him afterwards."

"Oh, I see," I nodded and took a long sip of my club soda. "Were you at the Zoo on the morning of October 11?"

"Yes."

"Did you see Claude?"

"No. He liked to arrive early so he could..." sigh... "talk with people. People were important to him. He liked to stop and visit. He had signed in long before I did."

"Which was at what time?"

"Nine o'clock."

"When was the last time you saw him?"

"The week before..." She trailed off into a dramatic pause. "And we fought—just so you know."

She wasn't sure what to make of me. On one level, she enjoyed having an audience for her grief. On the other, she was eager for me to get to the point of this questioning.

"What did you fight about?"

"I don't know that it's any of your business. It was personal."

"I see. I understand you dated."

"What does that mean? 'I understand you dated,'" she hissed. Clearly I had stepped on a nerve. "What you mean is someone told you we dated. You mean Corinne Flaherty told you we dated. What business is it of yours? Or hers?"

The images of furniture flying through the volunteer office came to mind. I needed to ease into the topic.

"I'm just trying to establish what happened in his life during the days leading up to his death."

"I had nothing to do with his death. How could you even think that?" She was crumbling around the edges. "I loved him. He was the love of my life."

I handed her a napkin for the tears that were spilling. "I'm not saying that you did. In an investigation like this, I need to put together a picture of the person's life. I'm sorry if this is intrusive."

After a long pause, I took a different tack. "How long have you been a docent?"

"Eleven years."

"Do you take the school groups out or—"

"Oh no. I've got no patience with children," she dismissed the notion with a wave of the napkin. "I have a food prep shift and I give upper-level donor tours. I have cart privileges."

Not anymore, I thought. Clearly, she had swiftly rebounded from Corinne's bad news.

"That's great. That's why I volunteered in research. I don't think I could handle the herds of children either. I didn't much like kids even when I was one myself."

Her frown lessened.

"Is that weekends or weekdays?"

"Saturday morning food prep at Raptorama. I only tour upon request, and that's usually on weekends, but sometimes if they need me during the week I come in. Like the day Claude..." she sputtered. I waited a few beats for her to suppress another wave of tears.

"Interesting tours?"

"Sometimes."

"Do you have a favorite section of the Zoo?"

"I love the cats. And food prep. That's how I first got to know Claude. We got off to a bad start but got to know each other doing food prep."

"Oh, yes. He was into falconry?"

"Yes, yes. He used to tell me lots of stories about the old days when he used to keep a bird, when he was in college."

"Were you into falconry?"

"Oh, no. I just like the birds. They kind of scare me a little bit. I guess that's part of the allure."

"So," I ventured. "I guess Les could be a little difficult to work with?"

"Self-important prick," she chortled. "He is so condescending. As if he's a world authority on birds of prey."

"Well, he has been a bird keeper for 15 years."

"Right. In the Zoo."

"But he has birds of his own?" I said weakly, recalling Wiley's mention of the home bird. Despite Les's tendency toward cranky, and the possibility that he had killed Claude, I felt the need to defend him. His cryptic surliness seemed more genuine than Regina's showy despair.

"Claude traveled to Saudi Arabia—where they revere these birds. He had experienced true falconry culture."

"And Les didn't appreciate that."

"Of course not," she said, leaning in conspiratorially. "He was jealous."

I hate lying, and am not very good at it, but every once in a while when I'm inspired, I can get a good embellishment going on.

"To be honest, when I talked with him, I got the same impression. I know what you mean."

"Yes!" Triumphant. "A real prick king."

I ignored the Thai food image that surfaced involuntarily.

"Were you at the volunteer appreciation dinner in September?"

"You mean when that s.o.b. assaulted Claude?"

"Yes."

"No," she winced. "I was upset with him and told him I had a headache. So I stayed home."

"Why were you upset?"

She looked down at her hands in her lap. "Oh, one of the new female docents had been throwing herself at him during a committee meeting and I suppose I was jealous."

"I see. Did he tell you what happened?"

"No. A friend who was there told me."

"Did you see Les after the incident?"

"Yes. Briefly," she bristled.

"He didn't seem very upset about what happened to Claude when I talked with him."

"Oh no. Well, you know, butter wouldn't melt in his mouth. And like I said, he was jealous of Claude. Just like his father."

I had to disguise the jolt of excitement that surged through me as a cough.

"Do you know Max Moore?"

"Oh, no, but Claude worked with him for years. You know, he invented Povenda."

"Claude?"

"Yes!"

"You mean Claude worked with Les's father," I said, feigning ignorance. "I didn't know there was a single inventor. I always thought drugs like that come from a huge team of scientists."

"Well, of course they have a lot of testing and and lots of people work on developing it, but Claude really came up with the basic formulation."

"That's amazing!"

She was beaming on behalf of Claude. "He was so brilliant. And Max Moore was jealous of him. He tried to stop the clinical trials of Povenda."

"Why?"

"Out of spite."

"What do you mean?"

"He came up with some claptrap about there being possible safety issues—stroke risks or suicidal thoughts. But that's silly since one of the drugs in it is an antidepressant. Claude knew it was fine. And he was right. In the end, at least Max was enough of a man to acknowledge his error and bow out of the project."

This was an interesting interpretation. "Right. So, Claude knew that Les is Max's son?"

"Of course!"

"But he never brought that up over the course of their many—" I paused, trying to think of a neutral term, "disagreements?"

"I wouldn't know. I was rarely present when they met."

I let things settle and took a long slow sip of my club soda while I worked out how to ask what Regina's last big fight with Claude was about and whether he had by any chance left her any money. Then she jumped into the lull.

"You know," she began, carefully, and when I looked up at her she was looking at me intently. Earnestly even. "What they say about never parting in anger is true."

I put the cup down and donned my best eager-to-learn expression.

"I was angry with Claude because he wanted to get married."

My carefully orchestrated eager-to-learn collapsed into a blaring what-the-hell?

"You seem surprised. I guess you learned from your..." she paused to look for the right word, "research—that Claude was quite a Casanova. He was charming and handsome and lots of women were interested in him. He went out with many of my colleagues here. But I was the one who made him truly happy. And I didn't know why he wanted to ruin that by getting married."

"You don't think you would have been happier if you'd gotten married?"

"Of course not!" she said, as if I'd just suggested that wearing live minks on your head as an accessory made sense. "What we had was exciting because we knew that either one of us could leave it at any minute. Every time we were together was as magical as seeing some rare creature appear in your back garden and then vanish. You always want more and it's always enchanting because it's ephemeral."

Her eyes were welling again, but this time her expression was also welling with pain. I grabbed another napkin and handed it to her.

"I'm sorry," I said, suppressing thoughts of my own lost creature.

"He didn't understand that, and I was impatient with him," she said, dabbing at her melting mascara. "And I am not one for concealing my feelings."

We sat quietly for a little while before I took my leave of her, my scorned woman hypothesis in ruins. Even if she had done it, I couldn't imagine her being able to move the body without some kind of help—and she didn't seem like the type to hire a hit man. Crime of passion was more her style. Our unexpected heart-to-heart left me without much in the way of motive. If she had wanted his money, she would have married him and then bumped him off. I wondered if Junior could confirm the marriage proposal. As soon as I returned home, I got out the Post-It notes and added a few more details to the patchwork on the closet door.

162

19

Hounded

November 1, 2002

The instant Philip Landers opened the front door to his house, he knew something was awry. On the rare occasion that he got out of the council chamber in time to be home for dinner, he could expect an enthusiastic welcome from his two stepsons and a chaotic greeting from Romeo the dachshund. Today, there was silence.

"Honey?" he called cautiously. His wife was a chronic migraine sufferer, so silence often prefaced an evening full of excruciatingly careful interactions.

"Yes."

He found her seated at the kitchen table with a glass of white wine in front of her and a cryptic expression on her face. Her expensively-frosted hair was carelessly clamped on top of her head with a plastic claw clip and she was wearing a powder blue designer sweatsuit. She had applied make-up, so she must have gone out at some point. He approached and bent to kiss her. She stared straight ahead, and the hair clip rebuffed him from her scalp, so he planted his lips lightly on her forehead. Lately he had been noticing that the fine lines around her eyes and mouth were becoming more pronounced—especially when her expression was inert, as it was now.

"Baby, I know Romeo is the love of your life…"

He winced. Not even a prelude of some sort. Directly to the dog. Usually she would work her way up to the latest complaint about long-suffering Romeo.

"Oh, sweetness! He is not. You know you are."

"Well," a wry smile tightened the corners of her mouth. "As the case may be, he is getting more and more out of control."

"What do you mean?"

"Today he humped Chip's friend Bobby's leg while the mother was here, and she was appalled. I had to explain that he had been neutered, but that doesn't mean he won't try. Then Bobby wouldn't stop going on about the little red worm that was popping out of Romeo's 'wee-wee.'" She violently gestured the quotation marks at him.

"But he's just expressing his need to establish the territory as his. It's not sexual at all."

"Well, it sure looked sexual. Especially to Grace."

"Look, the boys are ten. At some point they are going to have to learn about the birds and the bees."

"So I was supposed to make Romeo humping Bobby's leg into a sex education lesson?"

"No, no. That's not what I meant. I mean, it will all be made clear eventually."

"And he ate another one of my shoes."

"I told you it's important to keep the closet door shut."

"Yeah, well he must have pawed it open, because I did shut it."

"Oh," he felt a small thrill that the dog was clever enough to figure out how to get at the shoes, but kept that to himself. "Which ones?"

"What does it matter? The point is that he is now actively seeking out my shoes in order to destroy them!"

He reached out to pat her shoulder, which was as rigid as a cinderblock.

"He has dementia. He has to go."

"Baby, he is only four years old, and we can work this out."

"Philip, the dog is a walking collection of behavior problems."

"Everyone has idiosyncrasies. You need to lighten up."

"He's not everyone. He is a dog. And they were $900 Prada pumps," she said, becoming shrill.

"Where are the kids?"

"They're having pizza at Bobby's. Don't use your political subterfuge on me. I know that's what you're doing."

"I'll buy you new shoes."

"I don't want new shoes. I want the shoes that your dog chewed up."

"Where is he?" he asked, taking the leash off the counter and slipping it into his pocket.

"Are you listening to me?"

"Yes. I hear you." He wanted to hide until this had all blown over. It usually did. When they had gotten married, Romeo was just a puppy and the boys loved him (though not nearly so much as he did) so Louise had been outnumbered. Now they had grown as tired of the untrained and seemingly untrainable animal as she, and seemed resentful because the dog apparently continued to occupy a prime position in their stepfather's affections.

Louise had never cared for the dog, but Philip, her mother reassured her, was a good catch and clearly on an upward trajectory from Santa Narcissa City Council to the mayor's office, the governor's mansion, and maybe even further. That would be worth putting up with a quirky little dog. But Philip refused to obedience train him, didn't want to suppress his natural behavior, even though she tried to make him understand that natural dog behavior revolves around social structure and rules.

Quickly, the quirks that had been cute in a tiny puppy became annoying in an adult dog. Although he had been fixed as soon as he was old enough, he seemed to need to assert his dominance all the time by mounting whatever he could wrap his paws around. He ate, or tried to eat almost anything, which made walking him (already a challenge because he had never been leash trained) an exercise in exasperation. Bounding every which way, he

165

exuberantly consumed everything from pinecones and paper cups to corn cobs, tree roots, and scat from myriad species.

"Have you fed him yet?"

"You are impossible!" She gulped the last of the wine and stormed off toward the bedroom.

Philip sighed and went to the refrigerator. Louise was omnivorous and quite a good cook. Whenever he had important guests over to visit they were always impressed with the food she prepared. On rare occasions Philip actually indulged, but for the most part he restricted himself to a limited diet. It was important that he maintain his trim and youthful appearance. Although he was only a year away from fifty (which caused him a mild panic when he thought too much about it), he was confident that he did not look much older than forty.

There on the top shelf, clearly visible through the pyrex lid on the big casserole dish were the remains of the opulent macaroni and cheese, rich and crusty, topped with buttered breadcrumbs she had made for herself and the boys the night before. Next to that was the braised lamb and rice that she made every week to please Phil and feed Romeo. He took that out and put it on the counter, scooped a carefully measured serving into a clean bowl, put the rest back in the fridge and retrieved his Svelte Chef meal from the freezer—a fat-free, gluten-free, reduced sodium, low carb, vitamin forti-fied kale lasagna that Louise had once compared with the color and texture of a florist's sponge. He took the plastic tray out of the box, peeled back a corner of the protective film and placed it in the microwave. He had to admit that the ersatz noodles, made from pulverized kale and re-hydrolyzed quinoa just couldn't maintain any textural integrity in the watery, saucy environment, but it kept hunger at bay and provided whatever percentages of nutrients he required that weren't covered by the protein shakes and fiber bars he ate every day for breakfast and lunch.

The familiar, wan, tomato-esque aroma began to seep out of the micro-wave as the little square rotated on the round glass carousel. While it finished, he cut up a small avocado to add to Romeo's food. Suddenly an impulse

166

overcame him and he indulged in a luscious, buttery, wafer thin slice, then wondered how many calories he had just added to his daily load. He'd take Romeo on the longer walk route, he decided. The bell dinged. He put the container of molten lasagna on a plate and took it with Romeo's dish to the back door.

"How's my boy? How's my super duper doggy dude?"

Being banished to the patio had made Romeo even more anxious than usual, and after peeing on all the objects he encountered, he set about chewing the end of the folded shade umbrella that lay in a corner. The second he had heard Phillip's car, two blocks away, he began pacing and yipping. After the humans finished vocalizing, he knew Phillip would come to the door. The poor dog was wagging his tail so hard he looked like he was about to snap in half.

Philip spent a few minutes patting and scratching Romeo, who, he couldn't help noticing, defensively, was not humping his leg. But he did seem to be having a doggy erection which retreated when he put the food bowl on the floor. By then, his lasagna had congealed enough to be safely eaten, and sitting at the patio table, he dug in while Romeo ate. Watching him, Philip's mind wandered.

He was not an animal person. Until Peter had given him Romeo, he had failed to understand how people could invest so much emotion in them. Peter had found the pup abandoned, and kept him for a while, until he realized that he was dangerously contradicting the DofA principle about not enslaving animals as pets. But giving up the dog to a shelter was out of the question, as was any other potentially public way of rehoming him. So he made a gift of him to Philip, who was touched and also apprehensive. His experience with animals extended only so far as the supermarket meat and dairy sections, and his interest in them had been limited to the challenges of eating them. They seemed to be full of cholesterol and saturated fats. The only meat he enjoyed eating had to be significantly abstracted from what it might have been like in life—partly because the uncleanliness of most creatures, and thinking about their less than sanitary habits, quelled his appetite, and also because the more processed and refined the meat or dairy was, the less fat and other unsavory ingredients it contained. Boneless, skinless chicken breasts were about all he could stomach. He preferred to get his protein from power bars. Even after Romeo came into his life, he could only cope with feeding the dry kibble. Louise made the lamb-rice mixture, which he handled very carefully so as to avoid direct contact.

Although she said nothing, he could tell it irritated Louise that he was so discriminating about what he would eat. Peter was pleased to an extent. Philip knew that it would mean more if he objected to meat for more ideological reasons, but Peter was content with his dietary aversion. And Phillip found that he had developed an unexpectedly deep connection with the dog, who was a living link to Peter. Romeo was just finishing his food when Philip's cell phone rang. A dual pang of excitement and anxiety surged when he saw Peter's number.

Philip was uncomfortable talking with Peter while he was at home, and Peter only rarely phoned him there, but it had been weeks since they'd seen one another. Successful compartmentalization of his feelings about Peter relied on spending enough time together. When they were apart for too long, the balance he maintained failed and he found himself unable to concentrate on maintaining his home life. He avoided analyzing too much exactly what it was he felt with Peter, which was not terribly difficult between the demands of serving on the City Council and the needs of his family. His relationship with Peter had to remain completely clandestine, and yet ironically, it was with Peter that he felt most free. He did love Louise, but in a practiced way. She was the perfect spouse for his needs as a public figure, and he wanted to love the boys, but they were still too foreign. And they were lingering in the resentment phase of this new family arrangement. Their bio-father remained an important part of their lives and so there were elaborate emotional obstacles to feeling like a fully blended family. His home life was a support system for his career, and sometimes he felt like he was living in a carefully scripted performance from day to day. His time with Peter was more real, more satisfying—though he couldn't really accept the idea of being gay. It was too jarring. Two other Council members were openly gay, and this public knowledge had not impacted their careers one way or the other. But his struggle was not with the professional implications. It was with the personal implications.

"Hello?"

"Phil?"

"Hi, Peter.

"What are you up to?"

"Oh, feeding Romeo. Decompressing."

There was a pause.

"Peter?"

"Yeah."

"Anything wrong?"

"I got something in the mail."

It was Philip's turn to pause.

"A photo."

"Of what?"

"Us. Together."

"Where?"

"The Resort."

"Who sent it?"

"It was anonymous. Sent from a mailing service in Las Vegas."

"What do they want?"

"Didn't say. There was nothing with it but a Post-It that said, 'I know about you.'"

"Don't handle it—there might be fingerprints."

"I know."

"What do we do?"

"I don't know."

"I don't want to talk on the phone."

"Where's your wife?"

"Brooding in the bedroom."

"What happened?"

"Nothing. Romeo ate another one of her shoes, and I guess his excited greeting offended one of the boys' friend's mother."

Quiet laughter.

"It's not really funny."

"I'm sorry."

"Well, actually, it kind of is, but Louise is not amused, so I can't be."

"Can you get away for a while this weekend?"

"I guess we kind of have to."

"We need to meet somewhere else."

"Of course. Where?"

"Let me do a little research."

"OK. Thanks."

"I love you."

"Yeah. Talk with you later, OK?"

"Sure."

Romeo had finished his food and had planted himself next to Phillip, leaning against his leg. Philip, his thoughts racing, wondering how someone had known that he and Peter were at Hidden Valley Resort, worrying about the possibility of blackmail, absentmindedly reached down, fondled the dog, and pulled the leash out of his pocket, making the telltale jingle. The prospect of a walk rekindled the frenzy of the greeting. Romeo yipped and bounced to his feet, tongue lolling out of the side of his mouth, spattering saliva onto Philip's expensive worsted wool pinstripe pants legs as he bent down to attach the leash. Powerless to do anything about the situation until he saw Peter and they could decide on a response, he decided a walk would be a good diversion. After opening the side gate, he stumbled after Romeo, who bolted for the street.

As always, it was a roller coaster walk with Romeo bounding every which way while Philip made ineffective efforts to reason with him. He paused and pawed at newly mulched parkway planters, mounted two dogs and a yard gnome bent over a wheelbarrow, picked up a pinecone and dropped it at Philip's feet, chased a squirrel to the extent that his short legs and the retractable leash would allow, and then discovered a pile of seedy coyote poop. Philip grappled with the lead and succeeded in pulling him back from it.

"No, no, no. You don't want that, Romeo. Icky, icky, ca-ca."

The dog paused and looked at him, head tilted as if questioning why.

"Come on, buddy boy! I know what I want... and I bet you feel the same."

Several blocks from the house, and on the other side of a figmentary boundary that separated Philip's tonier neighborhood from the slightly seedier arts district was the Pronto Pup hot dog stand. It was a tawdry shack with two windows where bored teenagers took orders that were prepared in the back by surly tattooed men in hairnets. Suffused with a potent blend of umami aromas, it was a colorful hangout for wannabe hipsters, upscale drug dealers, slumming college students prepping for a night of drinking in the evening or recovering from a night of drinking in the morning, and the occasional call girl. Sometimes, when Philip felt unsettled or out of sorts, as he did now, caught between the absence of Peter and the omnipresence of his family, the compulsion to eat something decadent was overwhelming.

It was past the usual dinner rush, so he stepped right up to the counter and ordered the Double Dare Ya Chili Dog for himself and the Hot Diggity Kiddie Pup for Romeo. He seated himself in one of the cheap plastic garden chairs on the patio and ate the drippy dog on the rickety table while Romeo made short work of the hotdog on the ground next to him. A lean, exotic looking creature of indeterminate gender sat smoking a clove cigarette in the corner between two dying pygmy palms in pots. When Philip had finished eating s/he swung his/her long gleaming braids over an olive brown shoulder and glanced at him with a knowing smile and a fleeting wink. Philip froze for a moment, then quickly got up and dragged the reluctant Romeo (who had been busy cleaning his nether regions) with him back out to the sidewalk and toward home.

The dog, sensing Philip's strange moodiness, was relatively subdued, zigzagging furtively from side to side, with only a few forays into shrubberies and under cars. Back at the house, Louise's anger seemed to have abated. She had unclamped her hair and changed into a Hawaiian print caftan that she often wore around the house. Greeting him with a firm hug before he could even release Romeo from the leash, she asked how the walk was.

"Good."

"Baby, I'm sorry about being so cranky. It's just so frustrating sometimes."

"I'll get you new shoes."

"I know."

Romeo, sated from the walk and the Kiddie Pup, retreated to his basket. Louise pressed herself up against Philip and then pulled back enough to reach up for a kiss. Looking down at her, the neckline of the caftan gapped and he could see she was not wearing anything underneath it. He reluctantly pressed his lips to hers.

"Let's kiss and make up," she whispered, one of her hands brushing the front of his trousers.

"Not tonight, honey," he said with a pained expression. "I have a really bad headache."

20

Playing 'Possum

May 10, 1977

"Hey there, Lez-terine!"

Les, distracted by the cellophane wrapper that stubbornly refused to peel off of the sticky, conical Astropop, felt his stomach sink. He looked up to find Bobbie Studley, Ned Burnett, and both dreaded Young brothers (Paul and Donnie) standing menacingly between him and his bicycle. This was what he got for not going directly home from the library.

"Oh, hey," he said reflexively, making furtive eye contact and instantly regretting doing so.

"Does your daddy call you Lez-terine?" Bobbie demanded with a cold grin.

Les pretended he didn't hear, fixed his gaze on his nemeses' sneakers, and attempted to circumvent them, but they shifted formation so that he was now trapped between them, a parked car, and a sycamore. He clutched the Astropop stick and wondered if the business end of the hard, glassy sucker was sharp enough to use as a weapon.

"Or does he call you Lez because you are really a Lez-bian?" Bobbie persisted with a chorus of cackling from the others.

These weren't new taunts. Les had heard them many times before. One of the most annoying things about the bullies was their utter lack of imagination. The illogic of accusing him of being a lesbian was particularly irritating, but he knew better than to emphasize the obvious. He had tried to make that argument once before and they had immediately seized him, decked him, and pantsed him.

"Well, I guess you are a guy," Bobbie had said, towering over Les and sneering down at his victim's vulnerable genitalia. "But you sure fight like a girl."

"Hey there, girlie Les," Bobbie shouted, moving closer. "What color panties are you wearing?"

Bobbie and his minions closed in and Les stepped into the planter bed. Feeling the big, solid tree trunk at his back gave him a sudden flush of confidence. He brandished the Astropop at Bobbie, who burst out laughing at what Les realized was a ridiculous and futile gesture. Ned sneered and smacked Les's hand so the candy flew into the air and shattered on the pavement. Les was bracing for impact with Bobbie's fist when a rustling broke out suddenly above him. Before anyone could figure out what was happening, an opossum tumbled out of the canopy. The agitated animal landed on Les's shoulder, hissing and baring its array of pointy teeth. In a split second of inspiration, he grasped the opossum by the scruff of its neck, positioned it so that it was gripping his forearm and aimed it like an automatic weapon—fortunately he was wearing his heavy denim jacket, which was just thick enough to protect him from sharp opossum claws. He pointed the angry marsupial toward his assailants. A pungent smell erupted, an aroma somewhere between wet dog and mild skunk. He lunged at Bobbie and company and after some decidedly girlie shrieking, they were gone. Les put the opossum down on the ground and watched it scurry back up into the tree.

He bolted for his bike and hauled ass home. Safe in his bedroom, he chuckled to himself. He knew that the appearance of the guardian opossum was purely happenstance, but it sure did seem like a sign. His only previous experience with what he had always been told were mangy pests had been up-turned garbage cans and road kill. Later, he went to the library to investigate.

What he came to think of as his spirit animal was probably an adoles-cent, because it had been much smaller that what the books described as an adult opossum. He discovered that opossums have been around for at least 65 million years—since the age of the dinosaurs and long before people. Versatile and adaptable, they can eat almost anything and, he was surprised to learn, play dead as a last ditch defense—and they aren't "playing" anything. They basically faint when they cannot flee and fighting is not an option. Many predators that won't eat carrion are put off by the suddenly stunned quarry and avoid it.

That summer, though it meant a 40-minute bus ride, he started volun-teering at the local wildlife rescue station.

Contrary to myths of only children being self-centered, Les grew up as a full and equal member of the household, with requisite responsibilities and privileges. From the time he was big enough to help around the house, he did so, and his parents instilled in him the understanding that contributing to the household was part of his family duty. There was no bartering for allowance money. If he wanted to buy something, he could discuss it with his parents and if he made a convincing case for why he needed more Legos or an action figure, a bicycle or a microscope, he could have the item. If his case was insufficient, they patiently explained why. There were no limita-tions on books and purchasing them required no discussion.

Max and Mina were generous with their time and attention, and as a result, Les had no reason to pander for it. He enjoyed his own company, and lived in a rich world of imagination informed by science fiction stories, comics, and movies. He was bright and mature for his age. Other children were a bit of an enigma to him, and although he had a few friends among his classmates, he was just as content with the company of teachers and librarians. Which did not endear him to the bullies who saw him as a puppet of these authority figures. Harassing Les was the next best thing to political insurrection.

His parents were pleased with his developing intellect and character,

175

but distressed at the taunting he endured. They offered him the option of attending a private school, and were touched when he explained that there would be creeps at whatever school he attended, and at least he was familiar with the creeps at his school.

After he began volunteering at the wildlife rescue station, he really hit his stride. Everything about working there interested him. Of course, he always regarded the opossum as his spirit animal, but birds fascinated him, particularly raptors. After reading a mystery novel that revolved around a falconer whose hawk takes a dove that is carrying a sapphire in its crop, he became obsessed with falconry and found among the volunteers at the rescue center a sponsor who apprenticed him. He spent some of his time assisting the veterinarians at the station, and that sparked his interest in medicine. Before long, he also found part-time work at a veterinary clinic, and started volunteering at the tiny Santa Lucia Zoo and Gardens, which eventually hired him as an outreach animal handler.

The souring of Les began during his senior year in high school, with his mother's illness. When he came home from college on breaks, he could see her condition progressively worsen. His father seemed reluctant to explain what was happening to her, so she did. Over the course of surgery, radiation, and chemotherapy, he helplessly watched his mother cut, burned, and poisoned until she was a fragment of the person she had been. He knew that these were all measures taken to fight the invading illness, but she had always had an intense aversion to doctors and hospitals, and the irony of the situation was almost as devastating as the disease itself. His father tried to imbue her with his ornery fighting spirit, but Les knew that she had given up long before she died during his junior year as an undergraduate at the University of Texas at Santa Lucia. He had just completed his first year of veterinary school at Texas A&M when a fire broke out at the pharmaceutical lab where his father had recently been made a co-supervisor. Max tried to spare Les most of the drama that was happening at the lab. Between the death of Mina and the rigors of his studies, Les was only vaguely aware of the arson investigation that followed the fire. He knew the detectives had come by the house a couple of times, and he distractedly followed the news reports about the fire. When Max left Imperator and decided to move to California, where he had been offered a teaching job at U.C. Santa Narcissa, Les was angry and frustrated, not so much with his father as with the unreasonable forces of the universe. Max offered him the alternative of staying at Texas A&M to complete his degree, though Les knew that would mean taking on massive amounts of debt. His part-time work during college breaks would never cover all his expenses. So willingly, but not without regrets, he chose to move with his father and was elated to discover that Santa Narcissa had a zoo. He wrote to the general curator in advance and applied for the open animal keeper position before the dust had settled on his relocation.

Les had a love/hate realtionship with the big annual barbecue his father held every year. Being around a house and garden full of people was always a challenge. It wasn't that he disliked them as individuals. It was just overwhelming to have them all in one place. But the food was always superb (his father was a master of the grill) plus it was nice to have hang time with friends he didn't often see, and to see friends from work out of uniform. And there were never any awkward encounters with egotistical docents.

21

The Mulligan

April 29, 1981

Although he enjoyed playing golf very much, Wolf Faigl was not look-ing forward to accepting the invitation to join Claude Hopper for nine holes on Sunday. He would have to give his boss an answer no later than 5 p.m. Thursday, and every time he looked at his watch, all he could see was the countdown: T-minus 32 hours.

Things had been awkward between Claude and him for some time—pretty much ever since the new guy had started. Max Moore had been fast-tracked through the lab hierarchy by Claude's superiors, and, despite Claude's objections, a lab co-supervisor position was created for Max in order to "redistribute the managerial workload." Initially, Claude believed that it was part of a larger plan to bump him out of the lab. He had seen this tactic before. Bring in "fresh blood" with a new job title (and at a lower pay scale) and as soon as the newbie knows the ropes and settles in, let the senior go as part of a departmental restructuring. At first he was unfazed by the arrival of Max. He was privy to the big picture plans of the governing board, and his roots at Imperator Pharmaceuticals were deeply entrenched.

Then Claude began to suspect that Max had in fact been hired to spy on him.

Within a few months, it became clear that there were disturbances in Claude's well-ordered realm. He used a sticky note system to remember his many passwords—the arrangement of the notes on his desk blotter contained hints that only he understood. The notes hadn't been shifted, but every now and then something about them was not quite right. Additionally, files were not exactly as he had left them. Because staples and paperclips caused an annoying bulkiness on one side of the hanging files, he rotated the documents in a certain way to make all the files fit evenly in the drawers, and he had found one or two out of sequence. (Of course there had been instances when he had been pressed for time or short on morning coffee, and it was possible that he himself had misfiled them, but he couldn't be sure, and the discrepancies nagged at him.)

Wolf felt the shift in the social dynamic of the lab soon after Max's arrival. People continued submitting their official reports and paperwork to Claude, but had begun confiding in Max—about the lab, their ideas, and increasingly, personal issues. Technically, this had no bearing on the work. But business is as much about interpersonal connections as it is the chain of command, and this blossoming communication led to a sense of camaraderie that Claude perceived as a challenge to his control of the laboratory.

Before Max joined the staff, there had been no avenue for feedback. Claude monitored the work produced by those under his command, and on occasion his subordinates would make comments or offer suggestions that were helpful, but as a rule, decisions in the lab flowed from the top down. Toward the end of the second weekly staff meeting after Max's arrival, Max brought up the idea of starting "suggestion sessions"—informal lunch meetings where everyone could brainstorm and discuss lab issues and ways to perform more efficiently. There was an uneasy lull while everyone's gaze turned to the opposite end of the conference table where Claude sat. His expression became stony.

"And what purpose would that serve?"

Attention turned back to Max.

"Well, now, two heads are better than one, don't you think?"

"And too many cooks spoil the broth."

Max chuckled. "I see you know your old saws. But there's always room for improvement and I think it's good to try and incorporate different perspectives."

"Well, I think, Max, that a successful lab is an organized lab, and I run a tight ship here. I know that this concept of team-building is all the rage right now, but I believe in protocol. This lab runs smoothly because it flows in one direction only, like the human circulatory system. Now, I think we're finished here. Let's get back to work."

With no official outlet for expressing discontent, dissatisfaction manifested in strange passive-aggressive displays. The tiny kitchenette that was available to the lab staff was as white and sterile as a surgical suite. Claude personally saw to the cleaning. Shortly after the meeting in which Claude shot down Max's suggestion sessions, coffee stains—brown rings from the bottoms of sloshed coffee mugs—began to appear on the gleaming formica. Claude knew the culprit wasn't Max, whose coffee spills were largely confined to his office where he kept his own coffee maker. Additionally, he was all but certain that someone was pilfering his coffee creamer. He also began noticing discrepancies in the amount of postage used and the log where everyone was supposed to record all outgoing mail. In staff meetings, Claude's inquiries about these transgressions were met with blank stares.

Wolf was second in command at the lab and knew he was contributing to this tension. Max was easy to talk with and had a dry, disarming sense of humor. Breaking the ice in meetings and at lunches was effortless for him, and he could diffuse awkward situations with a few diplomatic phrases deftly deployed in a distinctive baritone tinged with a Texas twang. (Although the lab was located on the outskirts of Austin, only three people who worked there were native to the Lone Star State.) Compared with Max's benevolent chumminess, Claude's paternalism grated. Wolf found himself not only chatting with Max more than Claude, but feeling inclined to side with him in meetings, where Max's arguments were so much more compelling than

Claude's were. He could tell that this annoyed Claude, and so to assuage his guilt, he began overcompensating by launching into his work with inexplicable gusto—beating deadlines, planning proactively for short staffing over the holidays, oiling the bureaucratic machinations, and anticipating clinical problems. Except for the one big problem that none of them had anticipated.

When the the Federal Drug Administration (FDA) withheld approval of Povenda, Imperator's great white hope for capturing the prescription diet drug market, what was an uncomfortable work environment became very charged. Claude intensified his micromanagement while Max's imperviousness to Claude's pressure made him a sounding board for disgruntled staffers. When Max suggested to Wolf and a couple lab techs that they meet at the local watering hole for happy hour after work, nine staffers showed up and the venting was so therapeutic that "Unhappy Hour" became a weekly ritual, with or without Max. Claude eventually found out about these gatherings, but they were never spoken of in his presence so there was no opportunity for him to extract an invitation.

Wolf had had misgivings about the initial Povenda trials, but he successfully repressed these doubts. It took a tremendous amount of mental control, but he had learned how to prevent a notion from germinating into a full-blown idea. It was like meditation—learning to clear your mind of clutter. In this case, the clutter was paperwork pertaining to the Povenda studies.

One Friday afternoon when Wolf was on his way back from the kitchen, where he was careful to mop up his coffee spill, he heard the strained tones of an argument that was being reigned into a discussion. It was coming from Claude's office. Apparently he and Max were in a closed door meeting, only the door was not quite closed. Wolf lingered in the hall pretending to be intensely puzzled by a spreadsheet while he eavesdropped.

"So you're making this into an ethics issue?" Claude said.

"What else is it?"

"There is nothing unethical about allowing people to choose for themselves the risks they are willing to take."

"So you're saying that it's perfectly acceptable to sell cigarettes even though they are directly linked to cancer as long as they are labeled with a warning that they cause cancer."

"That's precisely what I'm saying. People have a right to make their own informed decisions. And we are not talking about cigarettes. Tobacco is a purely recreational drug. Povenda is an effective method for weigh loss, and the risk of adverse events from taking it is no greater than the risk of the co-morbid conditions."

"Yes, at one year of use."

"Look, Max, I understand that you're one of those do-gooders who doesn't trust people to make any decisions for themselves. But people believe in pills to cure their ills, and at Imperator, we have a vast array of compounds to give them what they want. No solution is perfect. Eventually everyone succumbs to something."

"That's a cynical way to look at it."

"No more cynical than assuming people are too stupid to determine their own fate."

After a long pause, the door suddenly swung open and Wolf leapt backward to avoid it, sloshing his coffee onto the spreadsheet in his hand, his shirt, and the carpet.

"Oh, Wolf! Man, I'm sorry," Max said, reaching out. "Are you OK?"

"Uh," Wolf felt himself flushing.

"Did it scald you? Do you need some ice?"

"No. I put so much milk in it, it's pretty tepid," Wolf replied, then looked at the big mocha blotch spreading on the floor. "Oh, no."

Max looked down. "Don't worry about that. It's just a rug. Do you need to run home and change?"

"That's OK. I have a spare shirt at my desk. Thanks."

"All right then," Max said, then added quietly, "See you after work."

After a time, it became clear to Wolf that Claude was evaluating his alliances in the lab. In the weeks following the debate he had overheard, he noticed Claude making a point of approaching staff individually, testing each with a battery of small talk designed to tease out attitudes about management at the lab and determine who was participating in the happy hour meetings. Never one for making waves, Wolf's first impulse was to maintain the status quo and support Claude. Yet Max stirred a long dormant sense of integrity in Wolf. He knew that the golf invitation was Claude's way of forcing his hand.

They met at the clubhouse at 10 a.m. and had drinks while they waited for their 11 o'clock tee time. It was a municipal course, and so lacked the amenities that Wolf found intimidating at other private and more exclusive courses—no valet parking, no caddies, and the clubhouse was informal, more like a neighborhood pub. Claude, for whom there was no such thing as casual attire, was wearing knickerbockers, an argyle sweater, saddle shoes, ascot, and cap. They made their way to a window table with a view of the dense planting of pampas grass that screened the Santa Narcissa Zoo deliveries entrance. Claude ordered a bloody mary and insisted that Wolf have something more substantial than a club soda. Not much of a drinker, the only item on the menu that sounded good to Wolf was a mimosa.

They had known each other since they were undergrads at Cal State Santa Narcissa, where they met when they were both assigned the same early morning shift working in the student cafeteria kitchen. Their friendship was definitely a case of opposites attracting. Wolf was earnest and idealistic, constantly exposing his vulnerabilities. Claude was charismatic, smart, and manipulative. He was the kind of guy who made you seem more interesting because he was your friend, and Wolf lived vicariously through Claude's adventures and conquests. Claude valued Wolf because he was a reminder of his own past and made him feel good about how far he had progressed in life. When Wolf came to work at the lab, they had not seen one another in years, and yet the friendship picked up right where they had left off—each of them slipped comfortably back into the roles they had played in college days.

"So where did you go on your vacation?" Claude asked, crunching into the celery stalk that garnished his drink. They'd had a similar conversation on myriad occasions. Wolf was a creature of habit, and he knew that Claude found this fascinating and somewhat repellant—like someone with a missing limb or a glass eye.

"Oh, Seattle," Wolf replied, sipping the mimosa, which was adorned by a lone raspberry bobbing helplessly in turbulent orange bubbles.

"Again?"

"Well, it's where I'm from. I've got family and friends there."

"So, what did you do?"

"Oh, you know. The usual. Hung out, talked, drank coffee."

Claude chuckled. "That's the thing about you, Wolf. You are so reliable."

"Um, thanks," Wolf said, thinking that at least "reliable" was more positive than "predictable," which is what his ex-girlfriend had claimed was his fatal flaw. There was a pause, and Wolf tried to become caught up in the baseball game on the television above the bar. He had seen guys in bars hanging out companionably, barely exchanging a word while engaged in sports on the television. But he had no idea who was playing or what was going on, and Claude was no more a team sport man than Wolf was.

"Tell me," Claude said, leaning in. "Where would you go if your folks weren't in Seattle?"

"I've still got friends there."

"OK," Claude replied with a bemused eye-roll. "Where would you go if you wanted to have an adventure?"

"I don't know." Wolf disliked vacations that lasted more than a few days because it disrupted the comfort of his routine.

"Come on. There must be someplace you've always wanted to see. London? Rome? Egypt?"

"I guess I'd go to Cape Flattery."

"Where's that?"

"On the Olympic Peninsula."

"Why?"

"It's the westernmost point of the contiguous United States."

185

"And again, why?"

"The Peninsula is beautiful. And I guess I'm kind of fascinated with boundaries."

Claude nodded with a wisp of a smile.

At last they were called. Wolf was relieved to finally get started on the game, and dismayed when Claude suggested they forego the electric cart and walk so they could get in a little exercise and chat.

They found themselves matched up with a couple of organic chemistry graduate students who could have passed for twins with their boyish features and tawny buzz-cut hair. They weren't wearing exactly matching outfits, though both had on brown polo shirts and khaki cargo shorts with gleaming white golf shoes. But one was Australian and the other was from Chicago, which made it easier to tell them apart. Both seemed awestruck to be playing with Imperator scientists. Claude fielded their questions, gave them business cards, and encouraged them to explore pharmaceutical research as a lively and lucrative future vocation. Once the game got going, Claude and Wolf managed to mostly keep their distance, which was easier since the bright young things—BYTs, Claude's term for newbies—had opted for a cart.

Golf is a game of etiquette and form, and the courtesies of play belied the awkward scenario unfolding between Claude and Wolf. While they waited for the BYTs to tee off ("Youth before beauty!" Claude had boomed at them) Wolf pretended to have something in his eye in order to avoid meeting Claude's gaze.

"How long have we known each other?" he asked, undeterred by Wolf's vigorous blinking and mugging.

"Um, let's see," Wolf replied, his eyes now actually watering as a result of his faux-futzing. "We met sophomore year. So that's—" he winced as he calculated, "about 24 years."

"Quite some time," Claude said as the first BYT swung and the ball shot sharply away from the green and skyward. They all squinted watching its upward trajectory and nodded as it bounced to a landing on the fairway.

"Longer than any of my marriages," Claude chuckled. "Actually, longer than all my marriages combined."

Wolf grinned despite his growing anxiety.

The second BYT had set up his tee and ball. He was mentally preparing, taking some practice swings, visualizing his shot, which, when he finally made it, was long, straight, and gently angled into the rough. Wolf was next. He selected a driver and tried to focus on the ball. His shot nestled on the cusp of the sand trap to the left of the green.

Claude placed his ball and tee midway between the blue markers with a motion that was as fluid as a dance maneuver and led right into a swing that sent the ball gliding—homing in on the cup, landing on the periphery right of the green. He and Wolf walked and waited while the BYTs tracked their balls. Wolf kept his eyes focused on the plush turf under his feet.

"What are you afraid of?" Claude asked.

"What do you mean?"

"What's your worst fear?"

"Fear?"

"Yes. You know, fear. Spiders, heights, flying, death."

"Fear."

"Right. You must be afraid of something."

"Yes. Fear."

"Ah. I see, Churchill fan."

"No. Herbert."

"Who?"

"Frank Herbert. *Dune*."

"What?"

"It's my favorite science fiction series. The books are set in a distant world where there's a holy order of women called the Bene Gesserit. They have a litany that they recite that's kind of the core of their belief system," Wolf explained, feeling himself flush at this exposure of something close to his heart. In the past, Claude had dismissed Wolf's interests as being nothing more than a symptom of his chronic nerdiness. But Wolf believed in the truths Herbert seeded in *Dune*. He gazed into the horizon and recited as he walked:

I must not fear.

Fear is the mind-killer.

Fear is the little-death that brings total obliteration.

I will face my fear.

I will permit it to pass over me and through me.

And when it has gone past I will turn the inner eye to see its path.

Where the fear has gone there will be nothing. Only I will remain.

He looked at Claude, afraid to find his friend smirking. Claude was looking at him pensively. "Well, then," he grinned. "May the force be with you."

The first hole had been an easy warm up. The second was longer, but not too complicated. The fairway had a slight bend to the left, but the sand trap was smaller and not so near the main approach to the green. The challenge was gaging the distance and calculating for the upward slope. The Aussie BYT, the more strapping of the two, hit a long, furious drive that overshot the green and vanished into the rough beyond.

"Do you know what I fear?" Claude asked.

"Nothing?"

Claude laughed sharply, and the Chicago BYT paused in mid-stroke.

"Sorry," Claude murmured to him, then turned to Wolf.

"Betrayal," he said after the sharp crack of the shot.

"Betrayal?"

"Have you ever heard the saying that all crime is theft?"

"No."

"It's true. A murderer takes your life. Thieves pilfer your belongings. Molesters steal innocence. And traitors rob you of your trust."

The third hole was shorter than the first, with a large sand trap and an ever so slight curve left. Claude birdied and finished in two strokes. Even the BYTs made par, and they were soon making their way to the fourth hole.

"Are you happy at Imperator?"

"Yeah," Wolf answered, but not fast enough.

"I sense some hesitation."

"No." The chuckle he intended to make light of the exchange sounded forced.

"Yes."

"It's just—" Wolf's mind was racing. He wanted to prove he was on Claude's side. "You know, the way Max was moved up—it seemed a little unfair."

"How so?"

"You're a great lab supervisor. He's kind of—redundant."

"And why does that matter to you?"

"Because," Wolf felt inspired. "If they can be unfair to you, they could do that to anyone. To me."

They wound up chit-chatting with the BYTs en route to the next green, which allowed Wolf a respite. He was playing well, but they were in the most challenging portion of the course. Twenty-six shots later, they were still at the fourth hole. One of the BYTs had to negotiate the sand trap and the other, unable to slice right, lost his ball in the water hazard between the fourth and fifth holes. After brief deliberation, he elected to take the penalty instead of wading into the pond. Claude dropped his club at the point where the ball went into the water and placed a fresh ball on the turf. Claude waited patiently, and Wolf uncomfortably, for them to progress to the green.

"Do you believe in an afterlife?" Claude asked. Wolf's shot placed his ball equidistant from the cup on the opposite side.

"Not really."

"What do you mean, 'not really.' That's like being kind of pregnant."

"Sometimes I believe that our life force may persist and that maybe an impression of our lives is carried on, like an energy signature. But mostly, I think we just die."

"So you don't want to spend the hereafter in some paradise teeming with virgins or in heaven with all your dear departed loved ones?"

"I don't think the afterlife would be like that."

"Why?"

"Because those are all earthly definitions of something that is inherently unearthly."

"OK. So what if your soul is recycled just like the elements in your body. What if, somehow, your life force continues?"

Wolf shuddered. "I'm afraid of coming back to a life that's worse than this one." Claude looked genuinely surprised.

"Not that this one is bad," Wolf stammered. "I'm not saying that. It just seems like I've come pretty far along, and the idea of returning and having to do it all again is sort of, I guess, depressing."

The fifth hole was even worse than the fourth with a sharp dogleg and a slope that made it difficult to calculate distance. Two sand traps nestled on either side of the fairway, one before the rise and one after. Wolf's shot was deep in the rough, though he was relieved to leave the others behind while he tracked his ball. Eventually, with two more penalties and bogeys all around, they converged on the green.

"Have you considered your own death?" Claude asked on the way to the sixth hole.

"Yeah."

When Wolf didn't elaborate, Claude plunged ahead. "I hope to die in an accident."

"Oh?"

"After all the studies we've done? Wouldn't you rather bleed out fast or have your head bashed in than go from some disease?"

"I was kind of hoping for sudden cardiac arrest."

"Hmm. That's a good one. But difficult to predict or plan."

"Yeah," Wolf concurred, not sharing his mental regimen of routinely visualizing his end in hopes of influencing fate. He had read an article in a psychology journal about an experiment in which two groups of basketball players were assigned different practice techniques. One group worked on free throws for an hour every day and the other group didn't physically practice, but instead spent 15 minutes visualizing successful free throws four times a day. In the end, the latter outperformed the former. Wolf hoped that by meditating on sudden cardiac arrest four times daily, he could actualize a quick end when his time came.

The BYTs were within earshot of this bit of conversation, and jumped in with their speculation about the likelihood of expiring while having sex.

The sixth hole, long and straight, with no traps or hazards was a breeze, and it was Wolf's turn for a birdie.

"What do you make of Max?" Claude asked as they approached the seventh hole.

"Oh, he's a good guy, I guess." Wolf felt a wave of anxiety well up in his gut like a pot of milk about to boil over.

"You think so?"

"Uhn," Wolf replied vaguely, and covered his fumble by turning the question back at Claude. "You don't think so?"

"You seem pretty chummy." Claude would not be thrown off stride.

"Well, you know, he's a supervisor."

"So you're saying that you talk with him because you have to?"

"Um, well, I can't not talk with him."

"What do you talk about?"

"You know, work."

"Where do you go for happy hour?" Claude's voice betrayed a shimmer of bitterness. Wolf knew he was on treacherous ground.

"Oh, different places," he lied to protect the sanctity of the watering hole. "Usually the Buffalo Bar at the Ambassador."

"Do you discuss work?"

"Not really," Wolf tried to make the discomfort work to his advantage, to make Claude think he was awkwardly confessing the truth rather than awkwardly lying. "It's more about personal stuff. You know, people like to talk about their kids and complain about their spouses."

His deception seemed to work.

"You think Max is good at his job?"

"Yeah?" Wolf answered as blandly as possible.

"Better than I am?"

"No," Wolf shook his head a little too emphatically. "No, of course not."

Though the seventh hole was short, the placement of sand traps made it challenging, but before long they were all bunched up at the collar and the close proximity of the BYTs interrupted Claude's line of questioning.

Eight was probably the most challenging. Shorter than four and five, but with a sharper dogleg and three sand traps, two of which were mere yards apart in front of the green. Even Claude had trouble here and had to focus more intently on play. Wolf had to hold back from jogging to the ninth hole, eager to finish, but Claude paced him with the BYTs hovering in their cart.

The ninth hole was probably the simplest of all—no traps and a straight shot. Claude and Wolf both birdied in two strokes.

"What's the difference between a whiner and a squeaky wheel?" Claude asked when they had all gathered at the tee box.

"Um, I don't know," Wolf answered.

"It depends on who's listening."

The BYTs assumed it was an in joke and laughed companionably. Wolf joined in late.

"I knew I needed to bring you on board the moment I settled in at Imperator," Claude said while the the BYTs packed up their clubs. Wolf made the mistake of looking up and making eye-contact.

"Really?"

"Oh yeah. I saw what the lab needed and knew you had the right stuff."

"Well, it has been a pleasure working with you," Wolf responded after a pause that was a wee bit too long.

"Same here."

Wolf nodded. He felt sweat rising. Claude had offered to buy a round of drinks and the BYTs had taken off in their cart toward the clubhouse.

"You know, I was just re-reading *The Inferno*," Claude said while they made their way back.

"Really?" Wolf tried to step up his pace and urge Claude along, but Claude would not be hurried.

"Yes. Have you read it?"

"No. Not really. I mean, yes. Sort of. Parts of it were in the anthology I had to buy for the English Lit requirement." He had in fact read it, but he was hoping by feigning ignorance to dull the point Claude was driving home.

"Well, there is a special place in hell for traitors."

"There is?" The foaming angst returned.

"Actually, the whole ninth circle of hell is devoted to traitors."

"Really?" Peripherally, he could see Claude looking at him. Desperate to avoid eye contact, he pretended to feel a rock in his shoe.

"Yes, and within that circle are four subdivisions."

"Oh?" His voice was strained.

"Yes. The first is for simple betrayals—like crimes of passion. It's named for Cain, who slew his brother Abel out of envy."

Wolf nodded. The clubhouse was near, but not near enough. Once there, he would be safe. There would be idle small talk with the BYTs. He would down a root beer and then make his excuse to leave. Claude was calmly continuing with his synopsis of hell.

"The next section is for those who betray a political alliance or their country. It's named for a Trojan prince who plotted with the Greeks. Sort of a Benedict Arnold situation."

"I see."

"Then comes the betrayal of friends or guests. This type of transgression was particularly abhorrent to Dante. But do you know who resides in the innermost circle of hell, with Satan himself?"

"Um..." Wolf knew, but did not want to say.

"Judas Iscariot," Claude replied, holding the clubhouse door open for Wolf. "It's the place reserved for those who have betrayed a master or benefactor."

22

Veteran's Day

November 11, 2002

When I got to the Zoo on Monday to meet up with Wiley and the gang, their two cars were pretty packed. I'm sure I could have squeezed in somewhere, but I felt awkward enough as it was, so I opted to follow along in my car and they gave me directions. Which was probably for the best anyhow—that way I'd be able to escape if things became too uncomfortable. I was armed with a new mini-cassette voice recorder that I had purchased just for the occasion. It was small enough to fit in my jacket pocket, and the enthusiastic young sales associate at the electronics store had assured me that it was super powerful and could probably record for, like, hours and totally pick up the faintest sounds and stuff.

I wound up parking three blocks away and even before I opened my door, the savory, succulent smell of smoke and meat crept into my car, triggering some primeval nerve center connected directly to my stomach. With my salivary glands all a-twinge I forgot whatever important thoughts I'd had about the case and scampered to catch up with Wiley and company.

Wiley wasn't kidding when he said that Max Moore put on a serious barbecue. The house was in an older Toyon Canyon neighborhood where the homes were sparse and modest, built before tract developments, and situated on enormous lots. Max's place was at the top of a long slope with a winding drive that cut through a slice of carefully preserved chaparral, shrubby with sage, sumac, and the area's namesake toyon, which was transitioning from flowers to berries—some already blushing red. Beyond the house was a California native plant garden; it was as if a section of the surrounding hillsides chaparral been organized into a formal presentation. The roof of a guest house was visible on the far side. Clouds of smoke were puffing up from nearby.

The main house was a low ranch-style affair, spacious but not showy. The front door was open and clusters of guests were milling about, some with drinks in hand, almost all carrying paper plates heaped with food. People were trickling back and forth between the back garden and the front yard, which featured an enormous coast live oak that offered shade to the guests seated in white folding chairs. I ran into Wiley and and a couple of his companions next to the large buffet table set up in the living room, just inside the front door. We nodded at one another then turned our attention to the opulent spread of food.

Few things are as sublime as pulled pork, smoky, moist, and tender complemented by the tangy sizzle of homemade sauce and a bowl of bright green sweet-tart coleslaw, cool and crisp, and big kaiser rolls with thin crusts and just the right amount of chewiness. Accompanying the main course were sides galore: fried okra, corn fritters, collard greens, black-eyed peas, cornbread, dirty rice, deep fried pickle chips, two kinds of potato salad (one with mayo and one without), chicken wings, hush puppies, spicy green beans, and catfish bites. Topping things off were about a hundred bottles of Shiner Bock in the fridge. I found a quiet corner in the kitchen at the end of a long counter where I could set my food and drink, away from buzzing guests, and got down to business.

At one point, coming up for air, I glanced across the way and felt a flush of panic. Les Moore was directly across from me just outside the kitchen in the hallway that led to the bathroom, talking with a man and woman who were arm in arm. He had a beer in one hand and was laughing at something one of them said. We briefly made eye contact and his expression curdled. Though the cricket honey incident had apparently been some sort of validation (according to Wiley), I was pretty sure that it wasn't enough of an endorsement to entitle me to be at his father's barbecue. I tried to pretend I hadn't seen him, but since I was standing by myself, in a corner with no cover and no companion, this ploy wasn't very convincing. So, I grabbed my plate and beer, then fled to the living room.

Wiley was nowhere to be seen so I wandered around pretending I was on my way to something or someone. Another round of food from a second, smaller table that was devoted to chips and appetizers plus another cooler of beer kept me busy for a while, but a bottle, a fork, and a plate demand three hands or a place to sit, and chairs were at a premium. I headed for the patio out back, but en route found a piano bench on the periphery of a conversation in the dining area. A wiry guy in khaki pants and a Rolling Stones T-shirt was in the middle of a story that a semicircle of four people were listening to in rapt attention. His head was shaved (and judging from the pattern of the dark stubble it was a pre-emptive strike against male pattern baldness) and he spoke with a hint of that peculiar New Jerseyesque accent that people from New Orleans have. He had a bottle of beer in one hand and with the other was gesturing evocatively with an unlit cigarette. He was in the midst of a pause for effect when I stealthily insinuated myself into his audience.

"You've got to be kidding," a woman exclaimed.

"I assure you I'm not," he said with a chuckle. "There I was at this gas station in the middle of nowhere in New Mexico, the wind whipping me with sand, and she's in the car insisting that I get her a box of mini-pads."

"The sand storm couldn't have been that bad."

"Have you ever been in one? A real one? Out in the desert?"

"Well, no."

"Trust me. It was bad. I had the hood on my sweatshirt up with the drawstrings pulled tight and I shifted my sunglasses around so one lens was forming a makeshift portal, and I had the sleeves pulled down over my hands 'cause the sand stung like a bazillion teeny BB pellets. I musta looked like a space alien with one eye in the middle of my head! After I finished gassing up the car, I bolted for the shop. And you know, I felt a little weird buying them, so to disguise the fact that I was buying mini-pads I got a bunch of camouflage items."

"Camouflage?"

"Yeah. You know, when the real point of your purchase is something kind of embarrassingly personal like condoms or hemorrhoid cream or a pregnancy test, you add all kinds of stuff so it's less obvious."

"Do you buy a lot of pregnancy tests?"

"No. I'm just using that as an example. So I got the mini-pads in amongst a bunch of stuff—Cheetos and lighter fluid and Windex and so on. I clutch the bag and make a dash for the car and when I get there, she's gone."

"No way!"

"Way! I looked around everywhere and waited a while in case she'd gone to the restroom, which of course wasn't the case or else I'da seen her getting the key. You know how gas stations always attach them to tire irons or hub caps to keep people from walking off with them."

There was nodding and murmuring of assent.

"So then I notice a little piece of paper sitting on the dash. It's a note from her saying sorry for the inconvenience but she had to go, and it was signed by her."

"Well, what happened?"

"I found out later—much later—that a friend of hers had coincidentally pulled into the station and she had recognized the car. Apparently she had kind of had it with me, though she never said a damn thing about being mad at me, and convinced her pal to drive her home."

"But how impossible is that? Didn't she live in L.A.?"

"Yes, and so did her friend. And they left me there with a bag of random stuff including a super-sized box of mini-pads."

There was laughter all around.

"What the hell did you do with them?

"You'd be surprised how useful they are."

I laughed with the rest of the crowd as he explained how mini-pads can be deployed to cushion areas on the inside of shoes that rub your feet the wrong way, how they can be cut into thin strips and used to pad cupboard doors to dampen slamming, or instead of the little felt pads under objects to keep them from scratching and slipping. He was describing how well they work for rubbing mineral oil into wooden cutting boards and salad bowls when I glanced out to the patio and saw an older gentleman in a straw cowboy hat who I was fairly certain was Max Moore. I quickly got up, dropped my empty plate in one of the many thoughtfully deployed garbage cans, grabbed a fresh beer and slipped outside.

Cowboy hat had vanished but the people he had been chatting with were there. The patio was about as wide as the house. It was roughly kidney shaped and surrounded by raised planter beds constructed from re-purposed coarsely cut blocks of concrete with green waves of coyote mint draping over the edges and artfully maintained ceanothus and toyon looming over it with dark green foliage and clusters of berries. Like one of those Renaissance paintings where the clouds part to reveal some luminous deity, the people grouped near one end of the planter parted to reveal Gladys Schmertz, possibly the unhappiest animal keeper in Zoo history.

During my time at the Zoo I had crossed paths with her on many occasions, but (blessedly) she never remembered me, so it was possible to maintain our relationship as one of nodding and waving. An unexpected perk of being a research volunteer was that in addition to gaining an endless number of fascinating insights about the animals you are observing, it was also possible to learn really great gossip. One goal of being a researcher was to not intrude on your subjects—you want them to behave as if you aren't there, Schrödinger be damned. And if you were really good, you could pull off what we used to jokingly call the English Butler Effect. (Speaking about his role as Stevens the butler in *The Remains of the Day*, Anthony

Hopkins once described the ideal butler as making a room even emptier by being there.) Sometimes it was necessary to stay out on grounds for an observation after the Zoo had opened to the public. It was often difficult to concentrate when squirrelly teens, packs of marauding school children, or obtusely intrusive adults turned their attention to you. So we all strived to become as invisible as possible—a skill that was equally valuable in the detective business. There had been a few occasions when I achieved this, and during one episode of invisibility, I overheard a conversation between a couple of Gladys's colleagues. They joked about her mood that day being "partly glowering" and then earnestly discussed the possibility of hacking into the human resources database and doctoring her personnel file so that she would be eligible for early retirement. The City of Santa Narcissa was at the time offering employees a limited-time early retirement option, but you had to be the right age and have clocked in a certain amount of time for the City. She had started a mere two months too late to qualify. Clearly they had not succeeded in their computer espionage plan, and Gladys was still slogging away at the Zoo.

It was too late to retreat to the living room. Surely Les was not follow- ing me, but the conversational currents had carried him there. His back was to the patio and he appeared to be embroiled in an animated discussion just inside the doorway. I turned to face Gladys and tried to position myself so that I was out of sight lines from Les.

"You know, everyone has it in for us." She looked pretty much the same as I remembered her—angular features that unfortunately settled into an annoyed expression when at rest. Her dark hair was more than half gray now and pulled back into a taut ponytail.

"What do you mean?" asked a gray-haired man with a Van Dijk beard and wearing a flamingo-festooned aloha shirt.

"The City Council is starving us to death by cutting our general fund allowance. The friggin' animal rights people harass us even though there are bigger, more high profile zoos they could hassle, because they know they can exploit the politicians. You don't see them going after the San Felipe

Zoo, do you?"

"Well, they are private. And they have way better spin control," someone offered.

"Spin control?" She replied indignantly. "It's all about money!" She slammed her beer down on the edge of the planter bed and it foamed up and erupted like a tiny volcano. "They just buy media. They can afford big shot lawyers to take on the animal rights people. Animal rights. Hah. If anyone is fighting for animal rights it's the people who actually work with them!"

"Well, they do at San Felipe, too," the man said. Gladys glared at him for a moment, but then continued undeterred.

"Yeah, but we don't make any more mistakes than they do, but we always get nailed. They just pay the fines, put out a press release about a cute baby something or another, and it all goes away. I know people there. I know what really goes on. One time they had a whole herd of yaks get out of their enclosure and no one ever heard about it." She paused, overcome by the injustice of it all. "Another time, wild squirrels that one of their keepers had been feeding regularly—what's wrong with *that* picture?—attacked a service dog."

"You're kidding."

"Would I lie about something like that?" she said in a drastic tone and stared at flamingo man, who shifted uncomfortably from one foot to the other.

"Uh, no?"

She was scrutinizing each member of her audience to tease out any doubters, and the urge to flee before the eye of Sauron fell on me was surging when I felt someone tap my shoulder. I turned to find Randall Wiley.

"You look like you need a fresh beer," he said with the fleetingest of winks.

"Yeah," I said, realizing that I had been nervously sipping and there was nothing but backwash left. "Yeah, I sure do."

"This way," he said and I eagerly followed. Glancing over at the living room doorway, I was alarmed to find Les watching me like a hawk. I quickly downed my backwash and, though it was pointless, lunged forward so that Randall screened me from Les. He led me around the corner to yet another cooler full of beers. We both refueled and started down a path that led through the main garden and toward another patio area near the guest house where the actual barbecue was located. It was screened by some tall shrubs, but the smoke drifting skyward was a dead giveaway.

"So you really work at Holcomb Gardens?"

"Yes."

"You like it there?"

"Oh, yeah. It's not particularly lucrative, but there's a lot of autonomy."

"What do you do?"

"I'm a senior gardener but I have a lot of creative latitude. I like to think of myself as a semi-curator."

"So what are you working on?"

"Have you been there?"

"I'm a member."

"Wow—that's great!"

He smiled at my outburst of geekish enthusiasm.

"Right. Well, I supervise some of the conservatory—the carnivorous plant collection and most of the epiphytes—but my main interest is succulents. And I'm curating a new garden called Magnificent Monsters."

"That sounds interesting."

"It is. Very."

"Where is it located?"

"Are you familiar with the Aubol House?"

"That big hacienda with all the artisan tiles and the reflecting pool?"

"Yes. They're going to open that up as an exhibit about the Holcombs, and one of the adjacent gardens is where the monsters are settling in."

"That'll be fantastic. I've always wanted to see the house. What monstrous plants have you gathered?"

"Well, it was pretty easy to come up with lots of 'monstrose' and 'ferox' plants that are all fierce and monstrous. But then once I started researching the plants, one thing led to another and I started expanding into others. Like 'demon plants.' It's amazing how many plants are satanic—devil's backbone, devil's claw, devil-in-the-bush—or love-in-a-mist depending on your outlook."

"That's awesome."

"Yes. Finding the sources of why particular plants are considered evil leads to some really obscure but interesting places. It's like playing telephone. But over the course of centuries, and across continents."

"Totally," he paused and turned to me. "You know about celery, right?"

"Celery? As in salad filler?"

"Yes. In the Middle Ages celery used to be known as Devil's fingers."

"I thought that was a fungus."

"It is—*Clathrus archeri*—but celery, as in the standard veggie tray veggie has also been called Devil's fingers."

"And it's demonic because..."

"Well, like you were saying, sometimes the rationale gets lost in translation." We continued walking. "Celery has been used by people since ancient times. Although up until about the eighteenth century, people only used the leaves. Kind of like parsley—and in a lot of old Roman texts the two are interchangeable. According to Greek folklore, it's associated with Archemorus."

"'Pre-death?'"

"Close. It means 'forerunner of death.' His real name was Opheltes. He was the son of Nemean King Lycurgus and Queen Eurydice."

"I thought Eurydice was married to Orpheus and had that whole underworld adventure."

"Different Eurydice. So when Opheltes was born, the king went to an oracle to see what his fate would be."

"Que sera, sera?"

He laughed. "Yeah, pretty much. The oracle told him cryptically (because that's how they rolled) that the kid would be fine as long as he didn't touch the ground before he learned how to walk. So I guess they were careful with the baby, but forgot to tell the nurse who tended him. This was during the Theban war, and one day some generals came along and asked the nurse where they could find water. So she put little Opheltes down on the ground while she pointed them in the right direction."

"Uh-oh."

"Exactly. Where did she put him, but in a bed of celery. And a snake came along and strangled him. Thus fulfilling the prophesy. So celery became associated with this bad omen. After Opheltes's death they referred to him as Archemorus. The king also started the Nemean Games in his memory. I've also read that this is why it was thought that celery seeds would only sprout after a trip to Hades—maybe because it takes a long time for them to germinate, so people thought the seeds had to travel all the way to the underworld before they were ready to sprout. I've never actually grown celery, so I'm not sure about that. In any case, ages later, when this story made its way to northern Europe after it had been Christianized, there were all kinds of problems with how it translated. You know Hades the god is sort of neutral, and so is the underworld because the Elysian Fields, where dead heros go, are there, but then it's also where people like Tantalus and Sisyphus were punished after they died. But in Europe it was interpreted as Hell. And then there was that snake."

"Of course."

"So that's how celery became associated with the devil."

"That's fantastic."

"There's an old saying in England that only evil can grow celery. Which is pretty funny. Whenever I see some elaborate salad chock full of diced celery, I have to laugh."

"Wow... I'll never look at ants-on-a-log the same way again." My thoughts were suddenly taking a detour into how I could incorporate Wiley's celery lore into my monster garden. "That is really fascinating. I would love to use that."

"Be my guest. There's no copyright on folklore."

"Yeah, but I feel like I should credit you somehow."

"Whatever. You probably would have stumbled across it yourself in a matter of time."

"Maybe."

"But you can't have all the evil plants growing together."

"No," I answered, tearing my mind away away from the Herbs of Hades concept. "And that's been what is challenging—but also fun. At first I thought it would just be one big garden, but the space is pretty large and by subdividing it into sections I can make micro habitats to suit the different groups. It turns out the hacienda has a large solarium that borders on the kitchen garden, which means I can keep some of the evil plants that need more humidity in there."

"How far along is the project?"

"I don't know. There's no concrete deadline. I would like to finish up all the plantings before the winter rains so everything can settle in. Then let it grow in for a while. I guess it could open next fall. There was talk of it being ready for next Halloween. I found a little company in Santa Barbara that sells amazing handmade stone garden statuary, and I blew a big chunk of my non-plant budget on replicas of little grotesques."

"Like the ones at Lotusland in that outdoor amphitheater garden?"

"Exactly! Though these are not replicas of those. These are more like Clive Barker garden gnomes."

Wiley laughed. "I'll keep an eye out for a Magnificent Monsters opening announcement."

We were approaching the barbecue pit. The smoke was gusting and Max Moore was armed with tongs and a brush dripping with brownish red sauce.

"So here we are. You know that's Max, right?"

"Yes." I had been enjoying the chat with Wiley and my developing beer buzz so much that I'd almost forgotten my ulterior motive. I took a deep breath, then reached into my pocket where I'd stashed the mini-cassette recorder and prayed I was hitting the right button to record. I couldn't very well take it out and check. Wiley probably wouldn't have cared, but I had decided not to tell Max.

"He's a good guy. I mean, hell, look at this spread."

"Right."

"Well, I'll introduce you and then beat it."

"OK," I looked over, reluctant to see him go. "Thanks."

He smiled. "Don't mention it. I hope you get more out of Max than Les."

"Me, too."

"Hey, Max!

He turned and smiled. "Randall! How the fuck are you?"

"Oh, you know, right as rain and horny as hell."

They punched each other jovially in the arms and erupted in hearty Man Laughter. I smiled politely and waited for it to abate.

"So you heard about Claude, right?" Wiley said.

"Oh, yeah. Damn shame. You know, we had our differences, but he was one of a kind."

"Well, this is Sandy Lohm. She used to be in research at the Zoo and now she's investigating Claude's death."

"So are you a cop or a private investigator?" he said, opening a fresh beer.

"Well, I used to be a PI. I've been summoned out of retirement for this."

"So then, you're a lady dick," he said with a mischievous grin that made me think of the Grinch when the idea of stealing the Whos' Christmas dawns on him. Wiley chuckled and excused himself.

I wasn't sure what to make of this. So I took a long swig of beer while I tried to come up with a witty retort. And failed.

"I've been told I'm no lady."

He smirked. "So what do you want to know?"

"Well, I understand that you knew Claude before he came to the Zoo."

"I did."

"How?"

"We both worked at Imperator Pharmaceuticals."

"In what capacity?"

"We were lab co-supervisors."

"Were you friendly?"

He took a sip of his beer and thought for a moment.

"I'd say I was friendly with him, but he was not friendly with me. I assume you've been digging into the past."

"I pieced together much of the story from Claude's files, which were meticulous."

"So you know the details of the lab fire."

"Yes."

"Well, that was an inside job."

"But it killed that lab tech."

"Yeah," he looked down at the ground and was silent for a while. "Poor Wolf. He was really in the wrong place at the wrong time."

"Did you set the fire?"

"Oh, hell no. That was a professional job."

"You know that for a fact?"

He held my gaze for a while, weighing something.

"Look. I've never discussed the circumstances under which I left Imperator. In fact, I signed a non-disclosure agreeement. So I'm telling you this because you seem honest. And because Wiley told me you're trustworthy. This is strictly off the record. I'm only giving you this information as a favor."

Pleased that Wiley had given me a good reference, I nodded and tried to exude honesty, though the tape recorder in my pocket felt like a brick of guilt and I hoped I wasn't blushing.

"Imperator hired me to spy on Claude. Of course, that only became clear after I took the job. I just wanted the supervisory post on my resume—and I really needed the bump up in income—but they were looking for someone to keep tabs on him. They suspected he was cooking the books. Well, they knew he was cooking the books because they asked him to do it. Not in so many words, naturally. Their instructions were swathed in plausible deniability, and he understood what he was being asked to do. But then the FDA decided to investigate. Natually, Imperator had a mole among the regulators and knew it was coming. Hence my appointment. They needed to confirm what Claude was doing, and to destroy the evidence. So I snooped on Claude and reported back to the mucky mucks—who shall remain nameless—until they knew the extent of his activities."

"And you never considered blowing the whistle?"

"Don't you get it? They set it all up—set me up to take the fall if I spoke up. They made sure that no one found enough solid evidence to pin it on me—unless I broke my contract with them. Wolf's death just gave them more power because, as I'm sure you know, arson is a felony, and a death that occurs during the commission of a felony is at least manslaughter, and there's no statute of limitations on that."

"Did they pay you off?"

"Not exactly. They transferred me to a less sensitive section of the lab while the investigation went on and the media speculated. Then, when the findings were inconclusive enough to not bring any charges against me, they made all the arrangements for me and Les to relocate."

"What about your wife?"

"She had passed a few years before this all happened," he said with a faint note of melancholy.

"So they sent you to Santa Narcissa and set you up with a new job? Like being in witness protection."

"Yeah. With the mob protecting you."

"And Les knew about none of this?"

"No. Well, he knew I wanted to get away from Imperator."

"Did you talk about the arson? I mean, how could you not?"

"He knew I was innocent of the fire, but he's a bright kid and he could see I was being marginalized by the company. He assumed it was because they doubted my innocence and wanted to get rid of me."

"So that was the end of your career in research."

"What career? Coming up with new drugs and then waiting for the marketeers to invent conditions for them to solve?"

"But you had been in the industry for years before you went to Imperator."

"Yeah. And the whole reason I took the Imperator job was because it was a notch up from what I had been doing at my previous post. I was at a different pharmaceutical company working on reformulations of the anti-depressants that were about to run out of patent so that they could keep milking them for more profits. That's what made me such a bright prospect for Imperator. Right before I took the co-supervisor job at Imperator, I was working on a feline formulation of Placidol for anxious cats."

"So you were disillusioned with the work?"

"Honeybun, being driven out of that job was a blessing."

"Did you know Claude was living in Santa Narcissa?"

"Of course I did. I talk with my son every week."

"That didn't bother you?"

"Why the hell would it? I'm not working at the Zoo."

"Was he aware of who Claude was when he met him at the Zoo?"

"Nope."

"And you had never mentioned Claude specifically?"

"Well, we're close and have always talked a lot. We were a household of two, so I told him about things going on at the lab, including my self-important colleague, but I probably only mentioned Claude by name a handful of times. He knew I was upset about Wolf's death. Les was obviously on my side, but he had his own life going on."

"He was in school?"

"Yep," he replied with a glimmer of pride. "He was was in grad school at Texas A&M College of Veterinary Medicine."

"Was he living at home with you?"

"No. He lived in college housing and came home on breaks and long weekends."

"How far was that from Austin?"

"A couple hours or so."

"Did he finish his degree before you moved to California?"

"No. No, he took a leave of absence to go to California with me, but then he never went back."

"Why?"

"It was expensive, for one thing. I'd paid for his undergraduate schooling, and he got grants and loans for grad school, but I was still helping out quite a bit. Leaving Imperator was a pretty big setback. My wife had been ill for a number of years before she passed, and the medical expenses were lingering. Once I got settled in out here, he found a job at the Zoo and then he got settled in, too."

"Did he talk about Claude to you?"

"Yep."

"What sort of things did he say?"

"Oh," his expression lightened and he chuckled. "Things I already knew to be true about Claude."

"Like what?"

"He was pompous and inflexible."

"And Les had no idea that you had worked together?"

"No."

"Were you never tempted to confide in him?"

"There was no point. He was annoyed enough by him without me giving him more reasons to dislike him."

"But he found out anyhow."

"Yep."

"How?"

"At the volunteer appreciation dinner in September. He overheard two docents talking about diet pills and Povenda came up, and that led to Claude because one of them knew all about his history at Imperator. Les figured it out pretty quick."

"So that's when he assaulted Claude."

"I think that's a little strong. He overreacted and took a swing at Claude."

"That's assault."

"Like I said. He overreacted."

"Did he tell you he'd figured out who Claude was?"

"Yes."

"How?"

"Like I said, we talk at least once a week and he point-blank asked me why I never said anything about having worked with Claude."

"And what did you tell him?"

"That it was all ancient history."

"Was he upset?"

"No. He had cooled off by then."

"Are you sure?"

"Now you just watch where you're stepping."

"I'm not implying anything."

"Like hell you aren't."

"OK. Well, it is an awkward situation. You've got to admit. To Les it must have seemed like Claude was the reason you lost your position at Imperator and he had to give up veterinary school."

"Look, it might have seemed that way to Les, though I really doubt you heard it that way from him. But I had been nudging him away from vet school."

"You had?"

"He's good with animals. And he's good with research. Take it from me—I know what good research demands. I spent a lot of time and energy chasing after the glory of being a physician. Then I found research. Of course I goofed a second time thinking I'd found my calling at Imperator. The love of money is the root of all evil, and money makes the pharmaceutical industry go round. I had hoped he would go into ecology and field biology. I think he's happier as a keeper than he ever would have been as a vet."

"He doesn't seem all that happy."

He laughed. "Yeah, well, like I said, he's a whole lot happier as a keeper than he would have been as a vet. There's certainly no love lost between Les and Claude, but if you think Les coulda killed him, you'd better think again."

"But it's no secret that they despised each other."

"Yeah. Right. It's no secret. Do you think Les would be that foolish? He might hate the guy, but I didn't raise some bonehead who doesn't know the difference between right and wrong and can't deal with whatever feelings he might have in a mature manner."

"They did have some pretty volatile disagreements. In front of a fair number of people."

"Yeah. Disagreements. People disagree all the time but they don't kill each other."

"But sometimes they do."

"Not Les."

I was stuck in a showdown.

"So you're pretty close to Les?"

"He's my only child. Of course we're close."

"Well, that's not always the case."

"It is the case with us," he glanced down at my empty beer bottle. "You need a refill?"

"Uh, sure." Actually, I was feeling lightheaded, but the desire to accept his offer and the desperate need for a prop won out. While he retrieved a couple beers from the cooler and opened them, I tried to figure out where to go next. He was oddly cranky but didn't seem really angry—like father, like son.

"Thanks," I said when he handed me the bottle. "Do you have any ideas who might have wanted Claude dead?"

Again, the gritty chuckle. "Nope." He moved over to the big barbecue—one of those made from a metal barrel that's been bisected lengthwise and hinged. A huge cloud of smoke billowed out when he opened it and turned the chicken halves, ribs, and tri-tip. The smell was tantalizing all over again.

"So what do you put in your sauce?" I said, my mind wandering to my stomach.

"If I told you, I'd have to kill you," he winked, and for some reason it struck me as being hilarious and I started giggling. Max gave me a double take, which made me laugh even more.

"Missy, you better make that your last beer for a while if you're driving."

One of the many downsides of socializing in the car culture of Southern California is having to choose between astronomical cab fares or the tiresome process of sobering up, which pretty much ruins the point of partying. Many of my colleagues actually believe that I'm in Alcoholics Anonymous because they never see me drinking at functions, but it's because I don't have a significant other to trade off designated driving duties, and I'm too cheap to pay for cabs.

"What do you do now?"

"Oh, I teach biology at U.C. Santa Narcissa."

"Is that where you were on the morning of October 11?"

He chuckled. "It was indeed. I was giving lectures at eight and ten o'clock in the morning to a couple hundred freshman biology students. Then I had lunch in the busy faculty lounge and talked with a steady stream of students during my office hours in the afternoon."

"Oh," I said, and couldn't refrain from adding "good."

Max grinned and shut the barbecue.

I chatted with him some more about teaching, Texas, and fine barbecue joints we had known, and he offered me samples of the various meats with sauce as he took them off the grill and piled them onto platters destined for the house. As is often the case, with the pressure of the formal questioning gone, he relaxed and shared a few insights about Les and his formative years—insights that made it even more difficult to see him bludgeoning Claude and dumping him in a compost pile.

Les was an only child, and a precocious one—the kind of kid who found it more important to be right than to be popular. Like his arch academic rival, Ted Masters, Les could be counted on to ace most every test. Unlike Ted, he refused to barter correct answers for playground protection and so endured the brutal (and obtuse) taunting that venal Ted avoided. Listening to Max, I had more than a few uncomfortable flashbacks to my own only-childhood spent haunting libraries, hiding from playground scourges, and fantasizing about the sweet revenge I would one day savor when my incredible future as a world renowned scientist was realized.

Eventually, I shook hands with Max and wandered off into the garden. In addition to the main pathway that Wiley and I had taken to the barbecue and Max were a couple minor, scenic paths that wound through the garden. I took one of these that led around to a little shaded area with a bench near a bird feeder. I sat to check the tape recorder. It was still running. I had successfully pressed record and it looked like I had a good 30 minutes. I was tempted to rewind and check the recording quality, but didn't want to risk someone seeing or hearing me. So I took the batteries out of the recorder (to prevent any accidental re-recording), stuck it back in my pocket, and looked up to find a scrub jay staring at me. He or she was a beautiful study in blue inquisitiveness, regarding me in that intent corvid way that seems to say, "Yeah, you've got thumbs and writing, but you're not all that." I was wishing I had my camera when I heard voices approaching on the main path.

"Hey, man. I said I was sorry."

"What were you thinking?"

"She used to be in research."

"I don't care. You had no business inviting her."

"Oh, come on. You said she was OK."

"Just because I said she was OK for putting up with the cricket honey gag doesn't mean I wanted to see her at my dad's house."

"He didn't seem to mind."

"Of course he didn't seem to mind. He's too polite to tell someone to get the hell out of his home when they were invited there. I'm the one who minds. If she was over here bugging him about Claude, I'll sue her."

"Les, you can't sue someone for coming to a barbecue. Even if you didn't invite her."

"Where is she? You were walking this way with her. Did you take her to my dad?"

I could barely make out Les and Wiley through the shrubbery. They were headed for the barbecue. My head was a little foggy, but the adrenaline spike from overhearing cranky Les helped clear it a little more. It was definitely time to leave. I could always hunker down in my car for a while to sober up before driving home. Cautiously, I made my way to the main path, checked to make sure it was clear, then hurried back to the main house. On my way out I noticed a table of desserts. As tempting as the pies and cobbler were, I made do with a big Texas brownie (easier to grab and go) and left. The sun had moved enough that the patch of shade around my car was gone, and I sat in it with the door open to let it cool off while I nibbled and thought about the case, making notes on the Post-It pad in my purse.

Les was still a definite possibility; Max less so. Being in a lecture hall in front of a full house of students was a pretty solid alibi. Plus I couldn't see how he would get into the Zoo without being identified. Maybe going to the Zoo and retracing Claude's steps would yield some insights. Maybe there was something to the photos Claude, Jr. had sent. It was going to take some effort to try and interview Philip Landers, but it could be worthwhile. And it couldn't be much more arduous than talking with Max. After all, Landers was a politician. Thinking about politicians made me think of favors and deals, and I wondered if maybe the solution wasn't a third party. It seemed a little far fetched, but it was possible that Les, or Max, or Landers for that matter, particularly Landers, might have hired someone to kill Claude. This was an interesting notion. Someone could have gotten in as an outside vendor—linen deliveries, tree trimmers, even a messenger service. But they would have had to sign in, and chances are someone would have made note of an away-team uniform. Sober and determined, I headed home.

The Path Not Taken

November 15, 2002

Claude had died on a Friday, so I wanted to wait until Friday the 15th to do my walk-through of his last day. That meant I could take advantage of three blissful days of perfect gardening weather. The mornings were foggy, cool, and not quite rainy—the type of weather that brings up the scent of damp concrete and leaves your car splotchy. Earlier in the year it would have been labeled "May Gray" or "June Gloom" because weather forecasters in Southern California feel the need to hype what few "weather events" we have. (It's probably the only place on earth where a wind storm needs to be branded with its own logo.) Afternoons were warm and crisp, and come the weekend, there was a chance of actual rain. Inspired by Wiley's celery lore, a whole new section of the garden was taking shape in my mind. A shipment of plants I had ordered the previous week had arrived, and I started working them into the landscape while I contemplated transforming the kitchen garden into the Herbs of Hades and wondered what other interesting lore Wiley might have amassed.

When Friday finally rolled around, I headed for the Zoo, arrived at the volunteer sign-in computer at 7:28 a.m., and waited seven minutes to be as exact as I could be about retracing Claude's day. At 7:35 I made my way out the back doors of the administration building and started down the stairs. Three keepers were going up the stairs and we exchanged hellos. I got to the sidewalk just as a big pickup truck clattered past. I didn't recognize the driver and he looked confused when I waved him over. He rolled down the window and squinted at me as if he were trying to place my face.

"Can I help you?"

"I hope so. My name is Sandy Lohm and I'm here investigating the death of Claude Hopper."

"Oh," he seemed startled. "I didn't know the guy."

"Did you know of him?"

"Well, I'd seen him around. He was kinda hard to miss."

"What do you mean?"

"Well, he was so damn friendly all the time, and he always wore those scarf things tied around his neck. It was almost impossible to avoid him."

"Did you ever talk with him?"

"No. Not other than nodding at him whenever he came around bellowing 'Top of the morning.'"

"I see. Do you come this way on a regular schedule?"

"No. I have to go out to the parking lot and check the drains right now. If it rains and there's stuff blocking them, the lot floods pretty bad."

"Do you remember the last time you saw Claude Hopper?"

"Well, sure. It was the Friday before they found him up at the compost yard."

"Are you sure?"

"Yeah. I was running late and had to pee before I went out to the parking lot to change some bulbs. I saw him when I was going up those stairs to the men's room. He was coming out of the building all chipper and stuff. He 'Top of the morninged' me and I was in such a crappy mood I almost kicked him."

"Did you notice which direction he went?"

"No, but there's nothing that way," he pointed forward, "but the security gate and the main parking lot, so if he was just getting here he musta gone up that way," he said, gesturing toward the service road leading into the main part of the Zoo.

"Great. Thank you so much. Your name is?"

"Don Wanderly. That's it?"

"That's all for now." I dug a small block of Post-Its out of my bag and jotted down his name and number, then gave him one of my cards.

"Hey, this is for Holcomb Gardens."

"Yeah. That's my real job when I'm not out detecting."

"All right. Whatever," he chuckled, and drove off.

So now I could place Claude in space and time on the day in question. I walked up the service road and made my way to Billy Goat Bluff. I spoke briefly with the keepers there. One of them had not been in that day and the other could not recall seeing him on that day in particular, though like everyone else, they could vividly recall his visits. But that didn't mean he hadn't gone past. It just meant that he had missed the keepers. I forged on, taking the public walkway through the Zoo. I had no luck at the African Savannah exhibit either. It was a large habitat and the staff area was far back, right up against the Service Road. If he came past on the public side, he would only have seen keepers if they were cleaning up right next to the moat between the barrier and the edge of the turf. I knew there was a gate hidden behind some ornamental grasses that led to a little access pathway to the keeper hut and made my way there. But again, no one here could recall seeing Claude on the day in question. I thanked them and went back to the public path. The main doors to the Reptile House would not have been open at that time of morning, and there was no way to access the off-exhibit spaces from the public side. So I decided I would check with the reptile staff on my way out.

On past the Hippoquarium and Rainforest Haven, I could find no one who had seen him during his last morning, which made it seem more likely that he had never made it into the main Zoo that day. But I didn't want to leap to any conclusions just yet. At Raptorama, I found Trixie Lockhart in for Les Moore. She was fresh-faced and young—surely not yet 30—with masses of blonde hair that she had restrained in a thick, gleaming braid. I introduced myself and she quickly washed her hands, shook mine, and led me to a small table with two mismatched plastic patio chairs in the kitchen area of the keeper shack near the cricket farm. I wondered if she had ever tried cricket honey.

"I was expecting you," she said, pulling out one of the chairs and indicating that I should sit.

"Oh?"

"Yeah. Les mentioned that you'd been by earlier. I figured you'd want to talk with me since Claude usually came in on my days here. You want a soda?"

"No. I'm OK, thanks. So you didn't see him on that last day?"

"No," she said and, frowning, took the seat opposite me. "Which was kind of strange. He was pretty punctual, and when he couldn't make it in, Corinne always made sure someone else could cover his food prep shift. I thought maybe he was sick or something and called in too late for Corinne to do anything about it."

"When was the last time you saw him?"

"Oh, whenever his last shift was before, you know..." she trailed off.

"Did you like him?"

"Yeah, I did. I know a lot of people found him annoying, but he was always so glad to be here. He really loved doing what he did, and that was pretty cool. I mean, most of us who work here like what we do. No job is perfect—there's always a certain amount of crap that you have to deal with. But if you enjoy the good parts enough, it makes the crap seem superficial. Or silly. But he had done all kinds of interesting things before he retired and came here, and even though he was kind of full of himself, I still enjoyed listening to his stories."

"Did he ever talk about his work on Povenda?"

"Hm. Sometimes. I know that was a big deal for him, but up here he tended to talk a lot about his travel experiences and all the amazing birds he'd seen."

"Did Les know he worked at Imperator, the pharmaceutical company that produced Povenda?"

"I don't know. Les was so annoyed by Claude that he just generally avoided him."

"Les seems really bitter."

"Oh, no. He's kind of a curmudgeon—just not really a people person. He loves his work. And if you've known him for a while—and I've worked with him ever since he started here—you can see he's just impatient with the song and dance you have to do sometimes to make things happen here. Claude was just the opposite. To him it was a game, and he was one of those extroverts who just thrives on interacting with people."

"But Les had gotten into veterinary school and was on his way to a degree before he came here, wasn't he?"

"Totally. When his dad left his job, Les had to put vet school on the back burner," she said. "Les had worked at the little zoo in his home town when he was an undergrad, and then after he got into Texas A&M for vet school, they were happy to have him back at the zoo on breaks. He had a work study job and got a great financial aid package but he still needed help and that was tough after his dad left Imperator. When they moved to California it was really all over. I mean, I guess he could have borrowed a ton of money and gone to school part time so he could get a job to pay his way, but I think he also wanted to be with his dad."

"Did his dad receive a severance package?"

"Yeah, but you know, Les's mom had been really sick for quite some time, and she died when he was still an undergrad. They weren't poor but they weren't exactly rolling in dough either. Les said they had to liquidate a bunch of assets that were in his mom's name and some joint accounts so that they could qualify for Medicaid. But there were still bills beyond that."

"And he never considered completing his degree out here?"

"Well, there aren't any good programs here in Santa Narcissa. He would probably have had to apply at U.C. Davis. I think that Les changed his mind about being a vet. Not that he would ever say this in so many words, but I've known lots of keepers who started off in veterinary school and opted out."

"Really?"

"Yes. I thought about being a vet, too. Majored in biology and worked at an animal hospital and a wildlife center with exotics during the summers."

"What changed your mind?"

"Well, it is super rewarding work when you can diagnose and treat a patient who is unable to tell you what's wrong. It really is a gift. But after a while you realize that a lot of the time you are seeing animals that are very sick, or animals that are afraid of you. A lot of the satisfaction you get is from making the owners happy—at least in the private practice where I worked. And sometimes that's awful because you know that what would be best for the animal is not what's going to make the owner happy. To be a good vet, you really have to understand that you may be caring for the animal, but the animal is an extension of the person, so it's really the two together that you are treating. I wanted to work with the animals, and that's what I do. It has its sad times, too. You can't have a living collection without having to deal with illness and death, but I get to see them sometimes all their lives—and the good times that come from that kind of connection definitely outweigh the bad."

"And you think Les had a similar realization?"

"Like I said, I don't think he'd ever admit it. Maybe not even to himself, but I see him when he's working with the birds. He's in his element."

"Thanks so much."

"Was that helpful? I don't feel like I helped you much with Claude."

"No, you were very helpful."

"Great! Well, if you have any other questions, you know where to find me."

I rummaged around for a business card. "Thanks. And if you think of anything else, here's my card. Feel free to phone me."

She walked me to the gate and I started down the service road. Unfortunately there was no sign of the Compost King today, so I had to hoof it to my next stop.

I had no luck with the reptile crew, or anyone else along the service road. No one other than Don Wanderly had seen Claude on his last day. So where had he gone after that? Was Don Wanderly the last person to see him alive?

Lost in thought, I soon found myself back at the junction to Billy Goat Bluff, where I was almost flattened by a bicycle messenger who came rocketing down the driveway that led to the graphics office. He had a large black poster tube strapped to his back like a quiver of arrows, and was encased in silver Spandex with the word "Mercury" emblazoned across his buttocks.

The graphics office was a small bungalow that I'd walked past many times but never entered. It was nestled between the service road and a small park-like area full of fiercely clipped hedges, picnic tables, and screaming children. With my heart still racing from my near hit-and-run at the bottom of the drive, I realized that it was the last building between administration and the pathway off the Service Road that led to Billy Goat Bluff. On a whim I decided to take a detour.

The office was a hive of activity that came to a crashing halt the minute I walked in. The supervisor, Doug Burroughs, was a trim, pensive man with a keen gaze. He was on the phone, crouched behind several precarious towers of reference books, folders, and assorted clumps of paper. I backed away around the corner and into the foyer while he finished his conversation. He seemed to be exasperatedly trying to explain that he had no insights into who the Sniper might be, and that he would do his best to repair the vandalized signs by the end of the week but could not make any promises. Apparently, I had missed the latest Sniper attack—this time the marmosets were the target.

He stood up to greet me between an ancient file cabinet with several tall stacks of magazines piled atop it and a wall of CDs in jewel cases. I silently prayed that the office be vacant in the event of an earthquake.

"Hello."

"Hi there. I'm Sandy Lohm, and I'm investigating the death of Claude Hopper?"

"Oh yes, we've been expecting you," he said and shook my hand.

223

"You have?"

"Yes. Ingrid Handy said you were working on the case and that we should cooperate as much as we can."

"That's great," I said, wondering if there had been a memo about my investigation.

"This is Rochelle," he indicated a tall, elegant woman behind a drawing table.

"And this is Ray," he gestured at the toothsome young man manipulating a complicated array of bat images on a vast computer monitor. Both nodded at me.

"So what time do you usually arrive here."

"All too late to have seen Claude if he got in before 8 a.m."

"That's OK," I started to reply when a loud crack on the roof caused me to start violently. "What the hell was that?"

All three were suppressing snickers.

"Oh, that was a golf ball," Doug answered. "We get those all the time. They don't always hit the building, but they frequently fly into this side of the Zoo."

"We collect them," Wray (I could now see the silent W on his name tag) offered with a wry smile and indicated the large bowls, jars, buckets, and cans of golf balls tucked into crevices around the room. "When we've accumulated enough, I plan to make an art installation out of them."

"One day when I was walking out of administration one of them ricocheted off the building and beaned me on the head," Rochelle added. "It left a pretty big bruise and I burned myself with the coffee I was carrying. I seriously considered suing the golf course, but I think golfers and their errant balls are covered by the 'Acts of God' clause in the insurance world. And besides, it turns out that the surveillance camera wasn't working that day so I don't think I could have offered any conclusive proof that the golf-ball was the culprit."

Suddenly everything else in the room vanished. "Surveillance camera?"

"Yeah. After a couple animal rights protesters broke in one night they

installed a bunch of them. Many of them are fake—just decoys to scare, uh,
I mean, deter people, but the one at the security gate where you enter the
service road is real and there's another functional one behind the administration building. It's disguised as a rock. But it doesn't always work. I guess
security had them put in, but no one could decide who should maintain
them—security, IT, or AV services, so the actual cameras sort of work at
will."

"Who would I see about getting a hold of those surveillance videos?"

"Gosh, I don't know."

"Probably security," Wray suggested. "At least they're the ones who
had them installed, so even if they don't keep the tapes they should know
who does."

"That would be a good place to start," Doug concurred, and the sharp
crack of a stroke out on the green across the way punctuated the statement.

"Thanks a million," I said feeling a surge of excitement at the prospect
of making progress in the case. I scurried off to the security office.

Officer Pinata greeted me with a wink and a "What can I do you for?"
I ignored the flirtation and explained that I was hoping to find whoever was
the keeper of the video surveillance tapes.

"Oh," he said, flummoxed. "What surveillance tapes?"

"There are video tapes from the surveillance cameras around the Zoo.
Wouldn't those be the responsibility of Security? They are security cameras."

"Oh, those tapes!" he chuckled. "You need to see Bonnie Brook in
accounting about that."

Had he not explained exactly where to go down the hall behind the
reception desk in the front office, I would never have found it. If you didn't
know that the wall of folding doors opened into individual offices, you'd
think they were simply storage units. Apparently, working in a sealed crypt
was the price for being authorized to handle Zoo cash. None of them were
labeled with name placards, but I could see that there were three sections.
As I approached the middle one, I could hear muffled shouting through
the door. I waited for a lull in the bluster, then knocked, which seemed to

trigger skirmishing noises—furniture sliding, a file cabinet door slamming, shuffling footsteps. Then the door wrenched open. A flustered, red-faced man with a comb-over that was more of a comb-forward—like those Napoleonic coifs where the hair is parted down the back and swept upward on the sides—stared at me.

"Yes?" he gasped.

"I'm looking for Bonnie Brook?"

"Well, you found her," he blurted, then lunged down the hall, leaving the door ajar.

The room was sharply bisected into zones of chaos and order. The side of the room near the door was scattered with old Post-Its, random paper clips, staples that had been pulled and allowed to range freely on the floor. Shelves packed with binders and journals covered the walls and a battery of file cabinets were all stuffed to overflowing. The woman on the far side of the office, presumably Bonnie Brooks, was crouched behind an eerily tidy desk that was set up face-to-face with a paper maelstrom that rivaled Doug Burroughs' desk in the graphics office. She had barricaded her territory with a row of ceramic pencil cups that were holding back the clutter. On her side, two piles of manila folders were stacked in columns rising at perfect perpendicular angles to the immaculate, white desk blotter and small bunches of forms, precisely paper clipped together, were aligned with the edge of the desk and staggered at what I'm sure were exact half-inch intervals. A pointy new pencil, a black ballpoint pen, and a red felt tip marker were positioned parallel to the phone, which gleamed with shiny black sterility on the corner opposite the folders. Behind her, on a long shelf was a museum of antiquated audio-visual gear that only a Luddite such as myself could appreciate: a gigantic TV monitor, a couple VCRs (one of which was a beta), a DVD player, a reel-to-reel tape deck, and a large cassette deck. All that was missing was an eight-track tape player. The walls were lined with rows upon rows of VHS tapes, each neatly labeled with meticulous, tiny handwriting. Distracted by the tape library, it took me a moment to realize she was staring expectantly at me.

226

"Hi," I said, offering my hand, which she took in a cool, limp grip. "I'm Sandy Lohm, a private investigator working on the death of Claude Hopper. I understand you're responsible for keeping track of the surveillance tapes from the cameras behind the administration building?"

She regarded me for a moment from behind round wire-frame glasses. She must have been far-sighted because they magnified her irises into enormous glistening gray orbs. Her dishwater blonde hair was pulled back and twisted into a tight bun that made my scalp twinge. She was wearing a stiff white shirt and a snugly tailored navy suit with brass buttons. An open 32-ounce can of Del Monte corn sat in front of her with a long-handled plastic spoon sticking out of it.

"What do you want?" she asked warily.

"I was hoping you'd have the surveillance tapes for the week the victim died–October 6 through 12. I understand there is a concealed camera behind administration in a location that might have recorded any activity that took place that morning."

"I see. And who do you represent?"

"Well, I'm a private investigator. Miles Patagonia asked me to look into the case."

"May I see your identification?"

"Sure," I said trying to keep the tart edge out of my voice as I dove into my handbag to get my driver's license. She inspected it closely, then handed it back.

"This isn't a private investigator's license."

"No. I don't have one currently."

"Then I can't help you."

"But the Zoo director asked me to conduct this investigation."

"Miles Patagonia personally hired you?"

"Well, he called me and gave me the assignment. Actually, he had his assistant have the assistant general operations manager's assistant call me and ask if I would take the case."

"Who's paying you?"

227

"I assumed the Zoo was footing the bill."

"Well, you'd better find out because unless the City hired you, I'm not obligated to provide you with anything and you'll need to get a warrant of some kind."

I was dubious about this assertion, but she seemed adamant and I didn't want to pick a fight.

"OK, well let's just say that Miles Patagonia, as a City of Santa Narcissa employee hired me on behalf of the City."

"I'm not going to help you based on some hypothetical authorization."

"I see," I said, recalling my conversation with Ingrid Handy on that first day. She had told me not to be concerned about my expired license. I took a leap of faith and decided to interpret that as meaning she was taking care of reissuing one for me. "Well, my new investigator's license is being expedited now. Once I have it, how would I access the tapes."

"Well, you'd need to go through proper channels and complete the appropriate paperwork."

"And where would I start with proper channels?"

"You'd need to go to Ingrid Handy."

Naturally, I thought.

"Are you sure I couldn't just look at the relevant tapes here? They wouldn't even need to leave your office."

"No. I'm afraid that won't work," she turned her attention back to the corn on her desk and proceeded to ignore me.

Officially dismissed, I retreated to the hallway, took a deep breath, and headed out to talk to the Hand.

It's not worth recounting the 37-minute verbal excursion I undertook in order to acquire the forms. Suffice it to say that I eventually found myself at the Wilderness Café studying the astonishing array of information and signatures I would have to gather in order to get the tapes. I sighed, uncapped my brand new Bic round stic GRIP pen, and plunged in. If I was lucky, I could complete it before all the administrators whose signatures and/or initials I needed, left for the day.

On Monday, November 18, I found myself back at the Corn Maiden's office armed with a sheaf of painstakingly completed forms. There was no sign of the exasperated office-mate, but the chaos on his side of the room had shifted since my last visit and I had to step over a row of dingy banker's boxes to present my offering. Bonnie Brook scrutinized every page with her owl-like gaze, then tapped them into a precise pile, which she stapled and filed in her desk drawer.

"All right then," she said, folding her hands in front of her on the desk. "The assistant general operations manager's office has assured me that your private investigator license is in order. Come back tomorrow morning and I'll have the tapes for you."

"What?"

"I don't have them here. They're in archive storage downtown."

"But they were just made about a month ago."

"Doesn't matter. I send them downtown every week. I don't have space to store them. The earliest I could have them is tomorrow morning. But you should call first to make sure they're here."

I phoned first thing in the morning on Tuesday and was informed that they wouldn't be ready for me until after 2 p.m., so to stave off the anticipation I headed for Holcomb Gardens and immersed myself in the monsters. Two more grotesques had arrived: a dandy magician with a goatee, an exaggerated top hat, and a menacing rabbit in his hand, and a Victorian nurse with severe hair and a huge hypodermic needle. I had just taken all the packing paper out to the recycling bin when ASAP showed up driving one of the electric carts equipped with a flatbed, from which he retrieved a box containing three potted plants. They were slim stalks about two feet tall with interesting scaly patterns on them and umbrella-like canopies of pinnate leaves above.

"Thandy! Theeth jutht got here. Thome one from the thoo thent them."

"Wow, thanks… " I quickly avoided addressing him by name, "… so much. Hey, how's that tongue piercing?"

"Itth thtill a little thwollen, but the doctor theth itth not infected tho it thould be leth tender in another week or tho. Thanks for athking," he smiled.

"Great. You can just put that down here," I said, indicating the nearby potting table. "Was there any paperwork with it?"

He handed me a delivery slip that he had signed. Apparently his actual name was M.F.K. Hunter—which left me wondering if his friends called him by any one of the names that the initials stood for, or if they just referred to him as M. The shipment had indeed come from the Santa Narcissa Zoo, but no particular individual was designated as the sender.

"OK. Thee you later," and off he loped back to the cart. I tucked the receipt into my pocket and looked into the box. Each of the three pots had a plant tag that read "Devil's Tongue (*Amorphophallus konjac*)." A note tucked into the box read in a spidery hand: *From Asia (Vietnam, China), max. height aprox. 4 feet, cold hardy, well draining soil. Interesting culinary, medicinal uses.*

Grinning and giddy, I moved them into the greenhouse and found a space for them, then hurried to my office to see what I could find out about the devil's tongue online. As I suspected, this *Amorphophallus* species is indeed a petite relative of the titan arum lily, which can grow up to ten feet in height. *A. konjac* tops out at about six feet. Its evocatively mottled main stem has earned it some interesting common names—snake palm, leopard arum, dragon plant. To others its massive edible corm (which can grow to the size of a large grapefruit) is its most impressive feature and it is also known as elephant yam. But "devil's tongue" and "voodoo lily" interested me most, and that moniker was inspired by its suggestive inflorescence, which resembles a really large, blood red peace lily. The maroon spathe or bract at the base of the bloom unfurls and out of it rises a fleshy three-foot spike that does not look entirely unlike the exaggeratedly lascivious tongues I had seen lashing out of the mouths of medieval demons in art history lectures. Like its titanic cousin, the devil's tongue it is pollinated by flies and emits a foul scent designed to lure insects in search of carrion where they can deposit their eggs.

Hours flew by and suddenly it was 2:15, and this time when I phoned

Bonnie Brooks, she had the tapes.

When I returned to her office she brusquely handed me a banker's box nearly full of battered VHS cases.

"Thanks," I said, taking the box from her. "This is a lot of tapes."

"They are from all the cameras for the time period in question."

"I see. Couldn't you just give me the tapes from the rock camera for the time period in question?"

"No."

I waited long enough to be sure that no further explanation was forthcoming, then asked if there was an index or key. She regarded me for a moment with the faintest wisp of triumph. "No, I'm sorry there isn't."

"But... " I began, but she had turned her attention to her lunch bag, from which she produced a can opener and a 32-ounce can of Del Monte corn.

"You can have them for 48 hours."

When I got home, Trudy and Bess had just finished unloading some groceries from their ancient Honda Civic. They waved and I nodded over the banker's box of video tapes that I had retrieved from my trunk.

"Hey there," Trudy locked the hatchback and came over to me. "Do you need a hand?"

"Nah," I said and lowered the box so that it was hip level and easier to hang onto.

"Whatcha got there?" Bess asked.

"About a hundred surveillance videos."

"Oh?" Trudy said, dying to hear more.

"Want some coffee?" Bess asked.

"Actually, I don't mind if I do."

"Come on in," Trudy held the front door open for me.

Bess and Trudy were also renters. Our mutual landlady had retired to the desert hinterlands of New Mexico many years before I moved in, and she was very happy that we all treated the property as if it were ours. When I offered to help replant the yard she gave us all her blessing. Ironically, my garden area is fairly small. I keep potted dwarf citrus trees and my personal collection of rare and eccentric succulents scattered around the south- and east-facing sides of the guest house. The main yard in front of the big house had been a miasma of ivy and heavenly bamboo. I cleared it and put in a dry garden full of Mediterranean herbs and flowering California natives to match Bess and Trudy's interior, which was part Italian villa, part Southwest mission, and all exquisitely tasteful.

The house was like an expanded version of mine, with the same details and, since we had similar taste in decor, general ambiance—though since, between the two of them, they probably brought in close to three times my modest income, the furnishings were considerably nicer than what was within my means. Their hardwood floors were covered with actual antique kilim rugs, and they had the space to accommodate dark, solid-wood barrister bookcases and a sumptuous leather couch that I sank into while Bess and Trudy puttered in the kitchen. Where my fireplace was faux, theirs was real with a deep hearth. They rarely used it, and it was generally filled with a couple big vases of flowers, usually freshly cut from whatever was in bloom outside. Television isn't a big part of their lives, so they keep theirs stashed in the guest bedroom, across from a daybed and a comfy chair. Filling the living room space where most people would park the TV is a 30-gallon fish tank occupied by a huge orange-and-black oscar fish. Bess is very much a dog person, but Trudy is allergic, so their compromise was Lurch.

Oscars are sometimes called "water dogs" or "river dogs" because they are so charismatic in their interactions with humans. Lurch can clearly distinguish between individual people, and hides from strangers. He lunges at Trudy and swims in excited circles and quivers when Bess approaches. After years of visits, Lurch seemed to be of two minds about me. When I leaned over the arm of the couch and peered into his watery domain full of chunky lava rocks that mimic a reef complete with a wrecked Spanish galleon, he lunged, "paced" a few times, paused to eye me, and then ducked behind a treasure chest overflowing with gold and jewels.

Bess returned with a thermal carafe plus three mugs and Trudy in tow with a tray of shortbread cookies.

"So what do you have so far?"

"Well, I've got a scorning lover, a resentful keeper, an estranged son, and a fetishy City councilman with or without his former-actor/animal rights activist paramour."

"Wow. That's a fantastic cast of characters!"

"Yeah," I said dubiously.

"What's wrong?"

"Well, none of them is entirely convincing as the killer."

"Tell me." Trudy leaned back in the chair and got comfortable.

I took a deep breath. "Where to start..."

"How about the scorned lover?" Bess eagerly suggested.

"Scorning, not scorned. It was she who did the scorning. She was in the same docent class as the deceased. I guess they were one of those hopeless star-crossed couples. He was quite the ladykiller, and by all accounts very full of himself. That kind of thing has its appeal. He had been quite an adventurer in the days of his youth and eventually served as a research scientist at Imperator Pharmaceuticals. He was on the team that invented Povenda, though as he told it, Povenda was his baby."

Both Bess and Trudy murmured their familiarity with the ubiquitous diet drug.

"She is something of a drama queen, and seemed to me to be capable of being quite manipulative. And jealous. So I thought maybe a lovers' tiff could have ignited some kind of crime of passion. They had a very tumultuous relationship, according to the volunteer director."

"Is Corinne still there?" Trudy interjected with smile.

"Yes. She's the director."

"She was a good egg."

I had forgotten that back in the day Corinne sometimes stopped by Trudy's New Year's Eve shindigs.

"Yeah. It was nice getting back in touch with her. And she had lots of helpful info about our main players."

"OK so get on with the scorning lover," Bess said impatiently.

"Right. So I guess it was very volatile and there were instances of public displays of animosity—heavy objects and sharp words hurled about. But when I interviewed her, she said their last fight had been because he wanted to marry her and she turned him down."

"They fought about that?" Bess said, incredulous.

"Yeah, and her rationale was so earnest and, I guess, quirky that I can't see her killing him. She's very much a tragic heroine, and she didn't want to marry him for fear of killing the tenuousness of their love."

"That's messed up."

"Hmmm. I don't know. It makes sense to me," I said, suddenly seeing my own scenario in a new light. I realized my thoughtful pause was running overtime when Bess tapped my knee.

"Sandy?"

"Oh. Sorry. Gathering a little wool."

"Huh?"

"Anyhow. She's also older and I can't imagine her lifting and dumping the body, even if she could have killed him."

"What if she hired someone?"

"That occurred to me. My gut tells me no."

"Hmmm," they responded.

"OK, so I want to hear about the fetishy City councilman," Trudy leaned forward. "Anyone I know?"

I smiled. "Yes, but I'm not telling who. You can make an educated guess after I'm done. So the estranged son (more on him later) approached me with some photographs that dear old dad took."

"If he was estranged, then how did he get the photos?"

"Apparently they reconnected after they both wound up volunteering at the Zoo. Claude had freelanced for the local papers and also celebrity gossip mags, so some of his work was public—nothing you couldn't find on the Internet somewhere, but some of the photos were clandestine shots of this particular councilman and a rather high profile animal rights activist in compromising positions."

"Oh?" in unison with synchronized eyebrow lifts.

"So this is the most recent line of inquiry. Even with security as reduced as it has been from the budget cuts and hiring freeze, I have a hard time imagining either of them getting into the Zoo before it opens and personally killing the docent. The activist (and I know you both have a pretty good idea who it is) would be a sore thumb, and the councilman has not been a friend of the Zoo in the past, so it would be almost as irregular to see him show up at the crack of dawn."

"Ah, but they probably have some helpful connections."

"That's more likely. But hiring a hitman to kill someone for you adds all kinds of complications to the mix. And I definitely believe that if it walks like a duck, and it quacks like a duck, then it's probably a duck."

"So how are ducks involved?" Bess asked.

I was starting to feel like an old timer, using all sorts of aphorisms that perplexed Bess and other young folk. Trudy came to my rescue.

"She means, sometimes the simplest solution is the correct solution." Bess nodded, but didn't seem convinced.

"Did you interview the activist and the councilman?" Trudy continued.

"Yes and no. It turns out that the activist received a copy of one of the photos that the estranged son gave me."

"Well that sounds like a good motive."

"Yes, only there was no money demand, just a note saying 'I know about you.' Also, the photo had been postmarked after the docent was dead. So that leaves me with the estranged son—with the emphasis on 'strange.'"

They both laughed and Trudy took advantage of the break to pour us all coffee refills. She asked if I thought Claude, Jr. sent the photo to the activist.

"I suppose. If he did, he did it after his father was dead, so that doesn't help make a case for the activist killing Claude. Even if he wanted to, Claude was already dead. He didn't really seem to care about the photo much. I think it would be more of a threat to the councilman than the activist, but the councilman didn't receive the photo."

"Have you interviewed the councilman?"

"No. I put in a call to his office, but it will take some persistence."

"And there's no chance that the estranged son did in the dad? It's not like that has never happened before."

"Yeah. Junior seems quite different from dad. I guess the parents split when he was just a toddler, and it wasn't particularly bad. Fatherhood disagreed with Senior, and since mom never talked about him, Junior was surprised to discover they had the same name and were both Zoo volunteers."

"That's a wacky coincidence."

"I'll say. But they seemed to get on well enough. Perhaps Senior had softened with age. After three marriages, and then a long run as a committed bachelor, he suddenly proposes to the drama queen?"

"So Junior's not really a suspect?"

"He lives pretty far from the Zoo and only comes in a couple days a week because of the travel time. Also, I think he must be legally blind without his glasses, and he isn't the most strapping specimen of manhood I've ever seen, so, as with the scorning lover, I have a hard time seeing him having the means to do it himself, and he works as a librarian so I can't imagine he has the resources to hire a hit man."

"Yeah, but you don't know. Maybe the mom struck it rich, or he's hoarding millions in the bank."

"Good point. But this is just where I'm at now, and where I think it might go. My gut tells me no on Junior. Though I could be wrong."

"So he's vengeful not toward dad, but toward the councilman and the activist because he thinks they did him in."

I smiled and touched my nose with my index finger. "On the nose."

"That leaves you with..." Trudy's brow furrowed.

"The resentful keeper."

"Why is he resentful?"

"Ah. That's why he's the prime suspect. He had motive, means, and opportunity—or at least more convincing motive, means, and opportunity than the others."

"Lay it on us." Trudy and Bess settled back together in the love seat and waited.

"OK. The keeper's father worked with the dead docent at Imperator. There was some problem during the clinical trials phase of Povenda. The docent was tampering with data to make it seem like the problem had been fixed, which the company knew about, but did not want the FDA to know. So when they got wind of an impending audit, they hired the keeper's father to spy on Claude and confirm the tampering, then once it was confirmed, they had the lab torched and threatened to pin it on the keeper's dad if he didn't keep quiet. So he was exiled. First to some obscure project at Imperator, shortly after which he was laid off. On top of this, the mom had passed away while the keeper was an undergrad, and they were still grappling with medical bills. As a result, the keeper had to leave veterinary school because he couldn't manage the cost on his own and dad could no longer help. Then the dad decided to move to California, and the keeper went with him. So they both wound up in Santa Narcissa, and he ended up at the Zoo."

"That's a hell of a coincidence."

"Yeah. But you know, I've seen weirder ones. So the docent winds up doing food prep for the resentful keeper, who eventually learns who Claude is, or was."

"Did Claude know who the keeper is?"

"He must have. The scorning girlfriend knew who the keeper's father is, so Claude must have known. But I think that just added to already clashing personalities."

"And the keeper had no idea who the docent was?"

"No. The events at the drug company took place years ago, and the dad may have mentioned the docent by name, but the keeper was never really privy to the exact details of what went on with his dad's work. All he knew was that there was a bad fire and the police questioned his dad, and then, due to some office politics, his dad was demoted and laid off."

"So he planned the murder and executed it by himself?"

"I don't know. I don't think it was premeditated. This seems to me more of an impulse. But he could have done it. He has the physical strength to have clubbed Claude, moved the body, and tossed it into a green waste bin. He was off on the day that it most likely happened, but he was in the Zoo to pick up forms in administration. So he was on grounds, if only for a short time."

"But for enough time?"

"I think so."

"So you have to track down Junior again and the councilman."

I nodded.

"You know, I miss these case studies."

"Yeah," I replied, "I guess I do, too."

Back at my house, I settled into my couch and opened the box, which didn't really contain a hundred tapes—there were only 26 video cassettes in plain white cardboard cases packed inside. Henry immediately rubbed his face on all four corners and then compressed himself into the shoebox-sized space left by the incomplete top row of tapes. I realized that the chicken scratch handwriting on the labels might as well have been actual chicken scratch. The runic letters appeared to be in some alphabet other than Roman italic. I phoned Bonnie Brook, who proved every bit as helpful as I anticipated, which is to say not the slightest. So, I fired up the television and the VCR, lured Henry out of his new nook with cat treats, pulled out all the tapes, stacked them on my coffee table, and started at random. Fortunately, they were all date and time stamped in familiar Arabic numerals so I could fast-forward and get through about four six-hour tapes in an hour. Most were the wrong location, but I scanned them while I fast-forwarded anyhow in case the tapes had been rerecorded and some useful bits remained. The relevant tape was in the middle of the pile. At the end of it, I finally saw what had transpired that morning, and the wide-angle perspective provided a full view of the whole bizarre sequence of events. After a fit of laughter, I fetched a beer and phoned Corinne. It was kind of late, but I knew she would want to know what I had discovered.

"So I'm done with the case."

"Already?"

"Yeah. I'm about to start writing up the report."

"And?"

"Brace yourself."

There was a pause. "For what?"

"A whole lot of paperwork."

"What happened?"

"Well, basically, Claude Hopper was a victim of red tape."

"What?"

"There's a surveillance video tape recording of what happened," I said with a heavy sigh.

"Come on."

"It's a very Rube Goldberg scenario that involves a bad golfer, an illegally parked truck, an equipment malfunction, a misplaced green waste bin, and really bad timing."

"This requires beer."

"I couldn't agree more."

At the Sasquatch Lair, I explained it all to Corinne. It's odd how a story solidifies in the telling. Each facet of Claude's history, under the scrutiny of my investigation, had resolved into other stories where they connected to the people around him. And yet, all the information I had gathered, all the dramas I had tapped into, were ultimately irrelevant. The actual story of Claude's death was a case of simple, stupid, happenstance: being in the wrong place at a precise moment. When I had finished the astonishingly short and bittersweet explanation of Claude's death as I had summarized it in my report, we sat and stared at each other for a while. During the lull, the waiter brought our drinks.

"That's it?" Corinne asked.

"That's it," I answered.

"You couldn't make that up," she said, extinguishing the marshmallows in her Happy Camper, then raising her mug.

"To Claude."

I clinked my glass to hers.

"To Claude."

24
The Deceased

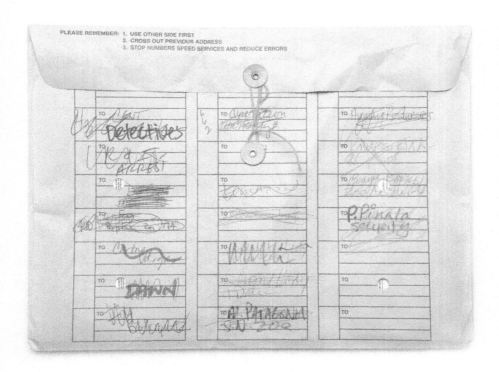

State of California	Please complete in triplicate (type if possible) Mail two copies to:		OSHA CASE NO.
EMPLOYER'S REPORT OF OCCUPATIONAL INJURY OR ILLNESS			
			FATALITY ☒

Any person who makes or causes to be made any knowingly false or fraudulent material statement or material representation for the purpose of obtaining or denying workers compensation benefits or payments is guilty of a felony.

California law requires employers to report within five days of knowledge every occupational injury or illness which results in lost time beyond the date of the incident OR requires medical treatment beyond first aid. If an employee subsequently dies as a result of a previously reported injury or illness, the employer must file within five days of knowledge an amended report indicating death. In addition, every serious injury, illness, or death must be reported immediately by telephone or telegraph to the nearest office of the California Division of Occupational Safety and Health.

1. FIRM NAME SANTA NARCISSA ZOO	1a. Policy Number A44-704	Please do not use this column
2. MAILING ADDRESS (Number, Street, City, Zip) 7924 ZOO PARKWAY, SANTA NARCISSA CA 90009	2a. Phone Number 500-5550530	CASE NUMBER
3. LOCATION if different from Mailing Address (Number, Street, City and Zip) SAME	3a. Location Code	OWNERSHIP
3. NATURE OF BUSINESS; e.g. Painting contractor, wholesale grocer, sawmill, hotel, etc. ZOO	5. State unemployment Insurance acct.no	INDUSTRY?
6. TYPE OF EMPLOYER: Private ☐ State ☐ County ☐ City ☒ School District ☐ Other Govt. Specify		OCCUPATION
7. DATE OF INJURY/ONSET OF ILLNESS 10/11/02	8. TIME INJURY/ILLNESS OCCURRED 7:35 am	9. TIME EMPLOYEE BEGAN WORK 7:35 am	10. IF EMPLOYEE DIED, DATE OF DEATH (mm/dd/yy) 10/11/02	
11. UNABLE TO WORK FOR AT LEAST ONE FULL DAY AFTER DATE OF INJURY? Yes ☐ No ☐	12. DATE LAST WORKED (mm/dd/yy) 10/11/02	13. DATE RETURNED TO WORK (mm/dd/yy) N/A	14. IF STILL OFF WORK, CHECK THIS BOX. ☒	SEX
15. HAD FULL DAYS WAGES PAID FOR DATE OF INJURY OR LAST DAY WORKED? Yes ☐ No ☐	16. SALARY BEING CONTINUED? Yes ☐ No ☐	17. DATE OF EMPLOYER'S KNOWLEDGE/NOTICE OF INJURY/ILLNESS (mm/dd/yy) 10/15/02	18. DATE EMPLOYEE WAS PROVIDED CLAIM FORM (mm/dd/yy) N/A	AGE
19. SPECIFIC INJURY/ILLNESS AND PART OF BODY AFFECTED. MEDICAL DIAGNOSIS if available. e.g. Second degree burns on right arm, tendonitis on left elbow, lead poisoning HEAD: CONCUSSION, HEART: HEART FAILURE		DAILY HOURS
20. LOCATION WHERE EVENT OR EXPOSURE OCCURRED (Number, Street, City, Zip) 7924 ZOO PARKWAY SANTA NARCISSA CA 90009	20a. COUNTY KORNE	21. ON EMPLOYER'S PREMISES? Yes ☐ No ☐	
22. DEPARTMENT WHERE EVENT OR EXPOSURE OCCURRED, e.g. Shipping department, machine shop DEPARTMENT OF THE ZOO	23. Other Workers Injured or ill in this event/exposure? Yes ☐ No ☐	GAYS PER WEEK
24. EQUIPMENT, MATERIALS AND CHEMICALS THE EMPLOYEE WAS USING WHEN EVENT OR EXPOSURE OCCURRED; e.g. Acetylene, welding torch, farm tractor, scaffold N/A		WEEKLY HOURS
25. SPECIFIC ACTIVITY THE EMPLOYEE WAS PERFORMING WHEN EVENT OR EXPOSURE OCCURRED, e.g. Welding seams of metal forms, loading boxes onto truck. WALKING		WEEKLY WAGE
26. HOW INJURY/ILLNESS OCCURRED. DESCRIBE SEQUENCE OF EVENTS. SPECIFY OBJECT OR EXPOSURE WHICH DIRECTLY PRODUCED THE INJURY/ILLNESS, e.g. Worker stepped back to inspect work and slipped on scrap material. As he fell, he brushed against sharp edge and burned right hand. USE SEPARATE SHEET IF NECESSARY. VOLUNTEER SUFFERED HEART FAILURE WHILE WALKING AND STUMBLED INTO VERSALIFT TRUCK, ARM OF WHICH FAILED → BLUNT TRAUMA		COUNTY
RESULTING CONCUSSION WAS FATAL PLUS		NATURE OF INJURY
HEART FAILURE.		PART OF BODY

ATTENTION: This form contains information relating to employee health and must be used in a manner that protects the confidentiality of employees to the extent possible while the information is being used for occupational safety and health purposes. See CCR Title 8 14300.29 (b)(6)-(10) & 14300.35(b)(2)(E)2. Note: Shaded boxes indicate confidential employee information as listed in CCR Title 8 14300.35(b)(2)(E)2*.

	SOURCE
	EVENT
	SECONDARY SOURCE
35. OCCUPATION (Regular job title, NO initials, abbreviations or numbers) DOCENT/VOLUNTEER	
37. EMPLOYEE USUALLY WORKS 4 hours per day. 2 days per week. 8 total weekly hours	37a. EMPLOYMENT STATUS regular, full time ☐ part-time ☐ temporary N/A seasonal ☐	37b. UNDER WHAT CLASS CODE OF YOUR POLICY WERE WAGES ASSIGNED N/A	EXTENT OF INJURY
38. GROSS WAGES/SALARY N/A $ ___ per ___	39. OTHER PAYMENTS NOT REPORTED AS WAGES/SALARY (e.g. tips, meals, overtime, bonuses, etc.)? Yes ☐ No ☐	
Completed By (type or print) CORINNE FLAHERTY	Signature & Title Corinne Flaherty	Date (mm/dd/yy) 11/20/02

Confidential information may be disclosed only to the employee, former employee, or their personal representatives (CCR Title 8 14300.35), to others for the purposes of processing a workers' compensation or other insurance claim; and under certain circumstances to a public health or law enforcement agency or to a consultant hired by the employer (CCR Title 8 14300.35). CCR Title 8 14300.40 requires provision upon request to certain state and federal workplace safety agencies.

FORM 5020 (Rev.7)   FILING OF THIS FORM IS NOT AN ADMISSION OF LIABILITY

Workers' Compensation Claim Form (ADR DWC1) & Notice of Potential Eligibility

If you are injured or become ill, either physically or mentally, because of your job, including injuries resulting from a workplace crime, you may be entitled to workers' compensation benefits. Attached is the form for filing a workers' compensation claim with your employer. You should read all of the information contained herein. **You should also keep this sheet for your records as well as all other papers related to your workers' compensation claim.** You may be eligible for some or all of the benefits listed depending on the nature of your claim. To file a claim, complete the "Employee" section of the form, keep one copy and give the original to your employer. Your employer will then complete the "Employer" section, give you a dated copy, keep one copy and send one to the Claims Analyst. Benefits can't start

until the Claims Analyst knows of the injury, so complete the claim form as soon as possible.

A private firm, Marx Bros. Business Solutions, Inc., will oversee the ADR Program. Marx Bros. has Ombudspersons and Nurse Advocates who have expertise and experience resolving legal and medical issues involved with workers' compensation injuries. The Ombudsperson is available to answer your questions, so do not hesitate to call. In addition, a Claims Analyst will contact you several times while your claim is open. It is the Claims Analyst's job to oversee the processing of your benefits. If you have questions regarding those benefits you may call the Claims Analyst or the Ombudsperson. Your Employer, the Claims Analyst, and/or the Ombudsperson will provide you with an informational brochure describing the ADR Program and the potential benefits. **Your claim is subject to the exclusive jurisdiction of the ADR Program created by ACW Local 127 and the City of Santa Narcissa. The cash payments to which you are entitled are no less than the cash payments you would be entitled to in the State system. IF YOU HAVE ANY QUESTIONS OR DISPUTES REGARDING YOUR CLAIM, CONTACT THE OMBUDSPERSON AT 1-877-555-7770 or your Claims Analyst.**

Medical Care: Your claims administrator will pay all reasonable and necessary medical care for your work injury or illness. Medical benefits may include treatment by a doctor, hospital services, physical therapy, lab tests, x-rays, and medicines. Your claims administrator will pay the costs directly so you should never see a bill. For injuries occurring on or after 1/1/00, there is a limit on some medical services.

The Primary Treating Physician (PTP) is the doctor with the overall responsibility for treatment of your injury or illness. Generally your employer selects the PTP you will see for the first 30 days, however, in specified conditions, you may be treated by your pre-designated doctor. If a doctor says you still need treatment after 30 days, you may be able to switch to the doctor of your choice. Special rules apply if your employer offers a Health Care Organization (HCO) or after 1/1/01, has a medical provider network. Contact your employer for more information. If your employer has not put up a poster describing your rights to workers' compensation, you may choose your own doctor immediately. Within one working day after an employee files a claim form, the employer shall authorize the provision of all treatment, consistent with the applicable treating guidelines, for the alleged injury and shall continue to provide treatment until the date that liability for the claim is accepted or rejected. Until the date the claim is accepted or rejected, liability for medical treatment shall be limited to ten thousand dollars ($10,000).

Disclosure of Medical Records: After you make a claim for workers' compensation benefits, your medical records will not have the same privacy that you usually expect. If you don't agree to voluntarily release medical records, a workers' compensation judge may decide what records will be released. If you request privacy, the judge may "seal" (keep private) certain medical records.

Payment for Temporary Disability (Lost Wages): If you can't work while you are recovering from a job injury or illness, you will receive temporary disability payments. These payments may change or stop when your doctor says you are able to return to work. These benefits are tax-free. Temporary disability payments are two-thirds of your average weekly pay, within minimums and maximums set by state law. Payments are not made for the first three days you are off the job unless you are hospitalized overnight or cannot work for more than 14 days.

Return to Work: To help you to return to work as soon as possible, you should actively communicate with your treating doctor, claims administrator and employer about the kinds of work you can do while recovering. They may coordinate efforts to return you to modified duty or other work that is medically appropriate. This modified or other duty may be temporary or may be extended depending on the nature of your injury or illness.

Payment for Permanent Disability: If a doctor says your injury or illness results in a permanent disability, you may receive additional payments. The amount will depend on the type of injury, your age, occupation, and date of injury.

Vocational Rehabilitation (VR): If a doctor says your injury or illness prevents you from returning to the same type of job and your employer doesn't offer modified or alternative work, you may qualify for VR. If you qualify, your claims administrator will pay the costs, up to a maximum set by state law. VR is a benefit for injuries that occurred prior to 1995.

Supplemental Job Displacement Benefit (SJDB): If you do not return to work within 60 days after your temporary disability ends, and your employer does not offer modified or alternative work, you may qualify for a nontransferable voucher payable to a school for retraining and/or skill enhancement. If you qualify, the claims administrator will pay the costs up to the maximum set by state law based on your percentage of permanent disability. SJDB is a benefit for injuries occurring on or after 1/1/90.

Death Benefits: If the injury or illness causes death, payments may be made to relatives or household members who were financially dependent on the deceased worker.

Discrimination: It is illegal for your employer to punish or fire you for having a job injury or illness, for filing a claim, or testifying in another person's workers' compensation case (Labor Code 132a). If proven, you may receive lost wages, job reinstatement, increased benefits, and costs and expenses up to limits set by the state. Even though your claim for injury must be pursued in the ADR program, you may not pursue disputes involving discrimination in the ADR Program. These disputes must be pursued in the State Department of Workers' Compensation

ADR Carve-Out Program: An ADR Carve-Out which is created through a collective bargaining agreement is an alternative to the dispute resolution procedures in the state workers' compensation system. The ADR program is implemented to improve the speed and quality of medical benefits, improve claim resolution time, reduce workers' compensation claim costs, and increase injured workers' satisfaction. Any dispute or problem must first be submitted to the Ombudsperson who will try to resolve it for you. If the Ombudsperson is unsuccessful, you will be advised of your right to mediation and the Ombudsperson will provide you the appropriate form to request mediation. If mediation is unsuccessful, the Ombudsperson will advise you of your right to Arbitration and provide you with the appropriate form to request Arbitration.

State of California

Department of Industrial Relations

DIVISION OF WORKERS' COMPENSATION

Employee—complete this section and see note above.

1. Name. CLAUDE HOPPER _____ Today's Date. 11/20/2002

2. Home Address. 425 MAPLE STREET

3. City. SANTA NARCISSA _____ State. CA _____ Zip. 90909

4. Date of Injury. 10/11/2007 _____ Time of Injury. 7:35 a.m. _____ p.m.

5. Address and description of where injury happened. ZOO
SANTA NARCISSA ZOO
2924 ZOO PARK WAY, SANTA NARCISSA, CA 90909

6. Describe injury and part of body affected. CONCUSSION - HEAD, SUDDEN CARDIAC ARREST - HEART

7. Social Security Number. *078-05-1120*

8. Signature of employee. *N/A*

Employer—complete this section and see note below.

9. Name of employer. **City of Santa Narcissa**

10. Address. **700 East Temple Street, Room 210, Santa Narcissa, California 90000**

11. Date employer first knew of injury. *10/15/2002*

12. Date claim form was provided to employee. *N/A*

13. Date employer received claim form. *N/A*

14. Name and address of insurance carrier or adjusting agency. *RELIANT INSURANCE*
City of Santa Narcissa, 700 East Temple Street, Room 210, Santa Narcissa, California 90909

15. Insurance Policy Number. *8675309*   Self-Insured

16. Signature of employer representative. *Elisia Hurley*

17. Title. *EXECUTIVE ADMINISTRATIVE ASSISTANT*

18. Telephone. *101-555-5505*

Employer: You are required to date this form and provide copies to your insurer or claims administrator and to the employee, dependent or representative who led the claim within one working day of receipt of the form from the employee.

SIGNING THIS FORM IS NOT AN ADMISSION OF LIABILITY WORKERS CLAIM FORM (ADR DWC1)

If you are injured or become ill, either physically or mentally, because of your job, including injuries resulting from a workplace crime, you maybe entitled to workers' compensation benefits. Employee: Complete the "Employee" section and give the form to your employer. Keep a copy and mark it "Employee's Temporary Receipt" until you receive the signed and dated copy from your employer. You may call your Ombudsperson at 1-877-555-7770 if you need help in filling out this claim form. An explanation of workers' compensation benefits and a brief description of the ADR program are included in the 2-page cover sheet of this form. Your Employer, the Claims Analyst, and/or the Ombudsperson will provide you with an informational brochure describing the ADR Program and the potential benefits.

PLEASE FAX A COPY OF THIS FORM TO THE OMBUDSPERSON: FAX # (877) -555-8436

245

REPORTING WORKERS' COMP INJURIES
SUPERVISOR'S INSTRUCTIONS

FOR INJURIES **NOT** REQUIRING MEDICAL ATTENTION:
(Or when the injured staff does not *request* medical attention)

1. Make sure area where injury occurred is safe.
2. Make sure simple first aid is administered as needed.
3. Immediately complete the "SN Zoo **Report of Injury with No Medical**" form. The original must be turned in. Copies can be made for the employee or the supervisor.
4. Complete the "**Supervisor Investigation Checklist for Employee Injury/Accidents**".
5. Submit the original of both forms TOGETHER to the Zoo Safety Office within two (2) days of the injury.

FOR INJURIES REQUIRING MEDICAL ATTENTION:
(Or when the injured staff receives any medical attention)

1. Make sure area where injury occurred is safe.
2. Make sure the injured staff member receives the required medical attention. Contact Security to call 911, if needed. If no paramedic/ambulance is required, it is the supervisor's responsibility to transport the injured employee to a medical facility.
3. **Call the Safety Office (ext 55279) and report the injury.** Leave a message, if needed, with full information. (Who, where, when, what, current status, etc.) An email is acceptable.
4. Complete the "**Workers Compensation Claim Form**" (Form ADR DWC1). The original must be turned in. Copies can be made for the employee or the supervisor. The employee completes the top portion; the supervisor completes AND SIGNS the bottom portion.
5. Complete the "**Employer's Report of Occupational Injury or Illness**" (Form 5020). A draft copy must be turned in to your divisional office within 2 days of injury. Your division office will contact Workers' Comp for a claim number, type the form and return it to you for signature. The **supervisor** completes this form. The original must be turned back in.
6. Complete the "**Supervisor Investigation Checklist for Employee Injury/Accidents**".
7. Submit the originals of the above three forms TOGETHER to your division office within 2 days of injury.
8. Once you know the medical status of your employee (off work, full duty, light duty), notify the Safety Office.

FOR INJURIES REQUIRING IOD TIME (Missed shifts):

1. The Safety Office must be notified by phone **IMMEDIATELY** upon knowledge of the employing missing a shift due to an on-duty injury. If it's a weekend, leave a complete message. (Ext 55279)
2. When the employee's status changes to Light Duty or Full Duty, notify the Safety Office by phone immediately.

SANTA NARCISSA ZOO
WORKERS' COMPENSATION
FORM CHECKLIST & ROUTING

NAME: *CLAUDE HOPPER*   CASE#: *206481 BSO*

DOI: *10/11/2002*   TYPE: *FATALITY*

....

EMPLOYEE RECEIVED NO MEDICAL ATTENTION:

☑ SN Zoo Report of Injury with No Medical

1. Complete with as much information as possible
2. Complete within one working day of knowledge of the injury from the employee.
3. Supervisor may keep a copy of the form
4. Submit the original to the Zoo Safety Office

☑ SN Zoo Supervisor Investigation Checklist for Employee Injuries/Accidents

1. Complete with as much information as possible, including the medical section
2. Submit the original to the Zoo Safety Office

Submit both forms *together*
to the Zoo Safety Office.

EMPLOYEE RECEIVED OUTSIDE MEDICAL ATTENTION:

❏ Call or email the Zoo Safety Office and report the injury (ext 44279)

❏ Form ADR DWC-1:
"Workers' Compensation Claim Form"

1. Form must be provided to employee within one working day of supervisor's knowledge of injury.
2. Supervisor must provide the employee a *signed and dated* copy within one working day of the receipt of this form from the employee.
3. Supervisor may keep a copy of the form
4. Submit the original to your division clerk *

❏ Form 5020:
"Employer's Report of Occupational Injury"

1. Complete a draft copy immediately upon knowledge that the employee sought medical attention.
2. Submit the draft to your division clerk. *
3. The division clerk will type the form, retrieve a claim number from Workers' Comp, and return it to you
4. Sign the form and return to your division clerk *

❏ SN Zoo Supervisor Investigation Checklist for Employee Injuries/Accidents

1. Complete with as much information as possible
2. Submit the original to your division clerk *

* Submit all forms **TOGETHER** to your division Clerk

❏ SN Zoo Injured Employee Change of Status

1. Submit first one to your division clerk with rest of package
   Complete form every time an employee's status changes (i.e. IOD to Light Duty, Light Duty to Full Duty, etc.)
2. Submit subsequent status changes directly to Safety Office

C. My Documents Vail Edition Work Comp Forms forms checklist.doc

Report of On-Duty Injury with No Medical

If you are injured or become ill because of your job, you are entitled to medical care with Workers' Compensation benefits from the city of Santa Narcissa. Completing this form notifies your supervisor of your injury and indicates that you are NOT requesting medical attention at this time.

You may choose to seek professional medical attention for this injury at a future date. If so, please contact your supervisor before doing so.

DATE OF INJURY: 10/11/2002

INJURED EMPLOYEE'S NAME: CLAUDE HOPPER

JOB TITLE: DOCENT   DIVISION: VOLUNTEER

SUPERVISOR: CORINNE FLAHERTY   EXT: X 55007

TYPE OF INJURY: Sprain (joint)   Strain (muscle)   Laceration (cut)
        Contusion (bruise)   Bite   Illness   Other: CONCUSSION HEART ATTACK

BODY PART(S) AFFECTED (ie: right ankle): HEAD, HEART

LOCATION INJURY OCCURRED (ie: camel barn): SERVICE ROAD

WHAT HAPPENED: HEART ATTACK PLUS CONCUSSION FROM COLLAPSED VERSALIFT TRUCK ARM.

WITNESSES: NONE (SURVEILLANCE CAMERA)

WAS ON-SITE FIRST AID GIVEN: None Required   Yes, by whom: N/A

I understand Workers' Compensation benefits are available to me and I choose not to seek medical attention (other than on-site first aid) for this injury at this time.

Injured Employee's Signature: N/A   Date: N/A

Supervisor's Signature: Corinne Flaherty   Date: 11/20/02

Supervisor: Return original to the Zoo Safety Office within 24 hours of the report of the injury.

SANTA NARCISSA ZOO SUPERVISOR INVESTIGATION

CHECKLIST FOR EMPLOYEE INJURIES/ACCIDENTS

EMPLOYEE NAME: _CLAUDE HOPPER_ DATE OF INJURY: _10/11/2002_

EMPLOYEE HAS BEEN GIVEN WORK COMP FORMS:

___DWC1 _X_ 5020

SAFETY OFFICER CONTACTED ON: _10/15/2002_

WHERE DID INJURY OCCUR:

SERVICE ROAD BEHIND ADMINISTRATION

TYPE OF INJURY (i.e. sprained ankle):

FATALITY

WHAT HAPPENED:

HEART ATTACK CAUSED SUBJECT TO STUMBLE INTO
VERSALIFT TRUCK WITH FAULTY ARM, WHICH
COLLAPSED CAUSING CONCUSSION

WITNESSES: _SURVELLANCE CAMERA_

PLEASE CHECK THE FOLLOWING :

FOR MUSCLE PULLS/STRAINS:

_____ Approx weight of item being lifted: _____

_____ Weight being lifted was not excessive

_____ Employee was following proper lifting procedures/mechanics

_____ Weight being lifted was excessive and assistance should have been sought

_____ Employee was stretching/reaching an excessive distance

FOR SLIP AND FALL INJURIES:

_____ Employee fell how far: _____ (Distance)

_____ Appropriate footwear was being worn (rubber boots, steel toed shoes, etc.)

_____ Shoe tread was checked after injury.

_____ Shoes were not appropriate, or tread was worn and needs to be replaced.
_____ Ladder (or like) was securely placed on flat surface

WORK SURFACE WAS:
✓ Dry, with no standing water
_____ "Just watered" grass
_____ Muddy, slippery, and/or standing water
_____ Uneven, potholes, and/or broken surfaces

FOR CUTS & LACERATIONS (circle one):

Yes / No PPE (gloves, glasses, etc) were worn
Yes / No Knife was sharpened
Yes / No Equipment guards were used

TRAINING: (circle one)
(Yes) / No Employee had been given instruction and/or training for task assigned
Yes / No Re-training is required

MEDICAL ATTENTION: (check all that apply)
✓ Employee did not receive/request medical attention
_____ Employee received on-site medical attention
_____ Employee sought walk-in medical attention on own
_____ Employee was transported to hospital by
      Security / Supervisor / 911 (circle one)
_____ Employee returned back to work the same day
_____ Employee returned to work the next shift
_____ Employee is off on IOD, starting: _____

RESTRICTIONS: (check all that apply)
_____ Employee returned to work with restrictions
_____ Employee returned to work with restrictions that can be accommodated
_____ Employee returned to work with restrictions that do not allow for continued work

ADMINISTRATIVE DETAILS:
✓ Job order(s) for defective equipment was submitted on: 11/20/02
_____ Job order(s) for change to a facility was been submitted on: _____

250

PLEASE WRITE ANY ADDITIONAL COMMENTS ON BACK

Submit to Safety Office <u>no later</u> than 48 hours after injury.

Submitted by: _Corinne Flaherty_   Date: _11/20/02_

ORIG March 2001
C:\My Documents\Worddocs\WorkComp\Forms\supervisorchecklistonepage.doc

Report of On–Duty Injury

SNZA VOLUNTEER

If you are injured or become ill due to your assignment, you are entitled to medical care with Workers' Compensation benefits through the Santa Narcissa Zoological Association. Completing this form notifies your supervisor of your injury.

(PLEASE PRINT CLEARLY)

DATE and TIME of Injury:
_10/11/02_ _7:35 A.M._

Name of Volunteer:
CLAUDE HOPPER

Type of Volunteer: ☒ Docent ☐ General ☐ Student ☐ Community Service

Please note that Animal Care Volunteers are CITY volunteers and not covered by SNZA

Division: <u>SNZA</u>

Area Supervisor: _LES MOORE_

ext: _55011_

Supervisor: _CORINNE FLAHERTY_

ext: _55077_

TYPE OF INJURY: ☐ Sprain (joint) ☐ Strain (muscle) ☐ Laceration (cut) ☐ Contusion (bruise) ☐ Bite
☐ Illness ☒ Other: _HEART ATTACK / CONCUSSION_

BODY PART(S) AFFECTED (i.e. right ankle):
HEART, HEAD

LOCATION INJURY OCCURRED (i.e. Lizard Grotto):
SERVICE ROAD BEHIND ADMINISTRATION

WHAT HAPPENED:
HEART ATTACK CAUSED DOCENT TO STUMBLE INTO VERSALIFT
TRUCK WITH FAULTY ARM WHICH COLLAPSED CAUSING
CONCUSSION AND DEATH

WAS ON–SITE FIRST AID GIVEN: ☒ Not Required

☐ Yes, by whom:_____

TYPE OF MEDICAL TREATMENT GIVEN: _NONE_

ANY FURTHER TREATMENT REQUIRED: ☐ Yes ☒ No

If YES, please explain:

_____
_____
_____
_____

WITNESSES:
SURVEILLANCE CAMERA _____

Injured Volunteer's Signature: _N/A_ _____ Date: _N/A_
Supervisor's Signature: _Corinne Flaherty_ _____ Date: _11/20/02_

Please **initial**:

_N/A_ I understand Workers' Compensation benefits are available to me and I chose **NOT** to seek
medical attention (other than first aid) for this injury at this time.

10.1991

Case # _____

Injured Volunteer's Signature: _N/A_ _____ Date: _N/A_

Supervisor's Signature: _Corinne Halutz_ _____ Date: _11/20/02_

SUPERVISOR:

Return ORIGINAL to SNZA's Human Resources,

and COPY to SNZA's Director of Volunteer Programs

within 24 hours of the report of injury.

10.1991

DETAILS: Based on a video recording of the incident, as well as interviews with various

staff members, the sequence of events began at approximately 7:40 a.m. on Friday,

October 11, 2002, after Claude Hopper had signed in for his volunteer shift on the

computer terminal in the Zoo administration offices. He emerged from the building, at

which point he greeted Equipment Operator Don Wanderly whom he passed on the stairs

as he made his way toward the service road. At that time, a golf ball shot over the tall

chain link fencing and the rows of trees that separate the municipal course from the Zoo.

The ball's trajectory was quite high and it fell at such an angle that it impacted the control

panel on the telescoping arm of a Versalift truck that had been illegally parked across four

spaces by Wanderly, who had left the truck in order to use the rest room in the

administration building. Apparently the Versalift arm was broken and the impact of the

ball on the control panel was sufficient to cause it to collapse just as Claude Hopper

passed beneath the bucket end of the arm. While under the bucket, it is clear from the

video that he clutched his left shoulder and arm, then staggered into the driver's side rear

fender of the truck. The bucket crashed down, hitting Hopper's head. He stumbled away

from the truck and off the edge of the road toward a green waste bin, just visible at the

extreme right edge of the video recording. The bin, a two-yard front-load Dumpster, is just over three feet tall with two hinged lids. The lid on the left was down and the one on the right was up. Hopper bumped up against the right end of the bin and appeared to attempt to steady himself against it. He then convulsed violently and tipped headfirst into the bin. In the video, his feet are visible for approximately 45 seconds while the seizure continues and over the course of it he sinks out of sight. The bin appeared to be partly filled because his movements cause tree trimmings and other plant debris to stick up from inside. It is the opinion of the Korne County Coroner that this is when he expired—though it could not be determined whether the cause of death was the cardiovascular event or the blunt force trauma to the head. Some 20 minutes later, the truck that picks up the green waste arrived. As is standard procedure, the truck operator used the automatic arms on the front of the truck to pick up the bin and dump the contents into the large container at the rear. It is not possible for the driver to see down into the bin as the arms lift and hoist it over the cab. According to the driver, after several more pickups, the load was taken to the compost yard, where it was dumped. Because Compost Yard Supervisor Randall Wiley was on vacation, a security officer unlocked the yard for the driver, though the officer remained at the gate while the load was deposited. Since the container was about one third full when the Dumpster with Claude's body in it was emptied into it, the heavier than usual thump of the body went unnoticed by the driver who also was not aware of anything unsual when unloading the truck. Upon returning from vacation, Wiley discovered the body and reported it to Zoo security on October 15, 2002 at approximately 8:30 a.m. The coroner has ruled this an accidental death, which is also the conclusion I have reached.

25

It's a Wrap

November 22, 2002

In the end, the Korne County Coroner's Office concurred with my report. Claude Hopper had died from either sudden cardiac arrest due to an undiagnosed congenital heart defect or massive blunt force trauma to the cranium. If one massive event hadn't killed him, the other would have—it was a chicken and egg scenario. In any case, the golf course was protected by an "Acts of God" clause in its liability insurance coverage, so I guess only God knows what really happened. Watching the videotape again frame by frame, I believe he felt the pangs of the cardiac arrest and staggered into the Versalift fender just as the damaged arm collapsed as a result of the impact from the golf ball. In either case, the conclusion was not wrongful death, but accidental death or natural causes. There was no way to determine if it was blunt force trauma, the heart attack, a heart attack precipitated by the blunt force trauma, or blunt force trauma caused by his staggering during the cardiac event.

I waited until Corinne had completed the appropriate paperwork to file my final report so I could submit everything together to the Human Resources Division and Miles Patagonia's office. She was just finishing up the morning meeting with the troops, explaining that, due to a new policy throughout the City of Santa Narcissa, all docents and volunteers would have to be fingerprinted for identification purposes. There were nods of acceptance, grumbling about unnecessary hassles, and a couple complaints about civil rights. While she smoothed the ruffled feathers, making it sound like it was no bigger a deal than taking care of a car registration or getting certified to drive the electric carts, I skimmed the newspaper.

Apparently the Sniper case had been solved as well. The culprit turned out to be a disgruntled graphic artist who had been laid off by the City during a previous round of budget cuts. Her downfall had been the Emei mustache toads. Unlike all of the outdoor exhibits she had sniped, which were easily accessible by reaching over simple barriers, to snipe the mustache toads' sign, she had had to precariously reach around and over a desert tortoise exhibit that was covered by filament netting. In contorting herself to attach the snipe, her cell phone must have slipped out of a pocket, through the netting, and into the faux-sage brush that lined the perimeter of the tortoise's habitat. She apparently did not notice it missing until Santa Narcissa police stopped by her house a day later. Keepers found the phone the morning after her visit and left it with the visitor information desk, but later that day, when the snipe was discovered, the tortoise keeper made a connection and it was all over for the Sniper. She was facing misdemeanor charges, and some hefty fines, but she had also received five job offers, one of which included a guarantee to pay any fines or legal expenses she had incurred.

After the crowd had dispersed sufficiently, I went up to Corinne.

"So, did you hear about the bench," she asked with a grin.

"Bench?"

"To honor the memory of Claude, Senior, and his love for the Santa Narcissa Zoo, Junior and the ex-wife have purchased a $50,000 commemorative bench with some of the Povenda money that Senior left to Junior. So that his name will live on outside the Volunteer Office."

"Wow."

"Can you believe it?" she chuckled and led the way to her office where two fat manila envelopes (one for HR and the other for Miles Patagonia) sat waiting for me on the corner of her desk. She handed them over with a wry smile. "It's like I have to walk past his specter every morning and afternoon."

"Well, at least it can't talk."

"I hope."

"Thanks," I said clutching the envelopes like a shield. "Sasquatch Lair— 5:30-ish? Drinks are on me."

"I'll see you then."

I added my paperwork to Corinne's paperwork and headed for the director's office, where I was sent to see Ingrid Handy, who informed me that my parking pass was ready and handed me an envelope containing a personal check from Miles Patagonia for only half the amount I was expecting along with a note that explained that this was because the incident had not been wrongful death but an act of God. She puzzled over my laughter and then asked if there was any reason that I might need to apply for an extension of the official long-term temporary restricted parking pass I had just received. I smiled and told her to have a nice day.

As I was leaving the administration building, I ran into Randall Wiley. He was carrying a ferocious pruning saw and a sheaf of multi-colored forms. There were oak leaves in his hair and he seemed mildly annoyed, but when he saw me he smiled and waved. I walked up to him.

"Hey, did you send me those devil's tongues?"

He laughed. "So all three of them survived the trip?"

"Yes! Thanks so much."

"I propagated a few from some corms that a colleague sent me. Mostly it was for my own edification—we've got nowhere to plant them out on grounds. Too dry here."

"Well, I can sure make use of them."

"Nice work on the investigation."

"How'd you know? I just filed the report."

"Word gets around fast here."

"Well, thanks, but it was kind of all for naught."

"Yeah. But at least the case is closed."

"If only someone had mentioned the surveillance camera in the first place."

"I guess."

"You guess?"

"Well, would it have made any difference?"

I considered poor doomed Claude with the ticking time bomb hidden in his chest, who had spent his last day on earth fulfilling his special purpose as a Santa Narcissa Zoo Docent, hero of his own epic. I thought about Regina Pearl, who believed that she had literally broken Claude's heart by declining to marry him, wallowing in the perfect tragic ending to her woeful love story. I thought about Les Moore and the cricket honey test I had passed, and Max Moore's escape from Imperator servitude. I thought about the success of Povenda, and the art of barbecue. I thought about Peter Manley and his quest to elevate our species beyond our animal instincts, a mission as noble as it is futile. I thought about how good it was to get caught up with Corinne, and to meet the Compost King. Clutching the parking pass in my hand, I laughed.

"Probably not."

"Well, there you go," he said with a note of finality and continued up the steps, papers rustling in the breeze. He paused momentarily as he swung open the door. "See you around."

"Yeah," I said, genuinely looking forward to the possibility. "Happy composting." Then I got into my battered Toyota and drove away.

26

Sweet Sixteen

October 11, 2002

Rick could not believe his luck. For months he had been scheming to kidnap Monica, and now all the circumstances were aligning in his favor. Friday, October 11 finally rolled around, and he was ready. He had borrowed his dad's golf clubs and packed them in the back of his cousin's minivan—a vehicle he knew she would not recognize. Monica's mom had excused her from school because it was her sixteenth birthday, and the plan had been to take her to the Department of Motor Vehicles office for her driver's test, then shopping. Rick and Monica phoned each other every morning before they left their respective houses for school. Even though he knew she would be playing hooky (with her parents' permission) he called her, and felt a little adrenaline rush when he knew she was awake. He feigned disappointment that she would not be at school, then headed for her house. Conveniently, her birthday fell before Daylight Saving Time set in, so it would be dark until almost seven o'clock, which would help.

Rick and Monica had grown up together. They went to the same elementary, middle, and now high school. Their mothers had met because they both

261

served on the Santa Narcissa Zoo Board of Directors, and the two families often socialized. Both were pleased when the two teenagers took a liking to one another. They were a good match, and the relationship was encouraged.

Monica came from a family of early risers, and Rick knew that they left the slider open in the morning so Mischief the cat could slip into the back-yard for her morning constitutional in the great outdoors and come back into the house at her leisure. He parked the van and left it unlocked, then crept around the side of the house. He smiled when he saw the fickle feline hesitating just outside the door before slinking inside. He waited, listening for voices. The bathroom, which is where she would be, was upstairs. The light was on and the steamed window was open just enough for him to hear the faint sounds of splashing water and her voice, singing enthusiastically along with that awful ABBA song she loved so much: *Knowing you and knowing me... uh-huh... There is nothing we can do...*

He hurried to the sliding door and peeked inside. Monica's dad was a contractor and usually was up and off to work early. Sure enough, there had been no truck in the drive. Her brother Lloyd would be at school super early for cross country training. Her mom was a part-time nurse and often worked the early shift. But not today. Today, she was in the kitchen frying things. The smell of bacon wafted and he salivated while he carefully, quickly darted past the kitchen doorway to the stairs.

She was drying her hair in the bathroom. The door was ajar and he crouched down and glanced quickly into the room, She had slipped into soft pink sweats and was brushing her masses of damp blonde hair while blasting it with the hairdryer. He had to strike while the iron was hot. The hood was tucked into his jacket pocket—a prop left over from the drama department production the previous spring.

When he sprang into the bathroom, Monica screamed and dropped the hairdryer, which continued running in the sink, then saw it was Rick. He was an inveterate prankster and had sprung numerous surprises on her since they were just kids. She hit him only somewhat angrily and cut off the drier.

"What are you doing here?" she hissed. Although her parents approved of Rick, she was quite sure that approval did not extend so far as welcoming him to her bathroom.

"Trust me," Rick said, quickly pulling the hood over her head.

"My hair!" she exclaimed and started to pull it off. But Rick grabbed her hands and held them firmly.

"Trust me," he said guiding her to the toilet. "Wait here."

She acquiesced and sat on the toilet lid while he went to her room to get some flip-flops for her to wear and check to see if the coast was clear. Shoes in hand, he waited in the stairwell for a few minutes wondering if he could sneak Monica out quietly and quickly enough, when he heard the washing machine buzz the end of a cycle in the basement. He gave himself a thumbs up and as soon as Monica's mom had gone downstairs to the laundry room, hurried back to the bathroom to fetch Monica and take her to the van, dropping the note he had written to her mom on the floor inside the front door, where he knew she would find it.

"What are you doing? Where are we going?" she asked as he belted her into the back seat. The side and back windows were tinted, so he hoped no one would see his hooded passenger. Getting arrested for kidnapping would certainly put a damper on his plans.

"It's a surprise," he said, fastening his seatbelt and starting the car. He pressed play on the car stereo and the sounds of ABBA filled the van: *I can dance with you honey, if you think it's funny... does your mother know that you're out?*

It was only a short distance to his destination. They were running a little late, but that was OK. The sun was only just starting to come up when he pulled into the golf course parking lot. Thankfully the surrounding park opened its gates early to accommodate joggers and hikers. The others were already there, and waved when they saw him turn into the lot. He parked alongside their cars, motioned them to be quiet, then got out and opened the back door.

"Where are we?" Monica asked as he removed the hood.

Shelly and Mike and Ken and Alexis all shouted "Surprise," and Rick

263

presented her with the box of jelly-filled donuts that Shelley had picked up for the occasion.

Monica laughed and hit him playfully. "Rick! My mom will be furious!"

"Sorry, babe. She's in on it, too."

"Oh my God. You are too much!"

He helped her out of the minivan, and the whole group sat at one of the nearby picnic tables to watch the sun come up between the trees. There was a big thermos of coffee to go with the donuts and afterward, a joint. Then the friends tactfully took off for school, leaving Rick and Monica alone.

"I told you I'd teach you how to golf, and today's the day," Rick said and kissed Monica. She tasted of donuts. He wanted to keep kissing her, but she hopped to her feet and started to clear the table.

"OK. Let's go!" she said. Vaguely disappointed, but happy to watch her bounce, he helped and then led her into the course.

The green was cool and crisp and the low sun made long shadows across the grass. A loud keening broke the quiet morning air.

Monica jumped. "What was that?"

"Oh, it's a peacock. The Zoo is on the other side of those trees."

"Really?"

"Yeah. Didn't you know that?"

"No. That's cool. Maybe we can go there afterward?"

"Maybe. You might have so much fun golfing that you won't want to quit."

She laughed. "Maybe. Show me."

He demonstrated how to hold the club and when she struggled to get the grip right, he moved and stood close behind her, reaching his arms around her to place his hands alongside hers on the club. She liked to look at his hands and feel his muscles tense along with hers as she swung. The shot was terrible—the power of his swing plus her hopelessly skewed aim—and sent the ball soaring off beyond the trees. He liked the way her body felt when she laughed. He had brought a bucket of golf balls, each one a chance to help her work on her form. Ball after ball, her technique did not

264

really show any signs of improvement, but then neither of them were really focused on that. Mule deer that had wandered onto the fairway from the surrounding chaparral to graze on the opulent grass paused to look up in alarm at every whack, but soon the shots were fewer and farther between until they stopped altogether.

Epilogue

There is an old proverb about five blind men, an elephant, and the truth that I modified to suit this story. Five blind elephant keepers are required to give a presentation to the Zoo Commission about the animal in their care. Each in turn steps up to the podium and offers his or her observations. The keeper who feeds the elephant says that the elephant is long and tubular, like a snake. The keeper who maintains the elephant's feet says the elephant is cylindrical and upright like a pillar. The keeper who takes blood samples from the elephant's ear for medical check-ups says the elephant is broad and flappy, like a tent door. The keeper who cleans up after the elephant, explains that the animal is warm and mushy. Since the reports all conflict, the City determines that there is no such animal as an elephant and suspends all the keepers for job safety infractions. The moral of the story is that truth (like beauty) is in the eye of the beholder. People who aren't looking for truth will never find it, and sometimes the truth eludes everyone.
—Rosana DuMas

Acknowledgments

Thanks to my parents, who taught me that work is only "work" if you aren't enjoying what you're doing; to my dad for all the stories he shared with me over and over again at my insistence (particularly *I am a Bunny* by by Ole Risom and Richard Scarry), and for the unlimited book allowance; to the many teachers who demonstrated how much fun learning is; to Lynda Watson for helping me get to Brown University and for being relentlessly upbeat; to Hjalmer Anderson whose insistence on understanding motivation and beats did not help me launch an acting career, but have been invaluable to me as a journalist; to Dean Carey McIntosh, who taught the satire seminar at Brown that changed my life; to the bullies who taught me early on that such behavior is the last resort of the powerless; to my friends who bravely kept me from throwing in the towel by gently nagging me to finish this book; to Rochelle Ritchie for the w(h)ine therapy; to Linda Anderson for the preliminary read-through; to Marlowe Robertson-Billet for the final read-through; to Andrew Lyell for myriad plant and golf insights; to Mike Maxcy and Jon Guenther for the excursion into falconry and for introducing me to the houbara; to Jeromy Chenault for thoughtful conversation about raptors and hunting; to Ian Recchio and the herpetology staff who have always graciously indulged my fascination with ectotherms; to the many fine editors with whom I have worked for demonstrating the art and science of refining verbiage, especially Ted Drozdowski, Jon Garelick, Charles M. Young, Richard Cromelin, Mark Kemp, Katherine Turman, Claire O'Brien, and Brenda Posada; to the authors who led the way, particularly Douglas Adams, P.D. James, Thomas Pynchon, A.S. Byatt, Dorothy Sayers, and Raymond Chandler; to Brown University and Harvard University, environments that nurtured my curiosity and made me proud to fly my geek flag high; to Mary Holcomb, who will never know how much those long summers spent foraging and adventuring in her wondrous garden would influence my life; to Woodland Park Zoo, the zoo of my childhood, and the Los Angeles Zoo, the zoo of my adulthood; to the Southern California Horticultural Society, the Theodore Payne Foundation for Wild Flowers and Native Plants, and all the gardeners who have ever revealed the tales that plants have to tell; to Michael Dee for many terrible jokes and excellent zoo yarns; to all the animal keepers who have ever shared the stories of the creatures in their care, especially Stephanie Zielinski and Bob Barnes, who, when I first started writing about the Los Angeles Zoo, recounted the saga of Sweetheart the polar bear, a story that has been a perennial inspiration.

I am grateful for Dr. Frans de Waal's 1986 paper "The Brutal Elimination of a Rival Among Captive Male Chimpanzees," published in *Ethology and Sociobiology*, for providing a model for the unfortunate events at the fictitious Eustace Scrubb Zoo (and Imperator Pharmaceuticals).

Thank you Michelle Leveille and ARTiFACT Graphics for allowing me the poetic license to borrow opossum moments and cricket interludes to make my narrative more intriguing, and for creating the brilliant cover art. Heaps of gratitude go to Mark Christopher Harvey for his important feedback, constant support, and for graciously donating his design skills to put the finishing touches on this volume. The two of you actually make me hope that people will judge my book by its cover. Thank you to illustrious former publications intern, field biologist, gifted storyteller, and bird nerd par excellence Angela Woodside for graciously proofreading my manuscript and sharing insights and suggestions for making the narrative clearer.

Art imitates life, and in striving to capture the harsh and hilarious reality of the bureaucracy that is such a pervasive part of our lives, I drew on episodes from my life as well as the vividly imparted experiences of friends and colleagues; however, any similarities between people and characters, living or dead, places, and events in this story and any actual people or characters, living or dead, places, and events are unintentional. The fictional city of Santa Narcissa and its zoo, including the staff, residents, and volunteers simply offer a convenient stage and cast of players to present an exploration of the perplexing relationship between natural law and human law.

Colophon

Unnatural Selection
A novel by Rosana DuMas
Published by Mollusc Media
Printed by CreateSpace, an Amazon.com company

Cover illustration by Michelle Leveille (artifactgraphics.com)
Linocut illustrations by Sandy Masuo
Santa Narcissa "Great Seal" designed by Kirin Daugharty
Cover and layout design by Mark Christopher Harvey / Fluxion Media (fluxion.net)
Typography is set in Baskerville

First Edition
Printed in the United States
10 9 8 7 6 5 4 3 2 1

ISBN 978-0-692-67907-4